Jak stared into the abyss

The abyss stared back. With a lurching fear, an emotion foreign to him, Jak felt the desire to throw himself off the edge and into the welcoming arms of…what?

Breathing hard, he hurriedly stepped away and looked up at the sky. It was cold and distant, yet reassuring compared to what he had just seen.

The land beneath the lip of rock had seemed to disappear beneath a blanket of darkness that had nothing to do with the absence of light. The darkness was almost a presence that seemed to have a life of its own, acting as a cover for what lay beneath it, and fiercely protective of its charge….

**Other titles in the
Deathlands saga:**

JAMES AXLER

DEATHLANDS®

Palaces of Light

A GOLD EAGLE BOOK FROM

W❖RLDWIDE®

TORONTO • NEW YORK • LONDON
AMSTERDAM • PARIS • SYDNEY • HAMBURG
STOCKHOLM • ATHENS • TOKYO • MILAN
MADRID • WARSAW • BUDAPEST • AUCKLAND

Recycling programs
for this product may
not exist in your area.

First edition May 2012

ISBN-13: 978-0-373-62614-4

PALACES OF LIGHT

With equal or even inferior power…he will win who has the resolution to advance.

—Ardant du Picq,
1821-1870

THE DEATHLANDS SAGA

This world is their legacy, a world born in the violent nuclear spasm of 2001 that was the bitter outcome of a struggle for global dominance.

There is no real escape from this shockscape where life always hangs in the balance, vulnerable to newly demonic nature, barbarism, lawlessness.

But they are the warrior survivalists, and they endure—in the way of the lion, the hawk and the tiger, true to nature's heart despite its ruination.

Ryan Cawdor: The privileged son of an East Coast baron. Acquainted with betrayal from a tender age, he is a master of the hard realities.

Krysty Wroth: Harmony ville's own Titian-haired beauty, a woman with the strength of tempered steel. Her premonitions and Gaia powers have been fostered by her Mother Sonja.

J. B. Dix, the Armorer: Weapons master and Ryan's close ally, he, too, honed his skills traversing the Deathlands with the legendary Trader.

Doctor Theophilus Tanner: Torn from his family and a gentler life in 1896, Doc has been thrown into a future he couldn't have imagined.

Dr. Mildred Wyeth: Her father was killed by the Ku Klux Klan, but her fate is not much lighter. Restored from predark cryogenic suspension, she brings twentieth-century healing skills to a nightmare.

Jak Lauren: A true child of the wastelands, reared on adversity, loss and danger, the albino teenager is a fierce fighter and loyal friend.

Dean Cawdor: Ryan's young son by Sharona accepts the only world he knows, and yet he is the seedling bearing the promise of tomorrow.

In a world where all was lost, they are humanity's last hope....

Prologue

"Time…time is a funny thing, my friend. Time is something that is the master of all of us. Even the greatest of barons who have ever walked across the soil that gives us what we laughingly call life is at the mercy of the ticking of the chron. Eventually we become part of that dust that we stomp beneath the heels of our boots. We're nothing when it comes down to it. We fuck and fight and think that we're really important, but it doesn't matter jackshit. Everything comes from the dust, and returns there sooner or later. What comes in between seems kinda important at the time, but all it really amounts to is our own sense of our self-importance. I guess some of us think we're more important than others. That's why some of us try to become better than others. Why some of us become barons, and waste our time trying to get somewhere, when at the end of the blacktop there ain't nothing but the same darkness that greets everyone."

Baron K frowned. In the darkness of the hut, it was hard to see if the grossly fat man seated in front of him was smiling. His tone betrayed nothing of the sort, but even in measured tones the weight of his words carried a reproach that the baron found irritating. Would the old man in front of him dare to be so dismissive of the efforts that had brought K to this point? Would he risk the wrath of the baron, and the violence that it could wreak?

"Careful what you say, Morgan. You have a great wisdom, but even so—"

"I could go too far, eh?" Morgan spit through the tangled skein of his gray beard onto the dirt of the floor. It was just the clearing of phlegm, but such was the aura of the old man that it seemed to carry greater import.

"I have seen men chilled for less," K replied, keeping his tone even.

Morgan fixed him with a gimlet eye that glittered bright, despite his age. He raised the paring knife that had been carving charred meat from the bone of an unrecognizable animal, and used it to gesture at the baron.

"Mebbe you have, at that. But I'm too close to the end of the blacktop for it to matter to me. So you chill me slow by your standards. Is that any worse than the certain knowledge that I have of the slow chilling we all endure? No—" he shook his head, his heavy frame heaving as he wheezed a chuckle "—let's face it, K. There's nothing you can do to bother me. And if you want to know what you've come here for, then you'd better get off that high horse you've ridden in on and start to listen. You want to know about the palaces of light. You think that's where they're taking them."

K tried to answer, but his throat was tight and his mouth dry. Constriction forbade him from breathing, let alone form speech. It was all he could do to nod dumbly. His own flesh and blood... He had to find where they were going and why. That was why he had to put up with the old man and his tongue, which by rights should be cut out and roasted like the meat he slobbered on.

Morgan sighed, tossing the bone over his shoulder and wiping the blade of the knife on his vest, which was unlikely to get any greasier than it was already. He chewed ruminatively on his bottom lip, his eyes glazing over as he stared into the distance. It was as though he was recalling something told to him a lifetime ago, and it needed immense concentration to plunge memory back through the years and pluck out the memory fully formed.

K thought about his daughter and felt the tightness in his chest as the pain of anticipation almost burst his heart. Even a man who could trample hundreds of lives beneath him in the quest for power had the weakness of tender emotion somewhere within him, and for someone.

When Morgan spoke finally, it was as though he were channeling something from the distant past, no more than a conduit for a dead and forgotten time. Which, in a sense, perhaps he was.

"All things come to pass. From sand to sand, they say. None proved that more fully than those who had the greatest tech of all human history, and did little with it other than create a blizzard of fire, ice and wind that lasted for more than three generations. Men who wanted to be gods, and created a tech that should have ensured their immortality, yet did little except wipe out the records and traces of memory that they wished to be commemorated by. Iron, or something, that was what they said about it. Doesn't matter. Point is, it shows that nothing lasts forever. But some things last longer than others. Last longer than memory.

"That's how it is with the palaces of light…the mysterious palaces of light as they used to call them back in the day. They were there for so long that people forgot just how they got to be there in the first place. But there were some old legends that survived. Whether they were the truth or lies, I couldn't say. I only repeat what I was told. One thing for sure, though," he said, slipping back into the faraway tone of a man who was reciting much of his text from memory. "It's always been a place where it pays to be fearful."

K felt his guts churn. He hadn't come from this part of the Deathlands, having spent his early years struggling out of a pesthole ville to ride with some coldhearts who preyed on convoys. It had been a hard and brutal training in the lessons of life, and he had acquired skills and a cynical, ruthless streak that had served him well when he ended up in a ville where the incumbent baron had grown fat, old and careless. Taking over had been a breeze, and he had used the superstition and fear of the people as a tool with which to maneuver his way to power. But the one thing he had never bargained on was that the superstition and fear was rooted in a sense of history. The words that Morgan now intoned brought that home to him, and clutched at his heart.

"There are those who say that the Mancos Canyon was gouged out of the rock by the thumbs of the gods. They needed somewhere to hide the demons that they had banished from the skies, and that was where they chose to leave them. Figures, when you look at how fucked the Mesa Verde is all around. Even before the shitstorms that the nukes brought with them it was still one hell of a place. *Hell* being the word. They say that the world was once a green and verdant vale— that's another one of those phrases that means something good, although I couldn't tell you exactly what it means." Morgan sniffed and shrugged. "Anyways, the Mesa has always been a place that the gods skirted around with no notion of ever visiting ever again. Man wasn't meant to tread there, but we did. Always have been some cursed souls who ended up there for want of anything better to do.

"Thing is, those who have wandered across the Mesa and not tumbled to their chilling when they reached the lip of the canyon have always seen the same thing. The mysterious palaces of light. Mysterious because they've been there since the dawn of time. Since before man, which kinda begs the question as to who the hell built them. Beautiful as they are, hewn out of the rock and shaped into buildings that have a light shining from them, they've been sheltered from everything that's ever happened in this world. Think about it, K," Morgan said softly, leaning forward so that his eye fixed on the baron, the paring knife emphasizing every word. "Even the nukecaust never touched these babies. That nightmare of howling winds and driving acid rains, the fire and the ice... It never touched them."

He leaned back and sniffed back a gob of phlegm, growling in his throat.

"'Course, there are those who say that there are no such things as demons. They say that there were men who lived long before the Indians who everyone took to be the real natives that came across from where the seas now run. These were men like those who lived on the old southern lands, the ones who used to worship the sun and ripped out each other's hearts to offer up. The kind of people you must like, K. But I tell you this—there are those who say that they built the palaces, yet they take no account of the fact that none of the temples and cities these men built looked anything like the palaces.

"Same way as others used to say that it was the Norsemen who built them. The ones who were supposed to sail on rafts across the raging seas centuries before the one called Columbo came and claimed the old lands, naming them Amerigo." He frowned. "Something like that." He shook his head as if to dismiss the confusion. "Thing about them is that, like the ones from the south, they couldn't have done it because they had nothing like it in their own lands. Besides which, they were coming from the far coast, and how the fuck were they going to get across the plains when all they could do was build rafts of wood that must have got them here more by luck than any kind of skill?"

K interrupted. He felt almost as if it was wrong to do so; his mouth, too, was dry with fear of what Morgan was leaving between the words. "If not them, then who? The demons of who you spoke?" he asked.

A smile, almost mocking, wreathed the old man's face. "You really believe that there are such things as gods and demons? It's all a story, K. Just a story. Evil comes from men, but perhaps—just perhaps—it's the case that the evil in men can somehow become instilled in a place, where it becomes magnified and acts as a draw to those who would think and feel the same way. Then again, mebbe I'm just plain wrong, and the story about there being gods who gouged the earth to throw down devils is right, and those devils built the palaces of light. One thing of which I'm certain, because it's the only thing that runs through every story I was ever told, is that the men who built those palaces weren't the Indians, nor the blond North men who were said to come before. These were men who came from a time before that, and had skills that could hew things of beauty out of ugly, harsh rock. That speaks of some power, some knowledge. And that's still in there, K. It ain't good, and it's always done nothing else but attract its like.

"The dark ones—be they a kind of power or gods and demons—have always protected the canyon. Through the days of skydark and right till now. And whoever lives there is evil. If not to start with, then it'll soon infect them.

"And that's where they're going, K. Into the heart of darkness and into the palaces of light. Remember, my baron, that not all light is good. The light that came with the nukes wasn't good. Mebbe this is that kind of light."

K was frustrated. He turned away from the old man, not wishing him to see the confusion that was written on his face. This talk of gods and demons was shit. But evil, real tangible evil that could infect a man, running from man to man like a disease. That was something he understood only too well. The palaces were places of legend. The legends were swathed in shadow, like the physical stones that hung over the canyon edge, protecting the palaces from the elements, just as they always had.

Hiding them from prying eyes—all but those of the most questing.

All but those, he hoped, of the ones he had sent to discover the truth.

Chapter One

Heat—dry and oppressive, unrelenting, bore down on them with every step the companions took. It was the kind of heat where, if they had any sense, they would seek out any shelter they could find and wait for the sun to sink in the sky, and the cool of night to start sweeping across the plain.

But the companions could only do that if they had time. And that was the one thing they were sorely lacking. There was no time for them to waste. The group they were trailing was obviously used to traveling in such conditions, and moved swiftly across the blasted and scorched plain. Swiftly enough to set a punishing pace.

"Oh, that we could have had the use of a wag," Doc bemoaned in a voice that was cracked and parched, both by the dry atmosphere and the effort of an enforced march in such conditions. "Even a gas-guzzler... a mere wooden effort on wheels, powered by nothing more than the power of a mule would have satisfied me. But no, we are to be denied even that Spartan comfort in the search for our prey. How, pray tell, are we to be in a fit state to face them when we eventually confront them when we have had to suffer such unendurable conditions?"

"Doc, if they were unendurable, you would have bought the farm, and I wouldn't have to listen to your interminable complaints," Mildred countered in a voice that was as dry as Doc's. Albeit that she had preserved hers by holding her peace for what seemed to be far too many miles while the old man moaned and droned on, his voice like the drip of water wearing away at her patience. At that, the fact that it made her think of water at a time when they were preserving theirs and putting aside thoughts of slaking their ravaging thirst was something that only served to increase her irritation.

"All I am trying to point out is that the baron may be rewarding us well for our endeavors if we achieve our goal, but he has not exactly given us the tools with which to finish the job." He paused for a moment, his head cocked in thought, much to Mildred's relief. Unfortunately, it wasn't to last, and before she had a chance to breathe a sigh of relief he had started again, albeit on a different tack.

"Strange, but by the Three Kennedys, that phrase strikes a resonant chord deep within the caverns of remembrance! Perhaps it was something that one of the three blessed ones themselves uttered at some point. Or some such personage, one who shared an exalted position similar to that—"

He was cut short with a sudden action. Mildred, realizing that his sudden ramblings, now that they had veered from the simple grumblings of before, presaged a descent into the kind of temporary madness that blighted his life—and therefore by extension hers and those of her fellow travelers—turned and slapped him across the face. Hard. She was about five yards from him, just in front, and so to achieve this action she had to spin and then take a step back that added to the momentum of her swinging arm. She caught the old man with a full and open palm.

In the quiet of the arid and deserted plain, with no sound from the others beyond the muffled padding of boots on hard-packed sand, the blow sounded large and shocking. Doc's head snapped on his neck, his eyes wide with shock and his jowls shaken by the impact of the blow. It resounded so loud in their collective silence that the others stopped to turn and face Doc and Mildred.

For a moment Doc stared blankly into Mildred's face. From his expression she couldn't tell if he would cry, yell, hit her or pass out.

He did none of those things. Instead, a slow grin spread across his face as he held a hand up to his stinging cheek.

"Madam," he said slowly, "there must be other, and perhaps better ways in which to bring a man back from the brink of the abyss. But I would doubt if there are any that would have such an immediate effect. Do you know, for a moment there I could hear myself and found it quite hard to credit the things that were coming from my mouth. It is very hard to describe, as though one is separated from oneself and observing from a distance. To be back in a place where the mind and body occupy the same place is a pleasure. Even if—" he added, looking around "—it is such a place as this."

The others had stopped to watch, taken aback by the sudden explosion of violence in Mildred's behavior. Doc's mumbling moan had become little more than a background sound to them, marking and punctuating each footfall. In truth, each of them was finding the going tough, and to waste time on the disjointed grumbling of the old man was more effort than they felt they could spare.

Now, almost forced into a halt by the turn of events, it became obvious that they had become mechanical in their actions, and for the first time in several hours under the baking skies they stopped to look at one another.

"He's right about the wag, though," Krysty said in a voice ravaged by the climate and by the lack of water. "At least we could have made some kind of shelter for the worst of the day."

Ryan shook his head slowly. To speak was a great effort, so he used his words sparingly. "Can't get too close. They're on foot. Too much risk of them seeing dust clouds if we used wheels."

Jak sniffed. "Get too far, lose touch."

J.B. cast a long glance into the far distance. Toward the horizon, it seemed as though the vista in front of them was devoid of life. Only toward the edge of land and sky, where the two met in an indistinct haze, was there anything that could in any way be construed as signs of life. Even then, the specks that moved in the sealike mirage of wavering light might have been nothing more than phantoms of imagination. Following the Armorer's gaze, Ryan could barely focus his only functioning orb on them. If he was honest, he knew they were real only because he had been tailing them for so long, and in an area about thirty miles back where there had been some jagged outcrops that jutted savagely from the earth to provide some kind of cover, he had been able to get close enough to take stock of the enemy.

"Should have taken them then," J.B. murmured, as though able to read the one-eyed man's mind.

Ryan allowed a grin to crack the previously grim set of his jaw. J. B. Dix had traveled with him for so long that each man knew the other's way of thinking.

"You know why we couldn't do that," he said simply, for the Armorer, as he was also known, was only too well aware.

"Yeah. Can't lose the captives. Can't return without them. And if we don't, then there's no point in us having come this far."

Ryan shrugged. There was nothing more to say. With a gesture, he indicated that they should start to move forward. Wearily, and with a resignation born of knowing that objective could only be achieved with further suffering, they began to move in a straggling line once more.

Ryan and Krysty were at the front, almost side by side. Jak came in their wake, with J.B. behind him. Mildred hung back a little, partly because she wanted to avoid the choking and irritating dust that they raised with their heels, and partly because she felt beholden to keep an eye on Doc. The old man—in some ways, and yet not others, as he was centuries old in conception yet had lived a span not much longer than any of them—was lagging behind. The ravages of his past experience made it hard for him sometimes to keep up in extreme conditions, his body having suffered at the hands of too many to sustain the levels of stamina sometimes needed. His tenacity, however, and sheer determination could sometimes equalize him with his peers.

As they made their weary way in the wake of the party they trailed, Ryan played over the options in his mind.

They had to have been crazy to take this one on. Sure, they needed the jack and the supplies that this would bring, but at what cost? It irritated him when they were reduced to hiring out their services like the mercies of the days before skydark. The highest bidder got the service, and screw what the mission may be. There were certain things that they wouldn't do. *Honor* might have been a word that had lost all meaning postnukecaust, but Ryan still had to be able to look at himself in a mirror and be satisfied with what he saw. In their own ways, all of them had codes that they lived by. And those codes were basically the same. It was one of the things that bound them together.

This job was different from most others they'd taken on. The way the baron told it, some coldhearts had taken all the children in the ville. Why was a mystery; how was an even bigger one. Despite his best efforts, Ryan had been unable to understand what had occurred. All he knew was that the baron was willing to pay them a lot of jack to rescue the ville's children.

While it was true that a ville was lost without kids—without the next generation a ville could do nothing but wither and buy the farm, at the mercy of an aging population and an outside world that grew progressively younger and stronger—still it was more than just altruism that had driven the baron's desperate bargaining. The fact that one of the kids taken was his own had a greater bearing on his willingness to give ground than perhaps his people would have liked, had they been privy to the negotiations.

The thing was, with his own kid being involved, he was willing to pay a lot to get her back. Conversely, what information was he holding back that might make them decide not to take the job? Ryan wondered.

How had these coldhearts taken the kids so easily? What danger did they really present?

Perhaps that was part of the reason that he was trailing at a distance: caution for his people until they had a real chance to recce the situation.

But it had better come soon.

LIGHT BECAME DARK easily in the barren wasteland. Heads down, focused on keeping one foot in front of another at a steady pace that ate up the ground, ignoring the thirst that gnawed at their parched throats, the companions didn't notice the passing of time. Suddenly the light around them became much dimmer, and the sands that reflected light and heat at them became much cooler.

"Dark night, how long have we been doing this?" J.B. asked in a voice that was barely above a croak. It was so quiet that it was hard to tell if he was talking to anyone in particular, or just to himself.

Nonetheless, Ryan opted to answer. Looking at his wrist chron, alarmed at how the heat and sweat in his eye made it hard to focus on its face, he said, "Too long, J.B. Hours. We should have taken a water break a couple of hours back."

"Mebbe have plenty time do that," Jak observed morosely, gesturing at the horizon.

Ryan followed the direction indicated by the albino teen. Although he could now see the group of people in the far distance much more clearly than a few hours previously, the horizon no longer blurred and obscured by the haze of the day's heat, the group was greatly diminished from the one they had been following up to this point.

"What the fuck…" he whispered.

"Unless they're walking off the edge of the world—and I wouldn't blame them if it goes on like this—then I figure that the plains must be about to take a huge dip," Krysty said with a wry twist to her tone.

"If that is so, then I would suggest we take advantage of the drop in temperature and step up the pace, lest we lose track of them," Doc suggested. "It would, after all, be a great pity to come this far only to lose them in a hole in the ground."

Mildred grinned. "Not like you to be understated," she said hoarsely, the smile cracking her dry lips.

Ryan, however, was in no mood to take such humor at face value. "Shit," he swore in frustration, "we'll take in some water, then try to step it up. I know you want to rest, people, but mebbe we'll get lucky and be able to take a break when we find where they've disappeared to."

The other five all experienced a sinking feeling in the pits of their stomachs when they heard what the one-eyed man had to say. Yet each of them had already steeled him or herself for the difficult trek ahead, knowing that it was necessary, and that Ryan only spoke what they all knew to be true.

Without another word, they took great drinks of water to rehydrate and fortify themselves before setting off in grim silence for the target.

The way ahead was nothing but a hard slog. They had to focus on getting to the target, and not waste time and energy on anything else. Even the encroaching darkness and cold seemed to be peripheral to the goal that filled their minds. But before the blanket of night finally descended, and they had only the pale wan light of a cloudless moon to light their way, Ryan was able to see that the last of the group of people ahead of them had vanished from view. How far was the horizon from where they were? Apparently, always the same distance.

No, he thought, shaking his head a little to clear the muzziness that came with fatigue and the chill that crept into their bones. The question was, how much land lay between themselves and the horizon at any given time? That was how far ahead their prey was from where they stood now. And if he knew that, then he could work out how long it would take them to cover that distance and so find out where that prey had gone, and how long until they could even think about stopping.

The figures rushed around his head, producing a different answer with each thought, and making him question his own sanity. And yet that futile train of thought served a purpose: the longer and more complicated the train of thought, then the more distance it ate up without his noticing the effort it took to drag his body across the arid plain, gray in the moonlight.

In their own ways, and with their own trains of thought, the others did the same. It was a way of shutting out the cold, just as they had tried to shut out the heat.

So it was that they came upon the fissure before they truly had a chance to register what was up ahead. It had looked like nothing more than a patch of ground that was darker than the surrounding area. It was only that the land beneath their feet grew less smooth, rougher and more broken, that the presentiment of any danger became apparent. The pale light of the crescent moon had been little enough, but somehow the land around had seemed to soak up what little light prevailed.

Another time, perhaps, any of them would have noticed. But, tired and worn by their self-enforced march, they were receptive to the change before it was almost too late. Ryan, still in front, had registered that the ground was less certain beneath his boots, but had put this subconsciously down to a minor change in the terrain than anything that should take his attention.

Perhaps it was the night around them dulling his senses. Perhaps it was the dehydration and the introspection that had enabled him to counter this. Perhaps it was nothing more than the tiredness that came from a day's march without any respite.

Whatever it was, it nearly cost him his life.

One moment the one-eyed man was wrapped up in thought, feeling and yet not registering the ground beneath his feet, the next, he was sliding forward as that ground gave way with an unexpected treachery.

Now the darkness around him made more sense. This was what the people they had been trailing had disappeared into: a fissure in the earth, running deep and almost sheer beneath them. Somehow they had wandered into a small ledge that jutted into space. Those who had gone ahead had known it was there, and had benefited from the light of day. For Ryan and his people there was no prior warning, and as his foot had come down on loose earth and started a slide, the momentum and weight of his body not only threatened to carry him over the edge and into the unknown dark below, but it also carried the risk of making the ledge crumble.

Krysty and Jak were nearest as Ryan's leg skidded from under him and he toppled back toward the ground. He would have yelled, if not for the fact that his throat was so cracked that little more than a startled croak would emerge. His arms flew out in an attempt to balance himself and spread his weight, to stop the ground beneath him giving way any more than it already had. Without his realizing it, this gave Jak and Krysty the help they needed. As his arms flew back, they were both able to reach out and grab hold of him.

Yet even as they did, both were aware of the earth beneath them trembling and starting to crumble. An ominous groan came from deep within the ground beneath their feet.

Mildred, J.B. and Doc were lagging behind a little. Although it gave them more ground to make up before they could be of assistance, it also gave them the split second they each needed to snap out of their respective reveries and take instant stock of the situation.

To be too close would be to risk their combined weight causing the unstable ground to break up even more. To stay away would be to leave Jak and Krysty to try to haul Ryan back while the rock splintered beneath their feet. They had to move in and lend support while staying back enough to stop the ledge turning to dust beneath them, and dropping all of them into the abyss below.

Ryan had no idea of what was happening behind him. He knew only that the ground was falling away beneath him even as he scrabbled with his boot heels to gain some kind of grip. Each frantic attempt to gain a foothold had only the opposite effect. At the same time, he could feel his legs start to slip and his calves cramp as the jagged edge of rock cut into them. At the other end of his body he could feel an ironlike grip around each wrist, and his shoulders strained in their sockets as he was grabbed and hauled back while his momentum sought to carry him in the opposite direction.

He stopped kicking, realizing that his efforts were counterproductive.

At his back, Jak and Krysty could feel the movement beneath them slow as Ryan ceased to fight. Now more confident, but still cautious in case they started a slide of their own, they began to move back slowly, one step at a time. They staggered their steps so that first Krysty, and then Jak, moved, causing the minimum of disturbance and impact to the fragile earth beneath them. Within a few steps, each felt another hand reach out and grab them in the darkness. Mildred took hold of Jak, and Doc assisted Krysty. Each allowed the others to lean a little of their weight into them, so that it took some strain off the ground beneath, and allowed the stress to be carried over a greater area of ground. At the rear, J.B. planted his feet firmly on solid ground and took hold of arms that were stretched out behind Doc and Mildred. Bearing their weight, he began to slowly shuffle back, taking the strain and helping them to haul back Jak and Krysty.

It was a slow and painful process. Sweating with the effort, despite the chill of the night, J.B. could only relax when he could see, under the wan moon, that Ryan was several yards from the edge, and was able to dig in his own heels and push back.

When they were all back level with the line of the crevasse, they collapsed onto the ground, breathing hard.

Ryan raised himself up on one elbow. In the moonlight he could see the inky blackness that was delineated only by the jagged line of collapsing rock. They had hauled him back only just in time. He could still hear the faint sounds of falling dirt and stone where small sections of the lip continued to fall away.

Just in time. Timing was everything. A few seconds and he would have been gone before they could reach him.

Timing was everything. A day either way and they might not even have been out here on this cold, dark night.

Chapter Two

"Tell me where they are, Morgan. Tell me what they're doing."

Baron K leaned into the fire, so that his face was reflected in the upward glow. Shiny, bright and expectant, there was almost something childlike about him as he asked.

The old man sucked his teeth, then spit to one side. "Wish it was that simple, Baron. But if it was, I would have seen them coming, known who they were when they arrived and been able to do something about it."

The baron shook his head. "When I look back, I should have seen it, too. It's not like it wasn't obvious that they were bad news. No, Morgan, they had a magic about them that was strong, and could mask a lot."

The old man cocked his head to one side as he considered the man who was nominally his superior. Not at present. Right now it seemed that the baron was looking up to him as a superior because of powers he appeared to possess. His faith was touching, if a little misplaced. Morgan mused that if he had been the kind of man who wished to gain and use power, he would have been able to use the baron's belief against him. For a man who had used a very physical and worldly grasp of power to gain his position, he had a vulnerable point that was unexpected.

But Morgan wasn't that kind of man. He considered that running his own life was enough of a struggle, let alone taking on the task of telling others how they should live. He also had what he considered to be a sense of perspective. And from that he knew that the baron had overestimated what he could do. The baron believed in magic and power that was beyond the physical and human. Morgan didn't. All those old stories were crap. It was true that he had a certain ability. He was a doomie, as he had heard others like himself be called. He could see things that weren't there, or that were happening some way distant. But he didn't call it magic. He came from a long line of those who carried the history of the time before the nukecaust. This role as a person who could recall the stories of the past gave him a kind of protection. He was treated with a kind of awe akin to those who could cure the sick. *Doctors,* as they called them once. With a wry twist of humor, he realized that he was one of the few who would know that word around these parts. Just as he was the only one who knew that doomies weren't some kind of supernatural beings.

But let the baron believe what he wanted. It kept Morgan alive and relatively safe.

It was true, though, that he did possess that kind of doomie gift that enabled him to see from a distance. If he concentrated, then he could see what it was that he concentrated his attention upon. Viewing remotely, as some had once called it. Or second sight, which seemed a stupe name to him, as he could barely see now that he was getting on and his eyes ailed him.

The fire wasn't really necessary, but it added a sense of occasion to what he did, as did the empty room and the silence around him. If he could shut himself off mentally, then he could do it anywhere. The most important thing about the fire was that it sent a shiver down the spine of the baron, and actually made him keep his big mouth shut. The worst obstacle that Morgan could face while trying to do this was to keep being interrupted by K's incessant questions.

So now, with the baron silenced by his own sense of occasion, Morgan was able to settle down, to relax his body from the toes up, and to blank his mind by thinking of nothing, just seeing the flickering flames in front of him.

He thought of the six people he had met all too briefly: the one-eyed leader and his wiry sidekick, the one with the stupe hat and the odd obsession with hardware. They were the kind of men you'd want on your side in a fight, though you might not want to be their friends in times of peace. The other four comprised a strange and motley crew. The red-haired woman was a doomie. That much he had sensed right away. That made his task easier, as he could focus on her. How it worked, he didn't understand, and didn't care to know. It just did. The black woman and the old man were really odd. There was something about them that seemed aged beyond their looks, as though they came from another time. He would have loved to have known their stories. They would have been well worth knowing to tell again and again. And then there was the albino. Not a youth to know in times of peace, like One-eye and the Hat. But different from them. He had an air of wildness to him.

They were brave. He had to give them that. He wouldn't have undertaken the mission, no matter how much jack was involved. When he thought of those they were chasing, a sense of cold, enveloping darkness came over him. Just letting that thought pass through his mind made him shiver.

Instead, he concentrated on the red-haired doomie. That was no great stretch, as to even let the thought of her beauty cross his mind brought the warmth flooding to his loins. He had to suppress a salacious smile at the thought.

Feeling more relaxed now, he began to get some impressions: faint at first, then confusing and jumbled even as they began to take shape. The agony of stretched muscles, and a feeling of danger—not hers, but of one close to her. The one-eyed man? He had sensed something between them, and now that seemed to be the overriding sense that he was getting.

It took greater shape, and he could see as though detached. Once inside her head and heart, it was suddenly as though he had been freed from this cage and was a bird flying high over them, seeing from above all that was going on. He could see now that they had wandered too close to the edge of a precipice when dark and fatigue overtook them. As he watched, he saw them pull One-eye clear. They were safe and he was relieved. For himself more than them, if truth be told. He didn't relish having to tell the baron that they had bought the farm before they had found their prey.

And he was pretty sure that they hadn't. They had to be on some kind of trail, as they had wandered into a region that he didn't recognize. The fissure in the ground into which One-eye had nearly fallen was something he didn't remember ever seeing in all his years. As to where the children and the darkling ones were... as a bird, he soared over the group that now lay exhausted but safe, and tried to stoop down into the fissure. He was looking for some kind of light. It was night, and they had to have some kind of torch to light their way, or fire to heat them as they slept. But no, there was nothing. No light and no sign of movement.

But he knew they were there, knew because he was forced to pull up and away from the deep groove in the earth, forced back by a sense of cold and black that was more than just the plains night.

Like a black claw around his heart, he felt it tighten and squeeze, making it hard for him to take breath. It seemed to last forever, that it would squeeze the life from him. Whatever it was, it didn't welcome him.

Morgan snapped back to the here and now, darting his eyes away from the flame, thinking now of how his bladder was bursting, and how he might piss himself with fright. The very physical pressure was the perfect antidote to that part of his mind that wandered far in the night.

Dragging in his breath sharply, feeling the smoky air fill his lungs as though it was perfumed, he felt relieved to be back in this realm. And still alive, at that—

at least, he did until he saw that K was staring intently at him.

"Well?" the baron asked simply.

Morgan considered this carefully.

"It is a long path, but as they come to the end of this road, they draw closer together until the point where they meet," he intoned after some consideration.

K nodded sagely, as though understanding every word.

Morgan breathed a sigh and hoped that Red and her crew would make better progress than he. Otherwise he might have to find the words to tell K something that he really wouldn't want to hear.

RYAN LOOKED INTO the abyss. It was hard to tell, under the pale moon, just how deep or shallow this crater was. It seemed to stretch as far he could see on either side of him, curving slightly to the left, but still reaching out into the darkness. Where it ended—if it did—he couldn't tell. One thing seemed certain: there was no way across unless you went down.

J.B. joined him at the edge, staring down into the black. He took off his spectacles and calmly polished them, as though the events of a few moments before hadn't occurred.

"They must have gone down," he stated simply. "No other way."

"But how?" Ryan mused. "Treacherous underfoot, and no path that I can see. Looks like a straight drop."

"Does in this light. But that's this light." The Armorer shrugged. "Can't see much in this. Mebbe it'll be different when the sun comes up. That'll be—" he tilted his wrist chron so that it caught as much of the moonlight as was possible, squinting to read the dial "—a good four hours. Can't do much till then. I say we get some rest. We need it."

Ryan sighed. "Four hours and we could lose track of them."

J.B. smiled wryly. "Kind of have now, Ryan. No light to show where they are, which way they've gone. What are we going to do? Stumble down and risk our necks and then either go completely the wrong way or run into them when we aren't prepared?"

Ryan's expression echoed his friend's wry tone. "I know, I know. Just seems like we're losing so much ground this way."

J.B. shrugged. "Mebbe... One of those times we can't do jack about it. Might as well grab some *z's* and wait till we can get a better picture."

Ryan clapped him on the shoulder. "Not what we want, but just what is, right? Sense like always, J.B."

They turned away from the edge. Now was the time to get some rest. Huddling together, for they couldn't risk the beacon of a fire, the companions bedded down for the remainder of the night. They had a routine that was always the same in such situations: however much time was left of the night, they would divide watch equally among them. Looking up at the position of the moon, Jak elected to take first watch. The darkest of the night would soon give way to the gray of predawn, and he was the best equipped to cope with the inky blackness of night. His red eyes were sensitive to light, but at a time such as this, they were the best adapted of all of them.

While the others settled and soon drifted into the uneasy sleep that came with night cold and the hardness of earth with no bedding to soften it, Jak settled down on his haunches to welcome the night. As the breathing of his friends subsided into the settled snores and soft grunts of rest, he was able to tune out those noises and concentrate on the land around them.

Even by night, not all was quiet. The companions had seen little in the way of wildlife and fowl during the day. Those few birds that had stamina to fly from distant eyries were content to circle at a great height, patient in the hope of fallen prey. On the ground, the heat and inevitable depth of any water encouraged only the most hardy of burrowing animals. Any aboveground dwellers who dared to encroach on the arid wasteland would soon scuttle back to their havens, or perish in the attempt. By day, few would venture aboveground, and even those that did would be wary of any who passed over their burrows. By night, it was a different situation. The cool air would draw them aboveground to forage. Their snufflings, the patter of claws on hard-packed earth, the occasional yowl of conflict, and pain or mating—perhaps both—were clear to Jak and proscribed a symphony of hidden movement.

The creatures were harmless, their musk faint and bespeaking of the distance they preferred to keep from the larger creatures they instinctively identified as a potential danger. Jak allowed himself something that appeared as only a flicker, a twitch, of the facial muscles, but was a laugh to all who knew him. Possible food, if he could be bothered to hunt them, but no threat.

Very well. There was something else that was bugging him that he could check out now that he was sure they were safe. While the others slept unaware, he walked to the edge of the crack in the earth. Mindful of his footing, he edged as close as he could to the lip, gingerly feeling for loose earth and rock. He found a path that was sure enough underfoot for him to reach the very edge, so that he could peer over and scan the width of the deep trench. With his eyesight being attuned more to the night than any of the others, he expected to be able to see more than Ryan or J.B. had a short while before. There was no fire to light the path of their prey, but the trail of a group of people couldn't fail to be read on such terrain. It would be impossible to move without leaving something in your wake. Maybe, if fortune favored them, he may even be able to make out something even blacker than the hole below: a darkness caused by a clustering of bodies.

Now on the edge of the abyss, he concentrated his attention on the space below, shutting out not just the sounds of his companions, but all the other noises of the night. Down there, somewhere, were enough people to be making some sound, to leave some indication of their position.

Jak stared into the abyss.

And the abyss stared back. With a lurching fear that swept over him like a wave, an emotion to which he was unaccustomed, he felt the desire to throw himself off the edge and into the welcoming arms of…what?

Breathing hard, Jak hurriedly stepped back and looked up at the sky. The night was ink-black in patches, dotted only with the distant diamonds of stars and the wan disk of the moon. It was cold and distant, hardly welcoming, yet somehow reassuring when compared to what he had just seen.

For the land below the lip of rock had seemed to disappear beneath a blanket of darkness that had nothing to do with the absence of light. It was like a presence that seemed to have a life of its own, acting as a cover for whatever lay beneath it, and fiercely protective of its charge. It was almost as if it had tried to strike out at him when he dared to look beneath it.

Despite the cold weather, Jak was sweating. An icy-cold puddle formed in the small of his back. He turned away from the abyss to see that Krysty had awakened, and was now standing, watching him. Her hair was coiled around her neck, in an almost mirrorlike imitation of the sweat at his own. Even in the dark of night, he could see the unease and fear in her eyes.

"Not look down there," he said softly. "Wait sunup." He walked back toward the sleeping group. If she was to relieve him, then he wanted to find the oblivion of sleep as soon as possible. As he passed her, she began to step toward the edge of the abyss. Jak grabbed her arm, pulling her back so that she turned around to face him.

"No." He said it simply and quietly, but there was a power in it backed up by the expression on his face and in his usually blank eyes.

Krysty tried to speak but nothing would emerge. It

was all she could do to shake her head before taking up her watch with her back firmly to the fissure in the earth.

Jak sank down gladly against the sleepers, welcoming oblivion....

BARON K SHIVERED as he recalled that day, shivered because he had no real memory of the day the children were taken. What had come before was still etched into his mind as though someone had taken a wag battery, cut it open and poured the gunk into his brain. And what had come after, when the whole ville had awakened from what seemed to be a stupor that could only have been induced by some kind of jolt was only too clear. But of that time—the time when the exodus had occurred—there was nothing.

And while Morgan stared into the fire, K brought back to mind the awful task of having to outline that moment to the one-eyed man and his crew as they had sat in front of him.

"You can't tell us anything? But you expect us to go after these coldhearts with no real clue as to what they can do." The man known as Ryan Cawdor had looked around at his people, all of whom were looking as incredulous as himself.

K squirmed. Part of the strategy that had made him a baron was to be in complete control of everything that went on around him. To admit that he hadn't been was almost like an admission of weakness. And weakness was anathema to him.

"The only way I can explain it is that it was like the

kind of sleep you get when you're exhausted...when you've been on the road for days, and you kept traveling until every muscle is at breaking point, and your eyes are out on sticks with the grit of the road rubbing them raw. That moment when you're just running on fumes one moment, and the next your body just gives up and you fade so quick you don't even know it until you wake up and it's dark, and your face is embedded in the dirt."

Ryan sniffed. The baron had a colorful turn of phrase, but it served its purpose. He knew that feeling. They all knew it.

"Okay, so you just nodded out," he said simply. "Your point is what? That these coldhearts drugged you in some way?"

The baron's laugh was cold and bitter, with no humor. "The whole ville? How would they make that happen?"

Ryan shrugged. "Could be easy enough, from what you say. Gather the whole ville together in one place, make like it's some kind of festival, and just spike whatever you're going to give them. Doesn't have to be anything mutie or some kind of weird shit."

"Doesn't have to be, but it probably was," K had said with a shrug.

Doc, at Ryan's elbow, indicated Morgan, who was seated by the baron. "I fear that perhaps you have been listening to your friend," he said in an amused tone.

Morgan glared at Doc. His eyes bore into him, and for a moment the scholar experienced a shiver of apprehension as it seemed that the grizzled old-timer was peering into his soul. Morgan smiled slowly and slyly.

"You know that I can't influence the baron in this matter, and you know that there are stranger things... what was it? On heaven and earth, Horatio, or something like that."

Doc looked uncomfortable. Yes, he knew that, but he was unwilling to accept at face value that K was right.

Maybe he was...

There was silence, broken eventually by the baron, who was hesitant as he tried to express what had happened, and what had led him to enlisting the outlanders on a task that he was so unwilling to undertake himself. Or to put his people at risk. When the outlanders had come their way, the ville folk had been suspicious. So soon after the ones who had stolen their young, it was remarkable that they had not chilled the newcomers on sight.

Yet there was something about the six people who had ridden into the ville in a battered wag that was on its last legs that set them apart from the ones who had come before.

"Listen, Ryan," K said carefully. "When they came, I should have read the signs. A bit of me did. But another bit of me couldn't do anything about it. Why the fuck was that? You tell me," he continued before the one-eyed man had a chance to speak. "All I know is that they did what they liked. In my ville. And then they took our kids. My kid," he said quietly, almost as an afterthought, but one that he deliberately downplayed. "I can't trust myself to follow them. I can't trust any of my people, much as I can any other time. This is…different."

"Then why us?" Ryan questioned.

K looked him squarely in the eye. "Because you haven't fallen under the spell. Because you're prepared…" He railed off, but seemed far from done.

"And?" Ryan said.

K shook his head. "Because you need the gold I'll give you for it."

Chapter Three

Ryan was the last one to take watch, and was still staring out across the wastes when the others had roused themselves and risen to join him.

Krysty walked over to him as he stood on the lip of the crevice, surer of his footing now that he could see the gaps between land and empty air.

"You see anything, lover?"

"Like what?" He turned and looked sharply at her. There was something about her tone that set his senses tingling.

She shrugged. "I don't know. Like a trace of where they went after they disappeared over the edge."

He said nothing for a moment, that single, ice-blue orb burrowing into her consciousness, probing that mind it knew so well. Finally, he said, "There are some tracks. They were careful, no doubt, but no one can be that careful. No one."

She nodded. "That's good."

"Something you want to tell me, mebbe?" he asked quietly. "About what you saw in the night?"

She grimaced. "I didn't see anything…not actually see…and I've got to be honest with you, lover, I didn't get so close. There was a way weird feel to it, and Jak…

Well, I don't really know what Jak saw, but it was something that wasn't just a bunch of coldhearts."

"This whole business has the ring of the macabre and mysterious about it," Doc announced, moving near and clapping his hands together as he did so. "I do so love a mystery, especially when knowledge of it could save my skin. It resembles some stories I used to read by a young man called Pope. Edgar Wallace Pope, as I recall. Liked a touch of the bizarre. A bit like these fellows we are chasing." Doc's tone, which had previously been jocular, now became somber, his voice lowering. "I really do think you and young Jak should share this with us, no matter how silly or odd you may feel about it."

"Doc's right," Mildred said, also coming near. "No matter how odd it is, even if it isn't spooky, the fact that they're making us feel like that means it's one of their weapons."

Jak had remained apart from the group, which had slowly clustered around Ryan. He was ruminative, as though weighing how to explain himself. He joined them, then. Looking away from them, he began. "Not sure how say. Deal with things in front you—hit man, chill mutie. Blades and bullets, know where are. Not with this. Shit scare kids with…didn't feel like that, though."

And so hesitantly, as the sun grew higher in the sky, Jak went on to outline how he had felt the previous night when he had tried to scan the dark, and how he had felt as though something was almost physically manhandling him. They listened in silenced until he had come to a halt almost as hesitantly as his beginning.

"Even if one does not believe in the supernatural," Doc said, "then there is the preternatural. There are powers of the mind that we have all felt, one way or the other. Indeed, our own dear Krysty is living testament to this. To suppose that there are others with a more enhanced power, who could strike fear in this way, is not such a leap. To purport to be an ancient evil as a means of clouding men's minds and gaining protection, that would be a simple expedient for such a power. I would venture to suggest that we proceed with nothing less than the utmost caution."

"I guess that goes without saying." Ryan grinned. Trust Doc to state the obvious, and in a way that used twenty words where one would do. But nonetheless, his central point remained valid. And as Ryan turned back to the narrow valley made by the crack in the earth, he knew that the people they were tailing had strengths that could put the companions on the last train west.

The fissure was unusual. It looked for all the world as though a fork of incredibly strong lightning had struck the earth and mined out a narrow and deep seam of soil. It was no more than fifteen yards across at its broadest point, the ledge that had nearly claimed him the night before being not so much an incursion into existing space as a curve in the trajectory of the seam, its width being the same even though the path suddenly changed. Now that they had good light they could see that it curved in a slow arc that took it beyond their view to the east and west. It was as if nature had decided to arbitrarily cut the earth in two, using this line as a crude division.

And yet there was something that was odd. At the edges of the horizon, where you would expect the curve to continue in a smooth arc, it suddenly seemed to cut sharply at an angle.

The Armorer had noticed that, and to his practiced eye there was something unnatural about the curve. Wordlessly, he took out his minisextant and took some readings by the newly risen sun. Then he sucked on his teeth, deep in thought.

"Something wrong, John?" Mildred asked.

"Could be," he said after a reflective pause. "This might sound crazy, but if you look at the distance between here and there, then there's no way we should be able to see those kinds of angles. What's more, where do they actually go?"

Ryan looked again. J.B. was right. The sharp bend in the fissure seemed to suddenly peter out into nothing before it finally hit the edge of the horizon.

"We'll follow the trail, such as it is, but we'll take it real slow," he said carefully. "There's something about this that's crazy, and not in a good way."

The path ahead of them seemed treacherous. The slope into the fissure was almost sheer, and it was deep. In places, it was so deep as to disappear into shadow. There were paths, but they were narrow and covered with shale. To try to descend them would take a sure-footed care that Ryan felt only Jak truly possessed. And yet the men they sought had made this descent with a bunch of children.

Was there another way? One they were missing? It certainly didn't seem so. Indeed, from the evidence of torn shrub and cleaned and skidded patches of shale, it would seem that there was a clearly defined route that they could follow.

"I'll take point," Ryan said. "Jak, you stay near the back, keep an eye on Doc."

Doc raised an eyebrow. "I feel somehow as though I should be insulted, my dear Ryan, and yet instead I feel a little reassured."

"More than I do, Doc," Ryan replied with a grin. "J.B., follow me and watch my back. If I go, grab me before it's too late."

The Armorer moved across Krysty so that he would follow Ryan down the path. To access it, they had to drop almost three yards onto a narrow ledge. Ryan looked over. It was no more than a yard wide, and while one side was sheer rock with only a few handholds, the other dropped off into space that was empty right down into shadow, the occasional jagged rock that broke the shadow being the only real indicator of depth.

"Here goes jackshit," he said with a sigh, gradually lowering himself over the edge until he was at full extension, his feet slipping on what little hold they could find, and his forearms taking the strain until he had to flatten his palms and let himself fall free a little way. He could feel the rough ground bite into his fingertips as they took his weight. With the pack that he carried, this wasn't inconsiderable, and as he took a breath, preparing himself for the next drop, he wondered how Doc and Mildred would cope. They were tough, but they weren't as physically strong as the others. With his head turned and his cheek pressed against the cold, dusty rock, he wondered if momentum would make any of them tumble back as they hit the ledge below, falling into space.

Fireblast, he thought. That was no way to think. Ryan spared himself one look down at the narrow ledge below, which seemed now to be too thin even to accommodate the length of his boots, before letting his fingers loose and feeling himself fall.

He scraped against the face of the rock, feeling it abrasive and hard against his skin. The uneven surface beneath his feet as they hit the ledge made him stumble and fall back. He put one heel back to steady himself, feeling it scrape the edge of the ledge and fall free into space. Barely able to take a breath, he thrust his torso forward so that he could equalize his balance, throwing himself into the rock, pulling that heel forward so that it was now on solid footing. For a second that felt like forever he held his breath in his lungs, feeling the blood thump around his arteries as he revelled in the fact that he had made it in one piece.

He stepped back as far as the ledge would allow and looked up. Above him, he could see the faces of the others, watching anxiously yet unable to do anything in the blinking of an eye that had yet seemed so long to him.

"Come on, we don't have time to waste." He grinned, making light of it.

Shrugging, J.B. slipped over the side and dropped down, allowing Ryan to steady him and so avoid the near disaster that the one-eyed man had faced. For Mildred and Doc, it was made easy by the assistance of Jak and Krysty up top, who aided them down to Ryan and J.B. Finally, when they were safely down, they pondered the way ahead.

The path was narrow and wound down into the valley formed by the crevice. Dark shadows enveloped it as it burrowed farther into the earth. Sparse scrub littered the rock-strewn pathway, and it was only this that marked the way taken by those they were following. It seemed a daunting path ahead. There was no indication of how much ground the other party had gained on them. Certainly, they were nowhere in sight.

The path wound down on a slight incline, moving into shadow. The companions started to walk along it, picking their way gingerly over the loose shale. The only consolation was that as the sun rose higher in the sky, they were in shadow and so protected from the worst ravages of the elements.

"How much distance do you think they've got on us?" Ryan muttered almost to himself. J.B., close on his heels as he had requested, sniffed ruminatively as he stared across the short yet infinitely deep space between one side and the other.

"I don't get it, Ryan. It feels all wrong. Never mind what Jak and Krysty were saying, thing is this—it was so bastard dark down here that there was no way they could have gotten that far in front of us before having to stop. Which means that down here, we should be able to at least catch sight of them. But where are they? They're nowhere I can see."

"No way they could have gotten across, either," Ryan mused. He stopped and looked into the darkness that seemed to swirl in the depths, having no real form. It was a disorienting experience and he quickly tore his vision away. "They must be in front."

"Yeah, well, they better not have gained that much distance," Mildred grumbled. "Or else they found some way off this path."

It was true. They had been walking on the narrow ledge for some time, and the lure of the endless drop to their right was calling to them, giving each the almost irresistible desire to throw themselves into the abyss. None would admit it, but it was all they could do to keep their vision focused on the shale path beneath and in front of them.

The call of the darkness grew stronger. Into each person's mind, unbidden, came a picture of what it would be like to throw himself or herself into the crevice. A despair at their progress swept across them like a wave. What point was there in going on when they couldn't see their prey? How far in front, how distant were they?

It was inevitable that, with this clouding their focus, one of them would stumble and fall. Almost as inevitable was that it would be one of the weakest of the group. And yet this was where fate had a surprise in store for them, for although Doc found his mind clouding, and his feet becoming heavy and cumbersome, it was J.B. who suddenly felt his combat boots slip on loose shale. Taken momentarily by surprise, he felt his leg shoot out from under him. He threw out an arm, grabbing instinctively for Ryan.

The one-eyed man felt J.B. pull on him, and he was thrown off balance. Beneath him, that which had once been solid was now almost fluid as it slid out from under his feet.

He heard Krysty and Mildred both yell, as he and the Armorer found themselves falling into space.

MORGAN WAS DOZING fitfully in the morning light as it penetrated the heavy covers over the windows of his hut. The fire had died down and was now little more than a few smoking embers and wisps of smoke, the smell of the sweet, burned wood permeating the room. The baron was hunkered down on the far side of the room, staring into the embers, lost in thoughts of his own. Since the moment the dark force had reached out and thrust him back, Morgan had been content to remain within himself. He might have had some small degree of power, but he knew that whatever was behind the people who had taken the children was far more powerful. Baron or not, he wouldn't risk going near it again. Tell K whatever he wanted to hear—make it up, if necessary. But he didn't want to feel that icy claw around his heart again.

"Don't hold out on me," K murmured without looking up.

Morgan looked across at the baron. Had K been watching him? Did he, in some way, have the power to see into the old man's mind? A power that he didn't, perhaps, even realize he had?

"Whatever you're seeing, I need to know. Even if you don't think it's what I want to hear. I won't hold you responsible. But I have to know."

I don't think you do, Morgan thought but wouldn't dare say.

Instead he said, "There's nothing to tell you. At the moment all is dark, as though there was some kind of blanket thrown over the glass."

K chuckled, albeit without humor. "You're speaking in riddles, Morgan. Don't do that. Speak plain."

"Very well." The old man sniffed. "There's some kind of power that's stopping me seeing clearly, but—"

"What is it?" K was electrified into sudden movement. With a speed that spoke of his strength, he moved from his haunches and across the room in one smooth movement, until he had Morgan's face in his hands. He was holding it up to whatever light he could find, trying to get a better view. For his part, the old man was making desperate gurgling sounds on the back of his throat, his eyes rolled up into his head so that only the whites showed, yellow and awful as the few shafts of light to penetrate the gloom caught them. Spittle rolled down his chin and into his beard.

"What is it? What is it, man? Tell me!" K roared, as if sheer volume would break through the barrier between them.

But Morgan couldn't answer. All intent of lying to the baron had been lost, and now all hope of soft-pedaling in an attempt to stay on the right side of the baron was also a cause that was given up. For Morgan had wanted to steer clear of the dark force that One-eye and his motley crew were pursuing. He wished them well, but he knew when he was facing something greater than he had ever believed existed. He didn't even care about the children. The ones he knew. Even the ones he cared about. Such was the fear that this dark power had instilled in him with one swoop.

Morgan wanted to steer clear, but the dark force wouldn't let him. It was almost as if it was sentient, seeking to use him as a tool, to scare the baron away from further pursuit.

Struggle as he might to deny it, Morgan was seeing what was happening to Ryan and his people. He hated it, for so many reasons.

But he couldn't deny it.

RYAN YELLED in anger and surprise. He was furious with the fates and with himself. He was certain that he had a sure footing, and that he would be able to take the weight of the Armorer as he reached out for him. It should have been simple to grab J.B. and stop him from falling. And yet the ground had seemingly given way beneath him, causing him to be dragged in the wake of his stricken friend. For the second time in less than twelve hours he felt that he was plunging to his doom, except that this time there was no one to stop him. Unlike the night before, the others were too far out of reach, being behind the Armorer as he was the first to take the plunge.

As he fell, weightless, in the air it seemed to him that he was falling at an infinitesimally slow rate. He felt as though he slowly turned in the air, away from the swirling and formless shadows below so that he could see the anguished faces of Doc, Mildred, Jak and particularly Krysty as they stared down, helpless. It was almost funny. They looked so ridiculous in that moment when Ryan knew even their pain and longing could no longer help him.

Maybe that was what did it. At that moment, when Ryan gave in to what he saw as his fate, and his inevitable end, it was as though he ceased to fall. He felt as though he was lying on static ground, as though J.B. was lying next to him. He turned his head and could see that the Armorer was level with him. Surely that wasn't right? Shouldn't J.B. have fallen first and been beneath him? The expression of bewilderment on his old friend's face told him that thoughts of a similar nature were crossing the Armorer's mind.

The others, looming over him, seemed to be closer than they had a moment ago. Too close. And the air, which had been whistling around his ears, now seemed so static and dry. Dusty, almost...

A blinding pain shot across his skull, running from the back of his neck, up and around so that it blinded his only eye, making him shut it tightly to try to stop the agony, which seemed as though it wanted nothing more than to take a physical form and force its way out through the socket.

He screamed.

And when he opened his eye once more, he was bemused to see that the others were, indeed, standing over him and J.B. Only instead of looking down at them, they were looking around.

Without even sitting up, he knew why. The hard-packed dirt was solid beneath him, and he could see from the periphery of his vision that they were on level ground. Level with where they had been before their descent. Raising himself on one elbow, he looked around. To his left, he could see the flat expanse of waste that they had trekked across the previous day. He recognized the scrub and rock they had used as landmarks to count off the miles.

They should be in the crevice.

But it was no longer there.

More than that, to his right, where there had previously been only the flat lands that stretched on the other side of the crevice, there was now a wall of rock that stood about forty yards high, on a steep incline, about three miles away. It was like an inversion of the crevice.

And maybe it was just as real?

"I don't know what just happened, and to be honest I don't really give a shit how. The real question is, what can we do about it?"

Ryan turned to the Armorer, who was sitting up, his arms clasped around his knees as he surveyed the territory. The laconic wryness of his tone belied the real urgency of his question.

"Keep going," Ryan answered simply. "I figure that we really were seeing them in the distance, and when they disappeared it wasn't down a nonexistent hole. It was behind some kind of wall they could put up mentally. Something that could get inside our heads."

"Curiouser and curiouser," Doc murmured. "Down

the hole and out of sight. Make something grow smaller and then make it grow bigger. Is it really that way or does it just seem to be that way?"

"Not make sense." Jak spit. "Have to go like real, then see. Just be ready for any shit."

"Looks that way," Krysty said slowly. "That crap that Jak and me were feeling last night… Mebbe that's the mechanism they use, a kind of super doomie power that can play on our fears."

"How know what scare us?" Jak questioned.

"Maybe it doesn't have to know us." Mildred shrugged. "Anyone getting this far would be exhausted, so a deep drop and a narrow path would be daunting. Like that wall is going to be bastard to climb," she added, indicating the distant barrier, which seemed to stretch across the horizon.

"Can't be that hard if it doesn't exist." J.B. shrugged.

Mildred laughed shortly. "Still hurt like hell to get down that nonexistent drop, didn't it? Wonder what we would have looked like to anyone watching as we went down an imaginary drop?"

"No more stupe than we'll look climbing an imaginary mountain," Ryan replied. "But if that's what we have to do—"

"That is if it truly is imaginary," Doc interjected. "There is, of course, the possibility that the abyss was a dream, yet the mountain is real. The one a mask for the other."

"You know, we could talk about that all day," J.B. said quietly, spitting on the ground in disgust at their impotence. "We're not really going to know one way or the other, even when we reach it. But one thing I can tell you for sure is this—the longer we stand around, the farther those coldheart bastards get from us, and the harder it's going to be to get the kids back and get our jack."

The Armorer was right. If they intended to finish their mission, they had little option but to continue regardless. And so they started forward again, in silence, hearts and limbs heavy, and all the time knowing that this was exactly the frame of mind that the clouding of their reality had been intended to produce.

Just how hard was it going to be if they had to fight on two planes simultaneously: the mental and the physical?

MORGAN'S EYES flickered, then rolled back into their usual position. He was surprised to find himself being cradled by the baron, and even more surprised by the distant look in the man's eyes. It was as though the hardened baron was a million miles away.

And then, as if suddenly noticing that the old man had come to, and not wanting to give anything away, the baron's worried mien suddenly hardened into its usual mask.

"What did you see, old man? Tell me," the baron snapped in a harsh voice. It was unnecessarily abrupt, and despite his best intent couldn't entirely hide the anxiety he felt.

Despite his own fear, exacerbated by the sudden intrusion of the visions he didn't want to see, Morgan felt a pang of pity for the baron. K wasn't a man he would have ever thought that he could have sympathy for, and yet he could see that the man had a… A what? A weakness? Was it a weakness to have feelings for your own flesh and blood? Perhaps it was if you were a hard-fighting and hard-fought leader of a ville. So, despite the stubborn streak of his nature that told Morgan to tell the baron to get fucked, in spite of any consequences, he took a deep breath and started to speak.

It was halting and confused as he tried to explain in words the things that he had seen and felt primarily as a series of impressions and emotions, but as he went on the baron's face changed yet again. He was absorbed by what the old man was telling him. It confirmed his worst fears about the powers of those who had taken the children. At the same time, it boosted his self-esteem. At the back of his mind, still there despite the fears for his own child, was the lurking fear that his judgment had somehow been in error when he allowed these events to happen. But after all, if a man of Morgan's undoubted doomie sensibility was easy meat to whatever was behind the intruders, then no one could hold him responsible and use that fact to challenge his position.

By the time the old man had finished, the baron had moved back and away, and was hunkered against the wall of the shack, elbows resting on his knees and chin in his hands as he focused on the story. Morgan, for his part, had moved in the opposite direction and had wiped the spittle from his beard. He turned to the barrel where he kept his own personal brew and scooped out a mugful that he downed in one swallow.

K didn't see it that way. As soon as he saw what the old man was doing, he sprang across the room, swiping the mug from the old man's fist in one smooth and swift motion.

"No," he yelled, "you're not doing that. I want you sober and awake so that you can tell me what's happening."

Mutely, Morgan followed the progress of the mug as it flew across the room, its tin body clanging as it hit the boards of the cabin floor, the fire hissing and flaring as a spray of alcohol swept across it like an incoming wave. He turned back to K and looked him squarely in the eye. When he spoke, it was with a hushed gravity that made the baron look away uneasily.

"You idiot. Do you really think that those poor bastards are going to be able to get your daughter back? You don't give a shit about the other kids. Why the fuck should you? Their parents wouldn't care squat about your kid, after all. But you should give it up, K. She's gone. And no amount of making me face going mad seeing what it can do and letting it get inside my head is going to make any bastard difference. Not one little bit. They're as good as chilled. And so is your daughter. The sooner we face it, the better. Whatever the fuck those coldheart bastards were who took her and the others, they weren't human. Mebbe once. Before whatever it's that makes the black fist got hold of them and changed them forever. Mebbe they still have some kind of humanity in them. But if they have, it's so buried that there ain't no way it's ever going to find a way out.

"Face it, K, she's gone. You lost. We all did. And those poor fuckers you sent after them with the promise of gold? They're gone, too."

Chapter Four

Doom. An overwhelming sense of it; a kind of despondency that weighed heavily and seemed to bodily add to any kind of forward momentum so that every step was a task that seemed almost beyond accomplishment.

So it was that they trudged across the hard and hollow earth toward the tower of rock that stood in front of them. It stretched across their vision in the same way that the crevice had but a short time before, and even appeared to curve at the same oblique and impossible angle as it reached the periphery of vision.

Each of them knew that it was an illusion. As they walked in silence they told themselves that, repeating it internally like some kind of mantra. It should have helped to reinforce the knowledge, and perhaps see the illusion crumble in front of their eyes. Yet the edifice remained solid to all appearances.

Krysty, who was the only one of them possessed of the kind of mutated sense that was in any way a match for the mind or minds that had created the wall, felt a despair that was unlike anything that she had ever known. It was more than just the sense that the illusion in front of them was stronger than they could defeat. It was as though the mind itself that had created this was thrusting tendrils into her own consciousness, attempting to find her weak spots and probe at her feelings and memories. To find out more about those who were approaching, perhaps? She wondered if the others were feeling this, or if it was something that was her own experience because of her mutie blood.

If it was her alone, then she had to be strong. She tried to think of anything that could blot it out and block the tendrils of despair with a wall of memory that was designed to combat the negativity. Back where she came from, in Harmony ville, those with the mutie strain and those without had always worked to further their own positivity, and she drew on these lessons.

But the toll on her was great, and the effort it demanded caused her to walk at a slower pace, and to fall back until she was lagging behind the others. Such was their own burden that they didn't, at first, notice. It was only when they were within a spit of the seemingly impenetrable rock face that Ryan turned back and noticed. He rushed toward her.

"Krysty, what…?"

She shook her head, flame-red tendrils of hair hugging the contours of her face. "Can't you feel it?"

"What?"

The woman smiled grimly. So it was just a mutie thing. She tried to explain, but the words came out halting and vague. It was like trying to capture a wisp of smoke borne away on the breeze. If she had but known it, she wasn't the only one having such problems in explaining what was happening to her.

"Can you shut it out for long?" Ryan asked with a calm he didn't feel. He was worried for Krysty, sure.

But he had the others to think of, too, and the safety of all his people was at threat unless she gave an honest answer.

Her twisted grin—half humor and half agony—was all the answer he needed.

"I can try, but every second is a battle. And I don't think I can win the war, Ryan."

He nodded grimly. "I know we're exhausted, people, but we need to get past this obstacle as soon as we can."

"For what, I wonder?" Doc mused. "Just what lies on the other side? Is it worth our effort, or should we perhaps just leave well enough alone and turn away? After all, do we really need the money?"

As he spoke, he could feel the waves of pressure recede slightly, so negligible as to barely be noticeable, and yet it piqued his curious nature, and he got to his feet and walked toward the rock.

"Perhaps it would be best if we just gave this up as a bad lot and walked away from it, maybe head off in another direction altogether," he continued with all the conviction he could muster.

Krysty, who had been kneeling as she tried to gather her strength, leaned forward. "Ryan, look."

Doc was walking toward the rock face as he spoke, and the sheer wall seemed suddenly to shimmer in front of him. For a moment, it became semitransparent. As though through a veil, they could see flat land beyond. A land that seemed to extend beneath a wall of rock that was, bizarrely, still there.

To each of them, it was apparent—if not clear why— that the rock wall was little more than an illusion, and one that it would now be easy to simply walk through as though it wasn't there. It was as if the consciousness that had created it was somehow impeded or lessened when they considered turning back.

Which, Ryan figured, kind of made sense if the mind behind this was building it as a defense. Why waste the energy it needed if the enemy was no longer a threat? Suppose it could see inside their heads, but had no way of physically seeing what they were doing? If it only locked onto consciousness, then perhaps it might be able to fool it for long enough to pass through.

Ryan stood and followed Doc on his steady progress toward the shimmering rocks. "Fireblast, we don't need this crap, Doc! You're right, mebbe it's about time we gave this shit up as a bad idea. It's not our fight, after all."

Krysty held back, unwilling to enter the fray as her psyche might betray the actions that Ryan and Doc were seeking to further. Mildred and J.B. looked on, uncertain as to how either of them would stand up to such scrutiny of conviction. But while they hesitated, for their own reasons, Jak walked forward to join Doc and Ryan.

"Screw this shit. Say we get fuck out, leave 'em to it," Jak agreed, his impassive visage giving away nothing of the inner turmoil as he sought to convince himself that he should walk away from a fight. It was something that he had never done, and in truth he had no intention of doing so now. Whatever had constructed the illusion of the rock wall didn't have to know that, though.

The three men advanced on the rock, their self-imposed conviction making the opaque now transparent.

Doc was the first to the surface that now shimmered and flickered like a light that was defective, there and gone in a strobe that was as fast as the blink of an eye. He indicated to the other two that they should stay, as with his other hand he stretched out and tried to touch the surface.

It gave in front of him like a pool of liquid that inexplicably remained on the vertical plane without flowing over him. His hand penetrated the surface without the kind of rippling that he might expect, for although it looked like an illusion of light, it felt as though he was actually plunging his hand into a wall of fluid. There was some resistance and give, and it felt as though the light was flowing and closing around his hand like a dense, viscous fluid.

"We cannot head back to Baron K and tell him that we have reneged on his mission," Doc said calmly. "I guess we shall have to proscribe a pretty big circle if we are going to avoid him on the way back, seeing as we'll be without his precious cargo."

As he spoke, he could feel the fluid grow lighter around his hand and arm. He was able to penetrate it with greater ease. Past the elbow now, and it seemed to be giving him less resistance with each moment. He had almost convinced himself that they would be turning back, so it was little wonder that the so-called rock was giving way. Indeed, so much had Doc convinced himself in his quest to break down the illusion that he had to remind himself to actually move forward: first one foot, then another, so that he was moving within the confines of the illusory rock face.

A moment of panic almost overwhelmed him as the strange semisubstance of the illusion hit his face. It was like plunging his head into a pool of molasses, thick and gloopy, sticking his hair to his head yet not actually making him wet. It felt dry and hot against his skin, which seemed the opposite of how it should feel, and for a second that panic was reinforced by the sudden fear that he may not be able to breathe. Yet, despite the feeling of being closed in by this elusive thing that was not, he was still able to suck air into his lungs. Dry and hot, but still oxygenated.

Doc felt confidence well in him as he took in a breath. He had it beaten, and he would be able to get through to the other side with ease. If he could do it, then that should break the illusion and allow the others—even Krysty—to follow with ease.

And yet, paradoxically, even as he thought this he knew that it was a major mistake. If whatever powered this illusion fed on their received thoughts to know how much power to put into the defense, then to think such a thing was to reveal that it was being deceived. And that way lay disaster.

Even as these thoughts flashed across his mind, he felt the illusion start to regain a kind of solidity that swiftly passed beyond the point it had been fixed upon when his hand first pushed into it. Now it passed from feeling like a dry mist around him to being like molasses again, and then to a state where it was more alarming. It began to increase in pressure around him, constricting his chest and making breath hard to take—not that this mattered, as the hot dry air became like dust that began to choke in his lungs. He felt his arms and legs become encased in something that was, bizarrely, both clinging and also hard around him. It stopped him from moving back to where the others were watching in mute and frozen horror. He could feel that, although it was impossible to see as he was now unable to turn his head.

Around him, the sky and land beyond the end of the illusory wall, which had previously been clear through the transparent and fading defense, was now disappearing as the air around him grew gray, shot through with red streaks of iron ore and sandstone as the rock started to attain the consistency of the land that it sought to copy. Even this was soon lost to him as the opacity grew to such a degree that it began to block out any light around him.

What would be worse? To choke on the air that had become dust, or to be unable to take breath because of the rock that hardened around you so that your chest was constrained, and the space around your mouth and nostrils became filled with the hard substance, allowing no breath to be taken, or even that which remained in your lungs to be expelled, so that they felt like they were exploding?

Perhaps it was the panic of the situation that flung Doc into such a place, but he felt strangely calm as he pondered this fate. If he was going to buy the farm this way, it would at least give him a conundrum in which to pass his last few remaining seconds.

But if Doc had resigned himself to his fate, the same couldn't be said of his companions. For a moment they were all frozen to the spot, stunned at what they were seeing. The rock seemed to darken and take shape around the old man, encasing him and gradually becoming more opaque so that his shape was becoming lost within it. It seemed absurd and terrible at the same time. The rock itself didn't exist, they were sure of that. And yet the mental construct that had formed it seemed to be so strong and vital in its force that it made the intangible solid to the extent that it had the physical force of the real thing.

It was Jak who snapped out of this trance first. The albino teen's hunting and survival instincts kicked in, overriding the shock that had momentarily stopped him dead. Without a word, he sprang forward, plunging himself into the rock.

Why it worked, he had no idea. In fact, the question didn't even occur to him. Jak didn't hesitate. And maybe that was the crux of the matter. He didn't give the construct a thought. Someone put it in his mind, and it wasn't really there. The logical knot that it was seemingly so solid as to be trapping Doc didn't matter. All that mattered was getting the old man out.

Jak felt the rock yield against him only with protest. It was like trying to push heavy rocks out of the way, yet these were rocks that had no edges. It was as though the sheet of solid rock in front of him moved and ground around the force of his momentum, yet didn't break up into rubble. He felt the pressure against his face and chest, closing his nostrils and constricting him. But where Doc had given in to this and accepted it, Jak wouldn't.

It couldn't be doing this, as it wasn't there. Simple as that.

This clear thinking seemed to have an effect on the illusion that the albino youth couldn't have foreseen. In truth, he didn't even notice it, so focused was he on his task. Pushing aside the hardness of the rock with what was little more than an effort of will, he reached out until he grasped Doc's shoulder. He shouldn't have been able to do that, as the rock was encircling the old man's form, and yet he felt the soft cloth of Doc's frock coat beneath his fingers. He clamped them down hard and pulled on the old scholar, to spin him.

Doc felt the hand and was puzzled. A hand through rock? Surely that wasn't possible. He was shocked more than any other emotion when he felt himself turn in what was, to him, a solid coffin, only to find that Jak's face was in front of his own. Bizarrely, and in a way that he couldn't explain, it seemed to merge with the rock that should have been there.

Dr. Theophilus Tanner was a man who was no stranger to madness. He recognized it. In the same way, as strange as this situation was, he knew that it was not insanity. On the contrary, it made perfect sense. His own belief in the power of the intelligence that created this illusion was now helping it to keep up that very thing. As a result, the only way for it to end, and for him to be saved, was…

"Hit me," he said to Jak. It came out cracked and barely audible, but it was enough. Jak looked into Doc's eyes, and even if he couldn't phrase exactly what he saw, he grasped it on an instinctive level. He pulled back his free hand and hit out. Even with the resistance, real or imagined, that the rock provided, he was still able to muster enough power to connect with Doc's jaw hard enough for it to make the lights go out behind Doc's eyes. The whites showed as they rolled up into his head, and he slumped toward the ground.

A ground that was now solid and unencumbered by the illusion of a wall of rock. It was as if, without Doc's belief—a belief that he had tried his hardest to deny but had, paradoxically, only reinforced by so doing—the intelligence that had formed the defense had nothing on which to build.

Ryan whistled softly. He turned and looked around at the other three, who were a few yards behind him. Krysty was still hunkered on the ground, while J.B. and Mildred had huddled together, perhaps unconsciously. Their eyes were fixed at a point beyond him; beyond even where Jak stood over Doc's inert frame, bending over him in solicitation now that the necessary force had been exerted.

Beyond the area where the rock wall had seemingly been, there was an expanse of bare and arid land, scorched and blasted by the hot winds of the nuke-caust and still enough of a hot spot for little other than some shriveled shrub to have prospered in the intervening years. And beyond this, where the land rose slightly in level until it formed a ragged lip, there was another chasm. It was a deep, wide split in the earth that extended for hundreds of yards. The shadowed contour of the rock face forming the far wall of the chasm could be plainly seen. It was a gash in the earth that ran in an irregular line, widening and then narrowing along its path. Unlike the earlier illusion, this had the random look of nature, and didn't veer off at strange angles from the periphery of vision. Unlike the previous chasm, and the mountainous wall, this had dust disturbed in eddies and whorls by the air currents that were stirred by the depths of what was, Ryan was certain, a canyon.

And, with a sinking feeling in his gut, he could have sworn he knew which one.

"Is that one real?" J.B. asked hesitantly.

Ryan swallowed the bile that rose in his throat and nodded.

"Yeah, that one's the real deal."

There was something in his tone that made Mildred look at him askance. "You sound certain," she murmured.

"Makes sense now," he said cryptically, shrugging. "I never really believed all those stories, but the look of that…and what's happened to us."

"Mancos Canyon," Krysty said softly. "I'd always figured that those stories were just that…not that there was any truth in them."

Jak turned back so that he was facing her. His brow was furrowed.

"Stories?" he queried.

"I fear I am with you on this one," Doc agreed. "You

speak of these as though they are common knowledge. Perhaps to you. But not to everyone."

"Sorry, Doc," Ryan said absently. "It's just that they were the kinds of tales that you spin around the fire at night, on watches, to stop yourself falling asleep unless you wanted nightmares."

J.B. walked past the one-eyed man and looked to the split in the earth that lay in front of them. He took off his fedora and scratched his head, lost for a moment in thought. Then, without looking around, he said, "Mancos, eh? Rumors have always swirled about that place."

Doc was becoming a little exasperated, and it was reflected in his tone. "This is all very well, but if there is some legend attached to this place that may, perhaps, have some bearing on what we are about to face, then I think that you should tell those of us who are not privy to the knowledge. It would, after all, help."

"I don't know if you could dignify it with the word *legend*," Krysty began reflectively. "The region got blasted in the nukecaust. So hot that no one could go near it for generations. But along the way there were those who wandered off the tracks and ended up here. Now mebbe you'd think that anyone who did that would end up as shriveled as an old man's dick that had been left out in the sun too long. If you did, then you'd be wrong. Most who disappeared into this region were never seen again. Those who were, well, when they were seen again, those who knew them said they were…different."

The way in which she let that last word hang in the

air made Mildred shiver. Different in what way? she wondered. More to the point was another thought, to which she gave voice.

"So you're telling me that we're headed into an area that is full of nukeshit still, and from which people either don't come back, or if they do they're not even recognizable to their friends?"

"Something like that," Krysty said in a tone that managed to be both flat and grim at the same time.

Mildred whistled. "Sounds like we're in for a real fun time."

"Quite," Doc added quickly. "But I think the real question for me is, in what way changed? Are we to expect that we will become in some way infected by radiation and covered with sores and distortion of the features? Or will we somehow develop some kind of mutation?"

"Like the ones that you think nearly caused you to buy the farm?" Krysty countered. There was an edge of hostility in her voice. "You think that because it's evil then it must be mutie traits? You think that's why these people—the ones who were seen again—were so changed?"

"My dear, I do not know," Doc said mildly. "That is the sole reason that I ask. Being mutie is not itself a bad thing. You must surely know me well enough by now to know that I would not countenance such a thought. But it would require a kind of power that is only possessed by those who are muties to achieve the things we have seen."

Krysty gave a short, barking laugh. "Guess you're

right about that, Doc. Mebbe that's why I'm getting so bastard defensive. Doomie sense is one thing, but this is more than that. Far more."

Mildred had moved forward so that she was standing next to J.B. "So what was it about those who returned that had changed?" she asked.

Krysty thought about that for a moment before answering.

"They had a darkness all around them. Not just in the way that their attitude to people they had known had changed. They seemed to relate to everything and everyone in a different manner. Even dogs didn't like them. Come to think of it, that's a good way to describe it. It was like they looked at those around them in the same way that everyone else looked at dogs."

"Another step up the evolutionary ladder, another link in the evolutionary chain," Doc mused almost to himself. "That is an interesting idea. Before the proliferation of fools tampering with nukes, and then the nukecaust itself did nothing more than prove the random nature of nature itself, there was an idea that those who had what we call mutie powers were some kind of preliminary breakthrough to the next step of humanity. So maybe, if those who wander this way survive and are changed by that which lies ahead of us now, maybe they feel that kind of superiority."

"I'll tell you what really worries me," Mildred added softly. "What if the reason they think that is because someone or something is telling them that? Where does that leave us?"

"Up to our necks in shit," Ryan stated succinctly. "That wouldn't be the first time."

"You know, we can sit here and wonder all we want, but the only way we're really going to find out is if we go and have a look for ourselves," J.B. said with a faraway tone that was reflective of the way in which he was looking to the horizon, and the gaping maw that split the land in front of it.

Ryan shrugged. His old friend was right, of course. They began the march toward what they hoped would be a real answer to all the questions that were bubbling inside them.

One thing was obvious from the start: whatever intelligence had been working on them, and however it had worked, that was now at an end. The land where the illusory rock carapace had stood was proof enough of this on its own. Where the land that had led up to it had seemed smooth and unmarked, now they could see that the land behind them was marked with tracks that were obviously other than their own—obvious because they now stretched across the space that had seemingly been taken up by rock before, and beyond that across the land leading toward the lip of the canyon.

J.B. looked up at the sky. There was some cloud cover, but it was high and thin, barely more than a haze in places. And hardly moving as it drifted slowly across the scorching sun. Down below, where they wearily and warily trudged across the hard-packed dirt, there was no movement at all in the air. It was still. Perhaps it had been that way for most of the time since the first scouring winds of skydark had cleared the land and left it to chill. Then, as his eyes scanned from the skies down to ground level, he could see the immutable proof of the land's still nature. The ground ahead of them was crisscrossed by trails. Some were made by human feet, others by the hooves of pack animals. Although it took a moment for the fact to sink in, he also realized that there were no wag or bike traces among the paths that had been trudged across the loose dirt. Maybe that said that the way down into the canyon—where, presumably, some kind of life was possible—was too narrow and precarious for such luxuries.

One thing was for sure: the tracks had been made over a long period of time. There was a massive amount of overlap, where one trail was crossed, often many times, by others. Some were ground deep into the dirt, impacted by repetition so that they ran deeper. But as the land around here was so arid, none seemed to have been baked into mud. Instead, they rested precariously on loose soil that should have made them things of an ephemeral nature. Their longevity said much for the bizarre conditions of the region.

And now they were adding to them. It would be simple for anyone to see where they had been, and where they were going, if they wanted to follow in their wake. But even as the thought occurred to Ryan, he realized that not only was there no place to hide out here on the flat, but whoever lived in the canyon would already know of their presence either because they had been alerted by the defenses…or because they were the defenses.

It was a chilling thought that they were walking

toward an enclosed space and people who were most probably aware of their presence, people who had cover while the companions were out in the open.

Perhaps it was his preoccupation with those thoughts that made the distance between where they had started and the lip of the canyon seem to pass by in less than the blink of an eye. Maybe, too, they had increased their pace with the knowledge that they were now within sight of their prey. For there was little doubt that the party they had been pursuing had descended into the canyon. There was a trail that they could follow plainly. It ran from the path that they, themselves, had traversed, and carried on ahead. The number of feet that had impressed upon the land was consistent—the children of the ville, and the men who had taken them.

J.B. thought about what Baron K had told them about the men who had come into the ville: how they had acted, how they had conspired to move themselves into a position where they were able to take the children with no resistance from the men and women of a ville that was renowned for its hard-bitten fighters. He suppressed a shudder at what Ryan had agreed for them to take on. It would have been hard enough to tackle them at any point on the route, let alone to follow them into their own territory.

His mind was still mulling that over when the companions reached the lip of the canyon. The strata of rock spinning away below them into the shadows were layered in geometric patterns that were awesome in their precision. The shadows, too, were layered in this way as shards of light caught on gleaming stone.

Yet that wasn't what immediately caught the eye. Certainly, it was something even more awesome— and yet completely apposite and bizarre—that caused Krysty to gasp, "Gaia, it's beautiful."

Mildred smiled wryly. "Yeah, but it's got trouble written all over it."

Chapter Five

Baron K was thoughtful as he left Morgan. The old man had recovered, but had been more taciturn than usual. After his outburst, he had refused to be drawn on what he had seen in his vision state. Even the direst threats that the baron could make—worse than chilling, the torture that preceded but stopped short all the time, suspending him on the edge of oblivion without ever taking the plunge—couldn't shift him from his silence.

That disturbed K more than anything. If anyone knew what he was capable of, then it was the old man. Trusted lieutenants came and went without much in the way of trust when you were a baron, but someone like Morgan—a seer whose insights were important, and whose cache with a sometimes disgruntled populous could never be an underestimated tool—was an invaluable ally, and as such would be privy to things that it was best others didn't know. Morgan had seen the worst of the baron, and he knew to what lengths K would go to achieve his aims. The old man had been smart in the past, and had known when to counsel and when to shut up and nod. Never had he been so—what was the word?—defiant.

Whatever the old man had seen, it had frightened him so much that he was prepared to incur the wrath of his baron rather than relive it. For it wasn't as if he didn't want to speak. It was stronger than that. It was as though to just speak what he had seen would bring it all flooding back in such a way that would drive him into the abyss of insanity.

K mused that he could make the old man talk. That would be easy. Everyone had his or her point of no return, after which their tongues would be loosened no matter what their threshold and their tolerance to pain.

But what would that achieve? Did he really want to hear whatever it was that Morgan had seen?

He reached his palace. His wasn't a rich ville, and in truth his home was only a palace in relation to the hovels that the rest of the population had for homes. K may be the ruler of this land, but it was a poor land in relation to much of the rest of the wasteland. The soil was poor for farming and the keeping of livestock, and much of the food they had came about as a result of trade. Not that they had much to trade with. When K had arrived here, it was a ville that was on the verge of extinction. Now it was barely alive and breathing. But it was there, crawling and scratching its way to some hope of prosperity.

It might not be much, but it was K's own. He had built it from nothing, and intended to keep it that way. To do so he had flexed considerable muscle. So it was that Morgan's defiance shook him on more than one level. It wasn't just the refusal, so out of character. It was also the fact that it reinforced that which he had been unwilling to face: his own uselessness in the face of this enemy. Rather than go after them himself, he had been more than happy—no, *relieved* was a better word if he was honest—to let the one-eyed man and his band of mercies go after the children. Even though his own daughter—the one thing he prized more than his own existence—was among the ones taken.

The one thing that K had never been—the only thing that his detractors couldn't hold against him—was a coward. Yet that was how he felt. He could try to explain it to himself in many ways: he couldn't leave his people at this time; he couldn't risk his best men and leave the ville undefended; he was sending the one-eyed man and his mercies as a scouting party for the real raid. No matter how he dressed it up, that sickness in the pit of his stomach remained. It was a sickness that was in part his own loathing of not going after the bastards in person and in part a dread admission of his own fear.

He waved away the servant who came to him as he went through the tarnished and barely disguised squalor of the old house that was his base. It was the largest and best preserved. That wasn't saying much when you looked at the rest of the buildings around, though. The ville was built around the remains of a small settlement that had serviced some nearby attraction for visitors on the days before skydark. That much was clear from the remains of an old display that took up part of the wing at the rear of his palace. That part remained unused, although at times he had gone in there and by lamplight had mused at the landscape described by the faded pictures and broken models that littered the unused rooms. Had the land around really looked like that? Shit, it had been so green. Just his bastard luck to come along when it was a dust desert.

The servant hurried away. Baron K wasn't a man to be disturbed when he was in a sour mood, even if it was a matter of great importance. In truth, nothing seemed that important to any of them since the incident involving the children.

K settled down to brood. Maybe he would find some answers as to why he had done nothing. Worse, as to why he hadn't even seen it coming at him like a bastard great bullet aimed between the eyes.

He started to think back to how it had begun....

"SIX OF THE BASTARDS, all weird as fuck, coming from out of the chill zone."

K stopped chewing on the stringy leg of mule that was marinated in grease and a few herbs. Food was never great in the ville, but at least his cook made an effort. She was better than most, and he could put up with her cooking as long as she gave him a blow job after the meal. There had to be something going for her. He could be an indulgent baron. And it had been the thought of this that had been occupying his mind while Higgins spoke. He hadn't, if he was honest, been giving the sec man his full attention.

The last sentence had caught his attention, though, and made him look up from the plate. He laid the shank down in its thin sauce and wiped his mouth with the back of a hand. Not that he gave a crap about manners, but it gave him a couple of moments to marshal his thoughts.

"The chill zone," he repeated in a flat tone. "But no one lives there."

Higgins shrugged. He was a big man, about six-four and 280 pounds, most of it muscle and a lot of it in his head. But he was loyal and—most important of all in the circumstances—he was just too damn stupe to lie. If that was what he'd seen, then that was what he'd seen, no matter how strange or even impossible it might seem.

K got up from the table and walked around to where the sec man stood. As he passed him, he clapped him on the shoulder. "Come on, Higgy, this I've gotta see."

Higgins grunted and nodded as he fell in behind his baron. He'd been a little nervous about reporting to K. When the eastern sector patrol had come back in on their mounts just before sunset and reported the distant group coming across the flatlands on foot, he hadn't been inclined to believe it, either.

Higgins had fallen in with K somewhere out midwest, when the two men had been mercies for hire. Higgins was a follower, not a leader, and had recognized the leader in K. All leaders need good, reliable muscle as backup, and so Higgins had made the decision to be K's right hand. It saved him having to think, which was something he wasn't good at. But by the same token, he wasn't a complete stupe. He wouldn't have stayed alive so long if he was. One of the first things that he had learned when he followed K to this pesthole and taken it over was that the lands to the east were beyond all life. No birds flew over them. No animals that you'd want to sink your teeth into, or meet on a dark night, lived on them. And no people. Sure, he'd heard the stories of those who had wandered out there and come back…different. But as he'd never actually met one of those people, or even anyone who could actually have claimed to have met one rather than just heard about it, he didn't believe it for a second. Just as he never gave more than that second's thought to what was out there. What the land looked like—shit, it could be flat, dead and dusty between here and the sea for all he cared, as long as he didn't have to go on it.

So when he figured that he should check it out before reporting to K, he felt fear in the pit of his stomach. It took a lot to shake it off.

He took his horse out slowly, and beat the bastard raw to get back quick. There were six men, of differing shapes and sizes, and they were coming toward the ville on foot.

As he followed the baron out on horseback once more, he felt the unease of a person who really didn't want to be doing what he was right then. But he had to lead K to them, make him see for himself.

They rode heavily across the dry and dusty earth for twenty minutes, raising clouds into the skies above them. There was no need for subterfuge, as it was plain that if they could see the oncoming party, then that party would have no trouble seeing them.

Visual contact was made after twenty minutes. That made them about seven miles out of the ville. Even in the fading light of evening, there was still enough visibility for the distant party to be a good five or more miles away. That would give K enough time to work out what to do.

He pulled his horse up, signaling to Higgins to do the same.

"What do you figure?" he asked. "It'll take them a good few hours to reach us. Gives us time."

"Plenty," the sec man agreed. "They ain't much farther on than when I last saw them. Whoever they are, they ain't rushing."

K looked ruminatively up at the twilight skies. The sun was now sinking, but even so it still burned in a sky that was devoid of all but the briefest of cloud cover. It had to have been bastard hot on that sunbaked earth. And they would have been marching all day. There was nothing before the horizon that could have given them cover, or from where they could have come.

The baron scanned the oncoming party: two of them were tall, one skinny and one a whole lot fatter—a lot like Higgy, he thought with a wry grin—and the skinny one looked like he was carrying something on his back that towered over his head, making him seem even more angular and accentuated. The other four were all around medium height, and three of them were stocky and not remarkable in any way. At least, not at this distance.

But that left one. And he was one weird-looking bastard, the baron thought, even as little more than a dot on the horizon. He was immensely fat, and seemed to walk with a rolling gait that made him look as though he was about to topple over with every step. It was only the momentum of perpetually falling that kept him moving forward. In fact, the only thing that seemed to keep him on his feet was the walking stick that seemed to extend from his hand like some kind of weird antenna, its point raising puffs of dust as it hit the ground. He walked slightly apart from the others, and K couldn't be sure if that was because he was the leader, or because the others didn't want anything to do with him.

He'd find out soon enough, but his instinct was already telling him which supposition was the answer.

"What are we gonna do, boss?" Higgins asked. He didn't really want to prompt K, or to push him. He knew what he was like, and a more irritable bastard you couldn't work under when that happened. Even so, the creeping fear in his gut was pushing him. He didn't want to stay here, and he'd be a whole lot happier when they got back to the ville, and safety in numbers.

K didn't answer for a moment. His instincts were telling him to go back, get a bunch of men and come back shooting. There was a pall of menace that hung over the distant group. And yet, even as his instincts yelled at him, another voice within him was telling him that they were just a bunch of people, too few in number to be a menace to his well-organized ville.

K pulled his horse around. "Let's get back and run up a little welcoming committee. Put the men on triple red around the perimeters, get the people ready, and we'll come back to meet them with six men at our backs. Armed."

Higgins grinned mirthlessly through cracked and stained teeth. That was exactly what he wanted to hear.

He pulled his horse around and took off in the wake of the baron.

They reached the ville to find that word of the men coming from the chill zone had spread like a disease among the people. Despite being told by Higgins to keep it to themselves until he had returned with the baron, the sec party that had made the discovery had found it hard to keep it to themselves, and the itching sense of excitement and unease that they felt at their discovery had soon spread among the ville folk. Most of the people in the ville had lived in the region their entire lives, as had their ancestors. More than K and Higgins, they knew that the chill zone was an area where life was almost extinct. What sort of men could come from there, or even just walk across its unknown length and stay in one piece?

It was a mark of the power wielded by K that he was able to silence the throng that had gathered around his palace. Briefly, he told them what he had seen, and just what he intended to do about it, ordering his sec teams into action around the ville while picking out half a dozen men to accompany Higgins and himself. He sent the team to get weapons from the armory he kept to one side of the palace, and directed the rest of the populace to form defenses. Even as he was doing this, a part of his mind was nagging at him. Wasn't this an overreaction to what was, when all was said and done, just half a dozen men on foot? Men who would doubtless also be exhausted after what had to have been a marathon trek. Yet there was something about the way in which his people responded that suggested they felt this apprehension, too.

He turned to Higgins as the crowd dispersed. The big man was sweating, despite the fact that the night air was now beginning to cool.

"Can you feel it?" he asked simply. And when the big man nodded briefly, he continued. "It doesn't make sense, but I don't want to take chances when it makes me feel like this. Lock and load, big guy."

Higgins nodded again, but this time with a weak grin. It had been a kind of catch phrase and private joke between them since they had first met, and its familiarity made them both feel better.

By this time, the crowd had dispersed, the sec teams had assumed their positions around the ville, and the six men had returned from the armory. Collecting their mounts along the way, they were now ready to go.

K turned to them. "Keep it frosty. There's more of us, and they're on foot, but don't take anything on trust."

The mounted sec men exchanged glances that mixed both surprise and shock. This wasn't what they expected from a baron best described, in the interests of their own safety, as driven and confident.

"I know," K said simply. "But this is the chill zone. I might not come from here, but I listen to my people." He stared at them. They returned the look with a ripple of understanding.

"Okay, then," he said, nodding, "let's get out and meet them."

They set out into the evening, the cooling air flowing around them as their horses kept up a steady canter. It was only a short while before the approaching party came into eye contact. Even as shambling shadows in the distance, they seemed strangely sinister, and it was with a sense of apprehension that the sec party grew closer.

K was a little puzzled by their behavior. With a mounted sec party headed toward them, which they had to have realized would be armed, you would have expected them to at least slacken off the pace a little, or to show some kind of sign of acknowledgment. Instead, they kept coming at the same steady pace, as though not seeing the sec party moving toward them. Or not caring, which, the baron reflected, would be a scarier prospect.

"Lock and load, but keep it casual unless they show the slightest sign," he called over his shoulder to the party at his rear. He liked to lead from the front, and in the same way he knew that he had no real need to issue the instruction. It was perfunctory. His men knew him, and they knew what they had to do.

K dragged his own Remington from the holster on the horse's saddle and slipped the safety, holding it barrel-up against his shoulder. It looked casual, but he was skilled and practiced. The longblaster could be leveled and the first round buried in a bastard's heart before he had a chance to take a breath.

Now that they were near, he could see that the immensely fat man with the cane had a brown derby on his head, almost white with dust. He also wore round glasses that blanked out his eyes as the baron rode close enough to be able to establish eye contact. The group at his rear was a motley collection. The stocky men were adorned with web belts of which they carried a variety of battered musical instruments, all of which had seen better days and clanged gently together in rhythm with their footsteps. They also had puppets of wood and cloth hanging from the webbing that crisscrossed their bodies. Carved of wood or made of cloth and stuffed, the eyes of the puppets stared sightlessly and chilled in a way that made K shudder.

Gathered just to the rear of these were the two tall men. The skinny guy had bug eyes that might have been due to the effort that he had to expend to carry the wooden booth that was on his back, or may just have been the result of madness from being in the wilderness too long. K wasn't sure, and he didn't care. He could just see that the faded paintwork on those portions of the booth visible was covered in strange stains that he couldn't—and wasn't sure that he wanted to—identify.

That just left the big guy that looked like Higgy— well, maybe not so much up close. Tight curls in his hair and beard gave him a deceptively angelic look, which belied his bulk. Just visible was the heavy pack that he carried on his back, but it was his clothing that was most remarkable—leggings, and a vest of patched and multicolored diamond shapes, hung with bells that jangled only dully, so clogged were they with the dust that also faded his clothes. His brown boots had bizarrely turned-over cuffs that only made him seem stranger. There were also the objects that hung from his belt, strange, shrunken objects that looked like dried fruit, and yet… K didn't want to consider the thought that suddenly struck him.

Indicating with a tilt of the Remington that his people should pull up behind him, the baron brought his mount to a standstill about a hundred yards from the oncoming party. It was uncanny the way they had just kept coming despite the approach of what was obviously a superior force. It was either a completely stupe action, or perhaps an act of supreme confidence. K couldn't be sure.

The mounted sec party came to a halt, dust settling around them in the darkening twilight. The walkers kept coming, until they were only a short distance away. Then, when they were close enough for all of them to make eye contact, the immensely fat man held up his stick so that it was raised above his head. At this sign, they came to a silent halt.

It was a strange and uncanny atmosphere as the two sides faced each other. K was unwilling to be the first to break this silence. Yet the wait was straining his nerves to breaking point. It seemed as if the fat man knew that. With an almost infinite slowness he removed his glasses and produced a handkerchief, with which he carefully polished the dusty lenses before inspecting them, nodding to himself, and placing them back on his nose with one hand while he pushed the handkerchief into the back pocket of his pants with the other. He looked up at the baron, head on one side, before sniffing and finally speaking.

"So…"

He let the word hang in the air for several seconds,

as if daring the baron to break in. But K kept his counsel. A crooked grin split the fat man's face. When he spoke again there was something in his voice—not an undertone, nor any hint of sibilance, but somehow it seemed to seep into K's mind, wrapping it up so that the trepidation that he was feeling was pushed to the very boundaries of his consciousness.

"So," he began again, "we have traveled far to drink your wine, and to provide for your edification an entertainment that will astound you and be fair exchange for your hospitality. What do you say?"

The baron, determined to remember the apprehension that counseled valuable caution, summoned up his will and as much phlegm as he could from a throat suddenly dry. He hawked a glob onto the dry ground, landing it at the fat man's feet.

"I say you've got a real strange way of talking. And of traveling. I dunno about any entertainment, and I don't even know what edifucktion is, but I'd sure like to know where the hell you've come from."

The fat man's grin grew wider at the baron's choice of words.

"You have no idea what you're saying. How close, indeed, you might be to a noble truth. But that is not for you to worry about. Our plight is our own. We merely carry it with us from ville to ville as we make our way across this rad-blasted land. Our sole aim is to make enough jack to keep alive so that we might carry on to the next ville."

"Why?" K asked, his tone hostile. Every fiber of his being was screaming at him that these weird crazies were nothing but bad. And yet somehow, even though he knew he should level the Remington and start blasting, still he couldn't bring himself to do it. There was something deep inside his head that was telling him no, a voice that he felt wasn't his own, and that he couldn't deny. A voice that grew, bizarrely and insidiously, wordless as it was, more insistent as he sat astride his mount, rooted to the saddle by the beady, short-sighted eyes of the fat man.

"We are traveling players, no more and no less," the fat man said with a shrug. He indicated those who were at his shoulder, causing them to genuflect awkwardly with a deference that wasn't matched by their demeanor. "We will entertain and bewitch you, and all we ask is that you feed and water us before we go on our way…perhaps allow us to rest for a few days before we put on a show that you will never forget."

There was something in the manner of those last words that made the baron's blood run cold. And yet, even as it did so, he found that he was opening his mouth and saying something that came as a surprise to him.

"Then you must come with us. We can house and feed you. We don't have much, but surely there is enough in our ville to sustain you. And it isn't often that we see anything in the way of entertainment. It'll be good for the people. Won't it?" he added, turning back to the men at his rear.

They all nodded. And as they did, it seemed to him that their eyes were clouded in some way, as though they were suffering the same sense of confusion that he was feeling. A confusion that meant he couldn't think with any kind of clarity. Even the words he had used seemed to him to come from another place. "Surely there is enough in our ville to sustain you"? What the fuck was that? What he should have said was "Get away from my ville, you weird fuckers, before me and my men blast seven shades of shit out of you." It was what he would have said, normally, but this wasn't normal. There was some weird shit going down here, and it was as though he was watching it from one side, as though he had been taken out of his own body and was now walking alongside the mounted men, side-by-side with the travelers, as they made their way in silence back to the ville.

As they approached the edge of the ville, he could see the darkness descend as the sun finally fell below the horizon. Slowly the lights of the oil and electric lamps that were dotted around the buildings began to flicker into life. But for a moment there was darkness on the edge of the ville, and in that he could see nothing but a portent. It was one that he found himself unable to act on, as he was being swept along by something that he didn't understand, and that he was powerless to resist.

Seeing their baron and the sec party he had rode out with return with the strangers, the people of the ville began to emerge from their secured places. They were still armed, but the weapons were at ease. They gathered and followed the party as it made its way to the center of the ville. Once there, the fat man turned to the baron.

"Pray introduce us to your people, K. We have much to show them, but as yet they do not know who we are."

It was only later—much later, after the event—that K realized that he hadn't told the fat man his name. That should have made him wary. But no, it didn't even register at that moment. Instead, he found himself telling the people that these strolling players had come to entertain them, and to teach them and to show them things the like of which they had never seen before.

As he spoke, he saw that the six moved among the ville dwellers, touching them, shaking hands, muttering in ears. Eyes that had been clouded with doubt were now clouded with something else instead. And as they did this, and as his people warmed to the newcomers, with their reserve weakening and their welcoming embrace enveloping the traveling players, so he, too, began to feel a sense of well-being—like a warm, white light—wash over him. Yes, these people were friends, and they should be welcomed.

What a crock of horseshit.

Except that this, too, only occurred to him well after the event.

When it was too late.

Chapter Six

The vista below them was breathtaking. Daunting, too, but that was something to be considered in a few moments, when the full impact of what they had seen had been given a chance to fully assimilate. Right now, the astounding beauty of what they could see had overwhelmed them all.

On the far side of the canyon wall, reached only by a series of twisting and narrow paths that slowly wound their way down the walls and across the uneven floor of the canyon, was a series of buildings the likes of which none of them had ever seen. They perched on a number of ledges.

The ledges on which these buildings stood were possibly man-made. Was it possible that nature had truly manufactured such a perfect platform for the foundations of such splendid isolation? The ledges came out from beneath the canopy of the rock face above for only the merest part of their depth. The majority of them were driven deep into the rock, providing shelter for that which lay beneath from whatever the elements might have to throw at them.

For Ryan, J.B., Krysty and Jak there was no way of knowing how old these buildings may be. Their knowledge of the styles in which architecture had changed

over the centuries before skydark ranged from sketchy
to nonexistent. There was no reason why it should be
anything else. For Doc and Mildred, however, it was
different. They had known the world before the nukecaust, and had histories that included a degree of edu-
cation that made them appreciate what they were seeing
in the context of a greater human history—a history
that made them all the more awestruck by what they
could see in front of them.

For these buildings were more than just roughly
hewn shelters in the shadow of an overhanging rock.
They were palaces of extraordinary beauty and simplicity of line that showed a taste and intelligence—a
culture—that seemed all the more remarkable for being
out here in the middle of nowhere.

There was little doubt that the buildings in front of
the companions showed a great intelligence, both in
design and execution. They were hewn from the same
rock that constituted the canyon walls around them and
in some ways looked as though they had been carved
out of the very face of the rock itself. And yet there was
an economy of line that showed an astounding use of
engineering in making the walls, windows and doorways run together in such a way as to make the buildings look both independent of one another, and yet also
so very much a part of an integrated design.

Despite the undeniable fact that they were of the
same rock as the walls around them, they had a smooth
and polished appearance that made them whiter than
the yellowing stone that framed them. It was as though
they had been relentlessly buffed and polished to a

glorious sheen. They seemed to reflect the sun that streamed into the canyon, taking, absorbing it and reflecting it back with a luminescence that made it seem that the buildings were less stone, more marble in their makeup.

They had to have been constituted of blocks and bricks that had been hewn from the rock and then carefully placed together. The buildings weren't of uniform height or width, with some having roofs upon them while others seemed to grow up into the rock that covered them, with no real indication of where the building ended and the canyon wall began.

The scale of the buildings, and not just their beauty and design, was also something that was enough to make them pause and gape in awe. By the size of the doorways and windows, and the occasional sign of life, it was soon apparent that the buildings were built on a magnificent scale. This was no mere ville, this was a city of such magnitude as shouldn't have survived the nukecaust: and, indeed, wouldn't have if not for the shelter provided by its location.

It was like a city glimpsed in a dream, a magnificence, simplicity and beauty that was a monument to the dedication, work and craft of a civilization long since passed.

It was a civilization that had a greater depth and intelligence than that which had been shallow and facile enough to be behind the disaster of the nukecaust. Doc and Mildred were certain of one thing, and the others suspected it. This city had been here longer than the few hundred years that covered the industrial revolution and the final capitulation of savagery over technology that had birthed the lands in which they now lived.

Its scope and beauty, the mystery of how it had come to be in such a place, and the intelligence that had conceived of it—these were questions that had no real relevance to them now. The only thing that really mattered was that the men they had followed, and the prey they had sought to recapture, had to have ended up in those mysterious palaces of light that shone magnificently in the early-morning sun. Whatever noble minds had given rise to these astounding edifices had long since been replaced by the more venal creatures that now used them as a domicile.

No matter how tragic it may seem, no matter how ironic or apposite, the only thing that mattered was to dismiss all from their minds but the attainment of their goal.

Not that this would be easy. Neither the dismissal nor the attainment.

"We're seriously exposed up here," Ryan said softly, staring down into the canyon. "If we're not going to be spotted, then we need to take cover."

Krysty looked at him wryly. "It's not like they don't know we're here. Look at the shit we've had to come through to get this far."

Ryan shrugged. "Sure. Something knows we're here, that's for certain. But is it some kind of weird shit thing that has power over the people down there, or is it part of them?"

"Not matter. Still enemy," Jak stated.

"I think I see what Ryan means," Doc said at length.

"If it is some kind of agent of influence, then it may be operating the defenses on a kind of automatic basis, and therefore would not necessarily mean that the men we are pursuing—nor, indeed, any of their companions down there in those magnificent edifices—may be aware that we are at their back. And so we can assume that they may have more regular defenses that we should also take care to avoid."

"That's a lot of assumptions," Mildred mused, "but I guess it can't hurt to think along those lines and keep it as frosty as we would normally."

"In which case," J.B. finished, scratching his head beneath the brim of his fedora, "we'd better get the hell out of sight before there are more people on the move than we've already seen."

The Armorer's words struck home. They had seen very few people up and about at daybreak, enough only to judge the scale of the buildings. At such a distance, and with so few eyes to train in their direction, it was unlikely that they had been spotted. But if any regular sec patrols should chance this way, or even chance to look this way, even at such a distance they would be highlighted perfectly against the empty sky behind them.

Swiftly, Ryan led them along the lip of the canyon. It was clear that there were well-established paths on this side of the abyss, just as there were on the far side, where the palaces lay. This much was clear from the way in which those paths that crisscrossed the canyon floor, running across the winding creek, meandered across until they ran out of sight beneath the overhanging lip where the companions now stood. From here there was no egress, but there had to be at some point. This would be where the abductors had taken the children when they reached the canyon the previous evening. It was just a matter of finding that point.

Traversing the canyon lip, and keeping low in case they could be seen from the other side, they soon reached a point where the lip of the canyon receded so that it was no longer overhanging. Instead, it now provided a short, sloping path down to a ledge of rock that was connected precariously to another that snaked at an acute angle. The dusty surface was tramped flat and worn in the center so that it formed a groove, as if it had been trodden over a long period by many feet.

This had to be the way, had to be the way taken by the party the previous day. There was nothing else that offered an obvious path.

Ryan paused. Steep and treacherous, the path brought the memory of the strange hallucination they had suffered so recently, which had seemingly ended with him plunging to his doom. That was a hell of a thing to have come into your head when you had to be so sure-footed, Ryan thought. Even more so when he considered how open to any potential view they would be, silhouetted against the rock face as they descended.

Krysty was at his elbow, looking into the depths of the canyon, and across to similar paths that scarred the rock face opposite.

"It's not like the dreams," she whispered. "This can

be sure underfoot. And I'll tell you something else. There must be cover along the way."

"Why do you say that?" he asked with a furrowed brow.

"Look," she said, indicating across the vast mouth of the canyon. Across the way, on the paths that proscribed similar trajectories, there were clumps and clusters of rock, some littering the paths before forming walls that would provide cover from probing eyes. Some of the rock had come from falls and splits along the rock face that had formed small cavelike apertures, which would also, if used wisely, provide cover.

Ryan's face cracked into a crooked grin. He felt better about this. If they could make anything similar on this side, then they could establish observation posts and work out just what their prey was doing, assess numbers and cultivate any weak spots. They needed any edge they could find.

Indicating to the others that they should follow him, Ryan began the descent. The first section of the path was steep, and he was cautious in case he gained too much momentum to make the sudden sharp angle of turn. The last thing he wanted was to tumble into the abyss. And, in truth, the residue of the vision in which he had fallen was still in his head, no matter how much he attempted to dismiss it.

He could feel, rather than see or hear, the others at his back. When he reached the turn, he could almost feel the extra depth of groove in the path that told of the efforts of the countless others who had gone before him, taking the care that he now exercised. Once he had got past that, and was on the other path, he almost breathed a sigh of relief. As he moved at an acute angle to the previous path, he was able to see them as they, too, took the turn. This path, although still descending at a steep gradient, was easier to negotiate.

Moments later, Ryan quickened his pace. The path was starting to level out, and they had reached a wider section that dovetailed with other paths that had either been hewn from or simply worn along the face of the rock. The way was clear for a distance, then clusters of rock blocked the way, some so long established as to have shrubs and grasses growing from beneath them, stunted and spiky in the rad-blasted atmosphere, hidden from the sun by being on the wrong side of the canyon. That might, he hoped, help them, for the sun rose and fell facing down on the side of the canyon where the palaces had been built. The side on which he and the companions made their way was in perpetual shadow, and he felt that could only be of assistance.

Beyond these sparse clusters, he could see that there was a cavern that fell back into the rock face. Its mouth was hidden in shadow from where he stood, which suggested that it might bore back some way into the rock, and provide them all with shelter. It would be perfect.

Ryan slowed to a halt, hunkering down in the sparse shelter of a rock cluster that had brown-green grasses sprouting from the cracks. He gestured to the others so that they should pull up behind him, crowding together as much as possible.

"Jak," he murmured, "you reckon you could get to that cave without being spotted and scope it out?"

The albino teen didn't answer for a moment. Instead, he squinted at the path in front of him, and then across at the palaces on the far side of the canyon.

"Mebbe," he said eventually. "Hard, not impossible."

And before Ryan had a chance to reply, Jak had set off. Moving swiftly and keeping low to the ground, he ducked when cover presented itself, then paused at those stretches that were open. Dropping onto his belly when he was as sure as he could be that there were no prying eyes from the far side, and that any chance of being observed was accidental and arbitrary, he slithered like some unholy cross between a crab and an eel across the dusty floor, so sure with his arms and legs that he barely raised any dust.

When he reached the mouth of the cavern, he disappeared from view before Ryan had a chance to really register that he had made the distance. He was gone for quite some time. Ryan said nothing while they waited. His tense silence was something that the others picked up on, and even the usually garrulous Doc maintained a tight-lipped silence.

Ryan hadn't realized that, in his anxiety, he had been holding his breath until he saw Jak's small frame emerge into the light, his white hair and skin thrown into relief by the darkness around him. The stabbing in his lungs reminded him to breathe, and he exhaled, almost light-headed.

Jak moved toward them as quickly as he had left. Keeping himself low and as concealed as was possible, he was back with them before Ryan had a chance to catch his breath.

The grin on the albino teen's face as he approached told Ryan all that he needed to know.

"Goes way back into rocks," Jak stated before anyone had the chance to ask. "Stand few yards in shadow covers you. Could sit all day and watch them, not seen."

Ryan's face split into a triumphant grin. He turned to the others. "I think we've got just the cover we need. Now we've just got to get ourselves in it without being seen."

The only way to get to the cave was to take the same route as Jak. As none of them were as lithe or as small as the albino youth, it became apparent that they would have to take considerable care if they weren't to be seen. A quick glance at the sun as it started to climb in the sky told them that they would have to move swiftly, in case those who lived in the shining palaces of stone along the opposite wall emerged to do morning chores. If they did, then the six people traveling the path directly across from them would be all too plainly visible.

Jak took the lead, moving rapidly to the first available cover. From there, he was able to get a better recce of any activity on the far side of the canyon. There was some movement, but it was soon apparent that those who were up and around this early were too engaged in their tasks to even look idly across the gap. Beckoning to Ryan to follow, he waited until the one-eyed man had joined him and then outlined his intent. He would proceed to the next point of cover and keep watch. He would beckon to Ryan when it was clear, and then

the one-eyed man could send across, one-by-one, the
other four.

It was a simple plan, but Ryan was happy enough to
let Jak take the lead. He had already scouted the route
they would have to take, and he could guide the other
four over the last stretch while the one-eyed man acted
as a point man and primed them.

J.B. went first, followed by Mildred then Doc,
and Krysty last of all. Ryan felt his pulse pound with
adrenaline as he looked up at the sun, then across to
the palaces of light beyond. The companions had to
move slowly in the sense that they were waiting for a
chance, a moment when there were no eyes on them.
They were moving quickly in the sense that they then
had to cover the ground fast. The tension between the
two things was causing him to fear for their ability to
make it unseen.

But his friends were good. They hadn't gotten this
far by being unable to adapt to any kind of terrain or
task if it was demanded of them. And even Doc, who
was the most erratic and by virtue of time trawling and
past injury the least supple and quick of them, buck-
led down to the task and sped across from Ryan to Jak,
listening hard and then falling to the ground, crawling when the moment came with a speed that Ryan
wouldn't have thought possible.

Even though there was more movement in the palaces opposite, and more outside, with every minute that
he could tick off on his wrist chron, it seemed that his
people had achieved their aim. Then came the moment
when he could no longer see J.B., Mildred, Krysty or

Doc as they were in shadow and cover. Only Jak was visible from the wall side of the rocks that he was using as cover. The early hour and the shadow in which their side of the canyon was perpetually shrouded had served them well.

Jak beckoned to Ryan, and he knew it was time. All other thoughts vanished from his head as he concentrated on making the gap between where he started and the point where the albino teen lay in wait for him. Keeping low to the ground, he headed for the next piece of cover, skidding on the loose soil as he came up to it and slowed suddenly, bringing himself to a halt beside the albino youth. Ryan was breathing heavily, and he realized that he had taken just the one lung-bursting breath as he crossed the distance.

He breathed deeply, consciously slowing his intake so that he didn't hyperventilate. Jak, seeing this, nodded slowly and waited, one eye on the wakening populace across the divide. When he could see that Ryan was ready, he indicated the path ahead of them, between the rocks where they stood and the mouth of the cave.

"Keep to ground and crawl. Path worn, fit into worn groove. Not much show then, and along there grass give cover."

The albino teen hunkered down then, as Ryan had seen him do with the others. As he crouched so that he could share Jak's perspective, it suddenly became apparent what he meant. Where the path had been in use for untold centuries, the constant use had worn a deep groove. It was, he supposed, much the same for any of the paths on either side of the canyon. It wasn't deep enough to completely cover anyone who would crawl in the channel, but it did provide some kind of shelter. What Jak had spotted, and taken advantage of, was the fact that on the lip of the path, as it petered out into space, tenacious grass had taken hold and now sprouted in sparse and browned tufts that had just enough height to make the difference between hiding and being seen in the shadows of the canyon wall.

Jak looked across, gauging the moment. "Now," he suddenly whispered hoarsely, clapping Ryan on the back in such a manner as to almost push the one-eyed man down into the dirt.

Ryan took this as his cue and used the momentum to propel himself forward as he hit the dirt, crawling on his belly with all the speed he could muster. It was only a matter of a couple of hundred yards at most, and yet it felt like the equivalent in miles. At every moment he expected to hear a shout from the far side of the canyon, or a volley of shots to indicate that his presence had been betrayed.

But nothing happened. Instead, he found himself reaching the gaping maw of the cave, hands reaching out to grab him like some obscene, tendrillike split tongue. It was only when he was safely in the shadows and he was able to clamber to his feet in the presence of his companions that he was finally able to feel at ease. Moving to the edge of where the light intruded into the mouth of the cave, he peered along the path he had just taken. He could see Jak watching and waiting for his moment. And then, with no warning and at a speed that was awe-inspiring, the albino teen dropped to his belly and slithered toward them like a white snake.

Once Jak was inside the cave and on his feet with the others, Ryan felt able to take a look across to the shining palaces of light on the far side of the canyon.

"We're here," he said flatly, "but that's only the first move. We have to get across to there. That'll be the easy part."

"An interesting definition of the word *easy,* if one looks too closely at how deep and wide this canyon is," Doc mused softly.

Ryan grinned. "Any stupe can cross a canyon if they have enough time and a sure foot," he said. "The hard part is getting across without any bastard seeing you do it. And that's going to mean a lot of patience."

J.B. sniffed. "Recce. Lots of it, right?"

"Got it in one," Ryan agreed. "We need to know how these people live, how many are there at a guess, what they do, what their habits are. If we're going to hit them, then we need to find their weaknesses."

"I wonder if they have any," Doc said. "If they had the power to cloud our minds, even one such as Krysty's—"

"But they didn't," Mildred pointed out. "Not completely. And that's where we can get them. They have chinks in their armor."

Doc brightened visibly. "What a splendid phrase, and one that I haven't heard for many a… I was going to say *year,* but I fear *century* may be a more apt word. What made you say that, my dear Doctor?"

Mildred shook her head. "I don't know. I mean

what I say, but I wouldn't put it that way, unless..."
She paused for thought, and when she continued, there
was a faraway look in her eye that gave pause to all of
them. "There's something about this place that's been
making me think about the past. Something familiar,
that I feel I should be able to bring to mind. I know this
place, or of it, from way back when...well, from before
the nukes came along and changed everything. It should
mean something to me. It's as though I have some sort
of mental block. Damn!"

Krysty stepped toward the light and looked at the
city on a ledge that lay across the canyon. As the sun
rose into the early morning and the first real heat of the
day hit the buildings, she tried to imagine what it would
feel like to be bathing in those rays instead of skulking
in shadow. While she watched, more and more people
emerged into the light. It was as though they had been
drawn out by the heat that hit them. The sun-bleached
stone on the magnificent structures seemed to shine
like polished bone or ivory as the rays of morning hit
them. The people who emerged into the new day moved
with a sense of purpose. There was nothing aimless
or unstructured about the manner in which they were
going about their business. In a matter of minutes, as
she watched, it seemed to her that this was a population that had a strong imperative to that sense of purpose that they showed. These were people with a fixed
routine that they practiced.

This was good. This kind of regularity, if studied,
was exactly the kind of thing that Ryan was hoping for.
Routine meant an unwillingness to change. It also bred

a kind of circular pattern to behavior that left gaps that had long since been ignored or forgotten, gaps or lapses in vigilance that would enable the companions to slip through those gaps, and mean that their own flexibility in combat could be used to counter the superior numbers.

It gave her hope that they could achieve their mission. And yet… She would keep her opinions to herself for the moment, but there was something about this behavior that also caused her to feel apprehension. Already she could feel her hair begin to tighten and coil to her scalp, and knew that it was rippling in waves of warning. There was an almost ritualistic air about the way in which these people were going about their tasks. She would wait and watch until she had seen more. Perhaps it would confirm her fears, or perhaps dispel them. She already knew which side of the argument she was coming down on, but maybe she was wrong.

Then closer scrutiny would reveal the rituals in greater detail. Their structure…and their reason.

Chapter Seven

Now safely ensconced in the cave, the companions settled to take watch in turns. It gave them a chance to rest after the trek to shelter from the sun, and to recuperate before they took some kind of offensive action. They would have to plan carefully, and marshal whatever energy they had to make an effective strike. To this end, rest was vital.

And so they took turns to watch and wait.

Mildred took the first watch. While the others gathered in the cool at the rear of the cave, some to try to grab some sleep and the others to merely rest, she hunkered down at the edge of the shadow cast over the mouth, and took note of all that happened in front of her. She knew that she would have to report it in detail when night came again and the city across the divide fell into the quietness of night. That was when the companions would compare their notes of the day to make a complete picture of how the city worked, and so make plans. Being the first to watch and wait, she would have the longest time of them all to remember. And yet she was content with this, for it would also give her the time to inwardly digest what she saw, and perhaps analyze it in a way that a later watch wouldn't give her. For she was haunted by the fact that she knew something of this place from her life before she was frozen and the nukes had come. Yet it remained tantalizingly out of reach.

But no matter; that could come later. She was absorbed in the activities that were occurring in front of her, and the makeup of the population, something that, it was soon becoming apparent, was oddly disproportionate. Children in any ville were at a premium. The effects of rad damage passed down through the genes had affected the birth rate. Some mutations survived and prospered, but many were sickly and survived sometimes only a few hours after birth. That was if the fertility of any potential parents hadn't been impaired in any way by that same rad damage. It was rare to find a ville where there were many children who were what she would have called healthy. In the kind of squalor and poverty that was now the norm, it was correspondingly the norm for infant mortality to be high. There may be no artificial birth control, but the rad-ravaged remains of Mother Nature had more than compensated for that.

But here? There were children and youths everywhere. As the morning came alive and the people on the ledge opposite began to go about their business, it became apparent that there were in fact more children than there were of what could be called an adult population. Her mind raced as she tried to make sense of this. Sure, these coldhearts had taken the children and the young from the ville of Baron K and marched them here. "Why" was something that they didn't know, and in truth hadn't given much thought to. Perhaps they should have. For the answer to that might also explain why there were so many young gathered here. At the back of her mind, nagging thoughts tried to extend tendrils of imagining that would link up and somehow connect with what she knew about this place. Yet for the moment, it remained frustratingly out of reach.

The older men and women of the ville were distanced by some way from the younger bulk of the populous. They were hardened and grizzled by their experiences. She could see that not just because her eyesight was sharp enough to make out some features, but because of the way in which they carried themselves. She had become an adept reader of body language since her awakening in Deathlands. It was one of the skills she soon found necessary to stay alive. And it was telling her now that these men and women had performed the same routines and rituals for some time. The routine was etched into the perfunctory way in which they moved, delineated or thrown into sharp relief only when one of the young didn't move in the proscribed manner, or did something seemingly out of turn. Then, there was a sharp flaring of temper resulting in a flurry of action before falling once more into the torpor of routine.

The young came out of buildings that seemed to act as dormitories, which were gathered in the center of the gleaming city. Those buildings at the edges served to house the older ones, who acted as guardians and patrons—but to what greater cause? Mildred wondered. Because it was soon apparent to her that they moved with a determination, one born of every action moving toward an end.

The young moved toward a communal area where they were served food from a large cauldron. From there, they moved back to the dormitory buildings. The mass of them moved slowly, so that by the time the last had been served, the first had emerged from the dormitories to clean their dishes and move on to their daily tasks. For the period that she was on watch, their duties seemed to be simple enough: cleaning, building, repairing the damage time had wrought to the white stone edifice of the city.

Yet surely this wasn't all that they had been taken for? Mildred was certain in her own mind that all of the young were abductees. If one set were known to be, then in such a disproportionate population chances were that most, if not all, had suffered the same fate. But if there was more than this, then what the hell was it? Before she had a chance to find out, she was relieved by Doc. But not until she had shared her bemusement with him.

Perhaps it was this exchange of views, and then again perhaps it was only his own instinct for dark doings that made Doc look at the events in front of him in a jaundiced light as he settled down to take her place on watch.

He supposed that he should be taking note of the comings and goings of the people, particularly with a view to establishing a pattern that could be exploited for weakness and an attack. But he would leave that to those who were best suited, such as Ryan, Jak or J.B. There were things about the way in which the people conducted themselves that suggested some kind of coercion or power over the younger people. It was the same thing that Mildred had picked up on, but filtered through Doc's brooding consciousness, a whole new set of possibilities opened up.

Mildred had intimated that the meals may have been tainted with a drug of some kind. It was possible that the coldhearts running the city may have supplies of old predark meds that could be put to this use. But they would need copious supplies to keep the numbers they had under them in line, and for an indefinite period. A herbal mixture was a possibility—certainly, he knew that Krysty had learned much of such things when she was growing up in Harmony—as was jolt, so prevalent across the continent.

Yet Doc was inclined to dismiss this notion. Little vegetation grew in these parts, as they had seen on their journey. The conditions were all wrong for the amounts of herbs that would be necessary. And it would presuppose the skills necessary to keep a herbal mixture at such a constant level of strength. In a similar way, he couldn't believe that a combo drug such as jolt was responsible. For a start, it would mean that these people, who seemed so intent on isolating themselves, would have to trade with the outside world to gain the necessary elements. More important, it was notoriously difficult to balance the elements that went into such a drug. And these young people showed every sign of being under a very steady—and pervasive—influence.

No. Doc was convinced, the more he watched, that the young people were under the influence of the mind. A kind of hypnosis or trancelike state that was reinforced by the use of ritual. He had seen this many times in his life. Indeed, he had been at the mercy of it on several occasions and no longer responsible for his own actions as a result. He knew how pernicious it could be, and how difficult to prevent. Add to this the power that they had already experienced on their trek to this place, and he had little doubt that this was what was happening.

What he could see did little to dissuade him of the notion. As he watched, he could see the young people go about their daily tasks with an air of ritual. Everything was done in a very deliberate manner, painstaking, almost. Motions were repeated with infinite care, as though every little movement was invested with meaning. Even the most mundane of tasks was performed as though of the greatest import. He had seen this kind of thing before, although when he had seen such things, they were usually within the context of what could be called ritual magic. Ceremonies and invocations.

But to whom? Or what? Ah, that was the question. Answer that, and you would truly know what you were up against. They had experienced some of the power that could exercise such a hold over the mind. Did it come from the adult population that held sway over the youth who toiled across the divide? Or was the adult population, too, in thrall to something older and perhaps less human?

Even as the thought crossed his mind, Doc felt slightly foolish. This was a visceral world in which only the corporeal could hold precedence. The idea of things that weren't physical having control over that which was tangible seemed beyond any reason. If he mentioned it without thinking carefully about the way in which he phrased it, he could easily find it dismissed as simply Doc having one of his mad moments.

And yet there was something about the architecture of the buildings opposite, the way in which they gleamed so highly in the sun, as though polished. The shapes were slightly off-kilter where they had been slotted into the gaps in the canyon wall. Their lines were straight, yet at oblique angles that seemed to make them loom out of the canyon even as they seemed to be secluded. The strange little windows and oddly out-of-proportion doorways seemed to give them a perspective that made them seem almost alive. Certainly, they didn't look like the architecture of any race that he could recall.

If there was an outside intelligence of some kind at work here—and why should it not be supposed, for it would not affect the fact that they would still have to fight the physical foot soldiers of such a force—then what was its aim? Why did it require so many people to do its bidding? And why, also, did it require so many of them to be so young?

There was something ominous about many of the tasks that they undertook, particularly the way in which they were constructing a kind of platform out on the lip of the ledge, in the center of the buildings. It was makeshift, and yet made with such care as to suggest a very definite purpose.

Doc was interrupted in his train of thought by the

arrival of Jak to take his place. Unlike Mildred, Doc kept his own counsel. As highly as he thought of the albino youth, he was far too prosaic a character to listen to Doc's notions without the likes of Krysty to act as a bridge between Doc's world and the one that Jak inhabited.

In the same way, the things that caught Jak's attention were very different to those that had absorbed Doc during his spell on watch.

Jak hunkered down and began to watch and absorb. His own highly developed senses—not mutie, but refined to a point that almost made him one with the fauna—began to tune in with the immediate world. The first thing it told him was that the area was almost certainly devoid of life apart from that which lived on the opposite ledge. Normally, the scents of any animals and birds, even those that may be nocturnal and so hidden away at this time of day, would begin to seep into his nostrils, his acute hunting instincts delineating them one from another. But here there was little to sort and identify, a few creatures that resembled rats, if the scent was anything to go by…and these were sparse. They lived on the meager grasses and the insect life that hovered around them. He guessed that the main source for maintaining the ratlike creatures was the detritus left by the people who lived in the shining houses. A grim flicker of amusement strayed across Jak's face as he considered what a finely balanced ecosystem existed on the ledge and in the canyon. By the smell of old food that was an undertone in the scents that drifted through the air, the rodents formed a staple part of the people's diets, roasted and stewed.

The people had to live on grasses and berries gathered from the floor of the canyon, the rodents they caught, and any supplies that they could take from passing convoys or villes they raided for their young. Jak knew that partly because he could smell that there was little other wildlife, and there was no scent of oats or wheat. But partly because he hadn't seen any riders leave the ville to go hunting, nor had he seen anyone leave to farm. There was also no sign of where anything was being cultivated, nor any indication of an area within view that could support any kind of agriculture.

Where Doc had dwelt on the idea of what might be powering the people of the shining city—an outside malign influence or their own belief in their power and possibility—Jak wasn't concerned with anything like that. He watched how the people moved and went about their business in a very different way.

They didn't move with any natural grace. Even the most unfit of the older people would still have a certain fluidity to their movements if they were in any way unimpeded. But they didn't. There was a certain jerk and tension to their movements that made them move as though they were marionettes on strings. Where Doc would deem this as being the sign of an outside hand, Jak looked at it differently. He had seen such movements before, particularly in animals that he had been hunting. There was a certain type of berry that, when eaten in any quantity, caused the muscles to jerk uncontrollably. Paralysis followed soon after, with a chilling at the inevitable conclusion. That was in small animals. Perhaps the men of the ledge city knew to avoid the berries, but they might have eaten rodents that had taken less care. Jak had seen villes where the poison of the berries had decimated the population when unwittingly eaten by the people through the meat they caught. Perhaps it was this. Perhaps it was something else.

Like Doc, Jak had been thinking of ritual, though his take on it differed from the old man's. Jak had seen villes where the baron had tried to rule with the idea of magic and some kind of power from beyond the physical realm. Maybe that was what these people believed in. Jak thought it was crap, but that didn't matter. What mattered was that they believed it, and they used berries and herbs to cloud their minds and reach states that they would call visions of the truth, and Jak would call simply dreams. And stupe ones, at that. Not that it mattered. All that mattered was that they would use these herbs and berries, and they would cause the same physical effects where they remained in the body. They would be slow and jerky. Easier to fight, then.

But that was the older ones. The younger ones— those who had been taken—moved in a very different way. Sure, they had a touch of the jerkiness that came from the ingestion—deliberate or otherwise—of the berries. But there was something else: they had a sluggish torpor to the way they moved, as though they were sleepwalkers, or their limbs were weighted down with rocks. No—sleepwalkers, that was more like it. They walked like they were asleep, or in trance, under the influence of hypnosis. It was a rare art in these post skydark days, but it wasn't unknown. He had seen it happen, and learned of how it worked from Mildred and Doc. They wouldn't, perhaps, see it as he would. They knew how it worked, but didn't have the closeness of observation.

So the young would be sluggish, but by the same token, they would do whatever was asked of them unquestioningly. Which made them, perhaps, the greater danger of the two groups.

He was still pondering this as the sun crept across the center of the sky, and Krysty came from the coolness of the cave to relieve him. He said nothing as he left his place to go back to the darkened interior, deciding to keep his thoughts to himself. There would be time enough to talk of these things later, when they compared their findings before deciding on a course of action.

As he neared the resting group, he was glad that he had opted not to speak, as the low sound of Mildred's voice grew distinct enough to make out words.

"And I knew that it meant something to me. It's just that it was so buried under all the shit that's happened that I'd forgotten about it, as though it happened to someone else. I wouldn't have recognized the land around here from all those years ago, but I doubt if anyone would. The mysterious palaces of Mancos Canyon, though—"

"That is where we are?" Doc interjected.

"Hey, you tell me where else I could find buildings like those right in the middle of a canyon," she answered wryly. "The Mesa Verde Park... Jeez, I remember that there were a lot of stories about those buildings. Some said that they were from the Native Americans, and others that they came from a time before that, when there were other races that roamed across the continent. Some said they were like the Mayans and Aztecs of the South Americas, and they had the same kinds of ideas about the sun and their other gods. There was only one way to make them happy, and that involved a lot of bloodshed and killing.

"Now some of that may be true, or all of it, or none of it. But it felt like the bit about the killing was right. This place looked amazing from a distance, but as soon as we went into Mancos Canyon, we could feel something. The air changed."

IF KRYSTY COULD HAVE HEARD what Mildred was saying at that moment—if it had been something more than a distant drone—then she would have agreed. For on her watch, she was witnessing something that made her blood run cold. Not just the act, but the manner in which it was performed, caused her sentient hair to curl closer to her scalp and crawl in tendrils around her neck.

It happened so gradually—perhaps even before she had come to the watch—that she didn't at first notice any change. The people on the ledge opposite ceased the tasks that had been occupying them for most of the morning. Now that the sun had crawled over the half-way point in the sky, it was as though they had been called to some kind of order. Gradually, they finished the tasks that they had been performing and began to move toward the area where the platform on the lip of the ledge had been constructed. They gathered around in a silent, milling throng, so that it seemed that everyone poured out from the palaces and onto the narrow strip of rock, jostling for a better position.

Just as it seemed that the platform was to be obscured by those around it, a pathway opened up, and an immensely fat man in a dusty coat and a stovepipe hat moved through the crowd, leading a tall, thin and blond young man by the hand. Even from where she stood, Krysty could see that the young man was almost stumbling over his own feet such was the trancelike torpor in which he seemed to exist. He wandered to the platform, watched intently by the crowd. There was something almost overwhelming about the silence, reaching out to her across the divide.

Guided by the hand of the fat man, the youth climbed onto the platform and lay on his back, almost falling over the edge as he stumbled on his way up. His complicity in being led into such a position was perhaps what Krysty found the most disturbing. She could see what was going to happen, so why couldn't he? And if he could, then what possessed him to be so compliant?

The fat man turned and began to talk to the crowd. Perhaps talk wasn't really the right word. He began a strange singsong chant, the syllables drifting across the gap between the two sides of the canyon making no sense. Maybe it was a foreign language, or maybe it was just the way in which he intoned the words that made the high, keening sound so incomprehensible on one level and yet so bone-chillingly understandable on another.

After finishing the chant, the fat man turned to loom over the platform, pulling a knife from somewhere within his dusty coat. There was an almost audible intake of breath from the gathered crowd—or was it, Krysty wondered, from herself?—as he lifted the knife above his head before plunging it down and into the breastbone of the blond youth. Eerily, the young man made no sound as the knife carved easily through his flesh, pausing only to stick on bone or cartilage before the fat man forced it onward with a grunt.

Although Krysty couldn't really have seen it in as much detail as her mind told her—not at such a distance—she could have sworn she saw the fat man reach into the chest cavity, pulling it open before plunging his fist in to grasp the beating heart, which he held above him, blood dripping down his arm and glistening in the sun, before thrusting the organ into his mouth while the crowd yelled a brief and yet oddly intense approval, which died away with an echo across the canyon.

"Fireblast! What kind of crazed bastards are these people?"

Krysty was so wrapped up in what was happening in front of her that she caught her breath in shock as she heard Ryan whispering at her shoulder.

"It's okay, lover," he said softly, "we're over here. Stay frosty."

"But what kind of coldheart weirdos are they that they can do that?" she said equally softly, shaking her head. "And what was that language the fat bastard was speaking?"

Ryan shook his head. "I don't know. Mebbe it's some kind of ancient tongue that goes back to when those buildings were made." He outlined for her briefly the memories that Mildred had shared with them while Krysty had been on watch.

When he had finished, she was nodding. "Yeah, some of that figures, I guess. Thing is, I can't work out why it's so important for them to gather together so many kids. It looks like they've been all over the Deathlands taking them. Why would they want to do that?"

Ryan snorted. "I have no bastard idea. Mebbe they sacrifice them every day like that poor kid."

Krysty pondered that. "Could be. They don't seem to look at it as anything other than a usual thing. Look at them now," she added, pointing across the divide. Ryan followed her gaze, and could see that even in the short time they had been talking the crowd had dispersed. The corpse had been taken away to be disposed of, and the platform had been perfunctorily washed down. Now, as everyone appeared to be going about their everyday business as before, lost in their routines, it was as though the dramatic gesture of a few minutes before had never happened.

"Can't be, though," she said on reflection. "They'd be slaughtering a shitload of kids, sure, but they wouldn't need as many as they've got there. There's something else, and we need to work out what it is."

'Why?" Ryan asked.

Krysty looked at him. There was something in the

earnestness of her gaze that chilled him to the bone as she said, "Because if we don't, then we won't know exactly what those bastards could do. And we need to know exactly what we're going up against if we're going to get Baron K's kids back. Mebbe free the others before they buy the farm."

Ryan nodded. "Yeah, guess you're right. Get back there and get some rest. We'll talk about it together when the sun goes down. Meantime, me and J.B. can sit out here the rest of the day."

When she had gone, Ryan sat and thought about what Krysty had said while he watched the people on the ledge opposite go about the rest of the day as though nothing untoward had occurred—mebbe for them it hadn't, he thought—in their ritualistic, almost hypnotic manner. The more he thought about it, the more he wished he could get inside their heads in some way, find what made them tick... That had always been one of the things that had given him an edge. And yet here he felt like he was blundering in the dark.

When J.B. joined him, the two men sat in silence for some time, watching the remains of the day ebb away. It was J.B. who finally broke the silence.

"Look at that," he said simply. But Ryan was ahead of him. Where the platform had been constructed, there was now an empty space. They had watched it being torn down and the pieces taken away without thinking much about it. But now, as the area became clear of debris, it was apparent that the space wasn't as empty as it had at first seemed. For in the area that had lain beneath the platform there was a circle constructed in the ground. It had been ringed around in rock, with a pattern running across it that—unless Ryan was mistaken—formed what he recognized as either a pentacle or pentagram. He knew of these from old predark books he had seen as a youth at Front Royal, and although he was unsure of which of the two it may be, he knew that either of them spelled trouble.

Now, as the final task of the day, the people of the mysterious palaces laid kindling and brush on the circle, laying it over with layers of wood that they then covered with a tarp to protect from the elements.

Ryan realized that the ritual slaughter earlier had been less of a regular event than a kind of dedication ceremony. They were building some kind of ritual beacon—for what end he couldn't comprehend—and the seeming ease with which the slaughter had been received had more to do with its purpose than its frequency.

That could only mean that whatever the circle and beacon were for, it was an event fast approaching.

They had to move soon, or risk losing all.

Chapter Eight

When K looked back, there was no way that he could understand how it had happened. More than that, he had no notion of how it could have gone on for so long.

Or did it? The whole thing could have taken days, months, years, perhaps. It had the unreal sense of time that happened with dreams. How long had those cold-hearts actually been in the ville? If he thought about it in one way, it seemed as though they had always been there. It was hard to remember a time before they had arrived, even though their arrival was etched into his memory. And yet the whole thing, while seeming to go on forever, had been over in the blink of an eye. It had to have been the way in which those bastards were able to mess with their minds.

That was his only consolation when he thought about his daughter. Amy was gone now, maybe never to return. Her mother was nothing to him. Chilled, long since, because she was nothing more than a pain in his ass. But Amy…

If it could be said that anyone had a redeeming feature, no matter how black and cold their heart, then the way that K felt about Amy was ample proof of this. He would do anything to get her back. And he would have, too. Despite the fear he felt about the way in which he had been so easily bested, and the men who had been able to achieve this, he would still have gladly charged into battle to win her back.

It was Morgan who had caused him to think better of that. The outlanders had gifts; the old man was able to see that. They would be a vanguard, who would either return with the children or blaze a path that would define the task ahead of a second wave.

Or something like that. But while he was waiting, all K had was the idea that he was letting Amy down. He should be the one going after his daughter, and not leaving it to strangers. He was pretty sure that there was an undercurrent of feeling within the ville that felt that way, too. He was their leader, and he should be leading the charge to get the children back. Sure, no one had actually said anything. If nothing else, they were too smart—or scared or both. But the feeling was there. It would rumble deep beneath the surface, maybe to build in pressure until it broke the surface like a steam geyser, scalding the shit out of anyone who got in the way. So he had to make sure that it didn't burst. Lance the boil and get the pus of discontent out. The best way to do that would be to get the kids back. And the best way to do that would be to find out where they had been taken, and then follow up on the mercies that he had sent to do the job. If they came back with the kids, then that was fine. If they didn't, then he had the backup plan—his own men, traveling a good distance at the rear of the six-strong assault party. They were to watch, wait, observe. If they had the chance, get the kids back and take the credit. If not, then act as an advance warning of the return. Grab the glory for the baron. He had the balls to do it, but the sense—for his people, of course—not to risk his own when there were others who could do the dirty work.

A wise ruler, who acted in the best interests of his people, or a coward who let others take the risks? He could present it the first way to the people he ruled and be pretty sure that they would believe him. Why not?

But it was in himself that he held the canker of doubt. No matter how much he rationalized it, or no matter even how much truth was contained within that rationalization, there was still that part of him, deep within himself, that believed the real reason was that he was scared. Scared like a little girl…like his little girl. Probably more than she was, if truth be known. He could face down any bastard with a blade or a blaster. Take him hand-to-hand and he would fight anyone who was stupe enough to take him on, and know that he could best them.

But this shit? This was beyond his understanding and his control, and that was what really frightened him. He had been hiding away since the strange outlanders had taken the kids, planning vengeance and their return, as he tried to present it. Yeah, right. The simple fact of it was that he was running scared of himself. Those coldhearts had hit him down to the core. How could he deal with something that was so unknown and so alien to him? And if he couldn't deal with that, then what the fuck else was there out there that could have the same effect?

K had ruled on his absolute belief in his own abilities. These were now shaken. And he was no fool. He understood that his ability to maintain command came from the power that he presented to those below him. His belief in that was central to discouraging any challenge. If that went, then any half-assed bastard could have a crack at taking down the baron. The truth was that these coldhearts who had come to the ville were way beyond anything that his own people could throw at him. But would he want to spend the rest of his days fending off challenge after challenge?

Screw that. He had to stop that before it could bloom. Get the kids back, make it look like his doing rather than the mercies, and assert his authority by slapping down any dissent as it happened.

But how to do that when he still felt this fear?

If time had seemed pliable like clay, then what else had been when the coldhearts held sway? If he could think back and work that out, then maybe he could understand. And if he could do that...

What had happened during that time? He sat in brooding silence, replaying the events and trying to sort out the jumble they made in his head.

After they had entered the ville, and he had led them to the center, they had soon been allocated quarters. The fat man had wheezed and grunted his way through an introduction that had seemed at the time to flow like honey from his tongue, despite the harshness of his voice as he tried to recover from the exertions of the long march. His words were like a serpent that snaked its way into their consciousness. The exact phrasing was something that eluded the baron as he tried to recall it. Why that should be was a mystery to him, especially as the import of those words was imprinted on his consciousness. Was it that the man had actually spoken very little, and that his meaning had somehow gone straight into their heads?

Maybe. He could recall that the fat man had told them that they were blessed, and that the sun was shining on them to have such delights in store. If they allowed the traveling players to rest awhile, and offered them food and shelter, then they would be rewarded with a show that wouldn't only entertain them, it would also explain the whole reason that they were on this forsaken dustbowl that was called Earth. The mystery of why life was such a long, hard slog with seemingly little joy or respite would be unravelled, and their place in the great scheme of things would become finally clear. It would be a reason to go on, a reason to give themselves up to what had to be.

For fuck's sake! K was disgusted with himself as, for the first time that he had dared to even consider what had happened, he realized what had been said. How the hell had he allowed himself to fall for such crap? Come to that, how come his people had likewise been duped? K only cared about what comfort and power *he* could get from the world around him, and he was pretty damned sure that the rest of his people felt that way. Life was too short to worry about other shit, and was soon gone.

Anyway, he would have to get past these feelings of disgust and disbelief if he was going to work out what had happened.

The strange party had been split up. There had been no shortage of the populace who had been willing to put them up and feed them, and this alone should have set all his instincts screaming. Normally, they would have moaned and bitched about having to share food, and not wanting strangers snoring, farting and shitting under their roofs. But on this occasion, the opposite had been true. It had been like some kind of bizarre slave auction. He had seen one of these once, over on the west coast, when he was running with a band of coldhearts who earned their jack by taking travelers and beating the crap out of them until they were scared of their own shadows. Then, when they would do anything that was barked at them, they were taken to a site where the rich barons of the coast bid big jack to buy these willing victims. They could do what they wanted with them— probably did, for all he knew or cared—and the pretty ones or the ones who looked like they could be blood sport fetched the biggest prices. When they came to the stands and were put on display there was a feeding frenzy as the rich barons surged forward, throwing wild bids to gain their favorites at all costs.

This had been more than a little like that, which was weird as there was no jack involved, and no obvious benefit to be derived from having the strangers in your shack, eating your food and sleeping in your bed.

But still, there had been places in the crowd where the people had almost come to blows as they vied for the favor of having the strangers stay with them. While this happened, and the baron's sec men had broken up the fights and tried to restore order, the strangers had stayed aloof. Was it just with hindsight that it seemed as though they had stood there with smug grins on their faces? K was inclined to think so, yet couldn't shake the feeling that they had been laughing at his people—and by extension, at him.

So eventually, the strangers had been allotted billets and had gone off for the night. The crowds had dispersed, and there had been dark mutterings from those who had been unlucky, and were left without a stranger in their house. Odd, but K couldn't recall discussing any of this with his sec men after the crowds had cleared. He should have. Normally, he would have. But this wasn't a normal chain of events, and although up to this point things were relatively clear in his mind, it was from here that it got really hazy.

He couldn't work out exactly how long they had been staying before the dark day's entertainment that was the precursor to abduction. It had to have been some time, as it seemed to him as though seasons came and went. And yet this couldn't be, as the passing of the seasons was marked by convoys that came and went, if not by the changeable weather, and there had been no convoys passing that way, nor any that he and his men had gone out to hunt down. This, along with an inventory of the supplies held in the ville, had shown him that it was unlikely that the strangers had stayed more than a few weeks at most. Weeks that seemed to stretch out into a pattern of repeated behavior that was nothing more than a continuous cycle, one that could, feasibly, have extended until the sun finally bought the farm and faded in the sky.

That was how it seemed as they went about their daily tasks, watched by the seemingly benign eye of their visitors.

Wherever there was something to be done in the ville, it seemed that one or the other of the newcomers was there to keep a close eye on the activity. Farming, maintenance, the manufacturing of clothing and bricks for the buildings—all of these were observed by the tall men, who walked from place to place seemingly appearing from nowhere to stand and watch silently before moving away in an equally wraithlike manner, suddenly not there where just a moment before they had occupied space. And yet they had elicited no dissent from those they watched. If anything, it seemed that the people welcomed them, as though it gave them some kind of comfort that they were under the protective eye of their new overlords.

Was that what they were? It had seemed that way to K at the time, and he had no reason to change that opinion now, even though the way he felt about that was completely different. At the time it had seemed perfectly reasonable to him, while now he marveled at the fact that he hadn't simply taken a blaster and blown them all to hell.

That had to say something about the way in which they had gained control over his people and himself. The fat man had seemed to make it his purpose to stick close to the baron. His wheezing breath and grunts as he sat were so imprinted on K's consciousness that he could feel and hear it as though the fat man were at his elbow, which was pretty much where he had seemed to be for the whole time. K ran the ville with a tight grip, and there wasn't much that escaped his notice. Infractions of the laws he made were treated with no mercy. His sec men would bring the perpetrators to him, and under his questioning they would soon confess to their transgressions. If they tried to hold out, then he would use torture to extract the truth.

While the fat man watched, both the innocent and the guilty had passed through the baron's hands. The fat man had watched impassively, the only indication of any feeling at all being an expressive nod and grunt of approval at some of K's more inventive methods. That should have been an indicator of some kind, but K passed over it quickly, preferring not to dwell on the possibilities of this considering that his daughter was now in the fat man's clutches.

The fat man had been irritating, looking back—though not at the time—but nowhere near as sinister as the pockmarked man who was laden with the dolls that formed a part of the marionette show that had presaged the blackout and abduction.

When K thought about it, he hadn't really noticed the man that much when he had ridden out to meet the strangers on their approach to the ville. Standing among the immensely tall and the immensely fat, his coat seeming to make him invisible beneath all that he carried, he had been a man whose face had been nothing more than a blank space. It was only when K noticed him hanging around the young that he began to take note.

Despite the fact that the coat and the marionettes attached to them had to have been heavy and stifling in the heat of the day, the pockmarked man always carried them with him. He loitered where the children worked and played, a faint smile always hovering at the corner of his lips, his eyes darting from one to the other as though sizing them up in some way. Now—hellfire, now everything seemed to scream at him for his lack of action—he could see that the man had been assessing how they would transport so many young people, and whatever means of persuasion they would need. And at any other time he would have called the man a sicko freak and cut his nuts off before ramming them down his throat. Now he could see that what the man had on his mind was something far worse than any sexual abuse—if there was anything that could repulse the baron more. K was a coldheart bastard, sure, but one who had lines over which he would never go. That was where the chilling started for him.

It shook him to the core to realize that he allowed the man to watch the kids. Worse, when he recalled the way that they would sometimes stop what they were doing and talk to the man, ask him what he was doing, and then the way in which the man would stoop and talk to some of the dolls that hung off him, bending an ear as if to listen to any answer they might make, it made him feel as though he could puke. The bastard had been acting like the dolls had talked to him, enticing the youngsters to come forward and watch, to take part in his little game. He was winning them over so that when the time came, it would be that much easier to make them do whatever it was that he, the fat man and the others wanted.

Priming the whole ville so that when the day came, it was all so easy.

However long it was since they had arrived, the strangers were no longer strange. They were a part of the ville as if they had been there so long that the whole place had grown up around them. They passed unnoticed, and the populace seemed almost oblivious to their existence, except in those moments when it suited them to be noticed. It was such that it was impossible to tell when it was that they decided that their moment had come. The first that any of the populace knew about it was when the sun rose, and the people with it. Although they hadn't noticed, they had started to rise earlier in the morning, and spend less time at night in the few bars that the ville had, getting wasted on the poor quality brew. Looking back, there was no reason for this sudden and strange abstinence. It just happened. Like so many things. The influence of the strangers was subtle and pervasive.

Maybe that was why K put up no resistance when he rose that morning to see that the middle of the ville had been cleared and transformed. Where once there had been the junk and detritus that went with the maintenance of the few wags that they owned, there was now a cleared and flattened space. The wags and the mechanics' gear that had littered the ground had gone. In its stead stood a cabinet, a display stage for marionettes that was high, proud and alone. In the morning sun, it seemed to loom over the ville, with no sign of the man who had carried it into the ville, or those who had traveled with him.

The first few people who came to the clear space were those whose curiosity overcame them. K included himself in this, and stood in front of the cabinet, looking up at its seven-foot height with a puzzled expression. Somewhere deep inside he knew he should be pissed about this. In so many ways, it was an insult and a liberty. But all he could focus on was the question of what was about to happen next. The curiosity overwhelmed all other feeling.

"Ah, that is what I like to see," the fat man wheezed as he appeared at the baron's elbow. K shuddered. He hadn't heard the man approach, and had no idea he was there until he spoke. "The baron should always lead his people from the front, don't you think?"

There was an undertone to the fat man's voice that should have made the baron want to smash his stupe face in, but instead he merely said, "What is this?"

The fat man clapped him on the shoulder. "The time has come," he said, then chuckled before turning away.

"Come, come, my people," he yelled. "It's time for us to reward you for your hospitality. We'll put on a show for you, the likes of which you've never seen before. This will be a show that will explain to you the mysteries of being. Come, come to the center of town, which will now be the center of the universe and the answer to every question you may ever have had."

K looked around him as the fat man called the ville to order. From every direction, the ville folk started to swarm into the clearing. It wasn't a large ville, but there were more people than could ordinarily be contained with comfort in such a space. Yet they seemed to fill it with ease. They were murmuring and muttering to themselves as they filed in, and yet were somehow strangely subdued. The strangers seemed to stand at every entrance to the center, looming over the crowd and grown to more than their normal size, ushering them in and directing them as though to some arranged plan. The only one who wasn't immediately visible was the pockmarked man in the multicolored coat. As K looked around, he realized that there were no youngsters among the crowd, although a space had been left in a tight circle around the cabinet. It had one open side, yet he could see that the other three sides had hinged panels, and he had little doubt that these would fall for the delectation of those who were gathered at the sides and back.

Now, in recollection, he was astounded that this had occupied his attention. Surely the thought that the young were somewhere under the obvious influence of the pockmarked freak should have made his blood run cold. But maybe that was it. Whatever had been screwing with his head had found it convenient for him to be so easily distracted.

While he was still looking at the cabinet, the pockmarked man led the children in procession into the space around the base of the cabinet. He walked with a strange gait, strides of varying lengths making it seem as if he was dancing. Certainly, it had the look of an old ritual move as he indicated to the youngsters that they spread themselves in the space left for them, and sit on the ground. This done, he disappeared into the cabinet, lost behind the faded panel of painted wood.

It was only at that point that K realized that the man's coat had been flapping loosely, and for the first time since he had been in the ville, he wasn't laden with the marionettes. K could only assume that they were already in the cabinet. But why would he take them off now?

Before he could dwell on that, his attention was taken by the fat man, who had seemed to sidle through the crowd and was at the front of the cabinet. No... Make that at the side, too... How was that possible? Just as there seemed more of the strangers than there had been a few moments before, standing at every juncture from the center of the ville, so it seemed that the fat man was standing on every side of the cabinet, facing the crowd and speaking in a voice that seemed to be fuller, deeper and carry more weight than the wheezing croak of a few moments before.

"My friends, you are here now to see how the world has worked, how it has always worked, and how it always will work. The truth of who has always ruled this universe, and the commands we must all obey if we are to see the light and live the eternal sunshine of their glow, in which we can only bask if we have the faith and ability to stand the pain and pleasure that knowledge of them must bring. Now, revealed to you today, my friend Mr. Jabbs will show you in marionette show how the history of the world had unfurled. When the bounteous knowledge that he bestows has been given to you, I guarantee that you will see the only way in

which you can make that future yours, and will give of
yourselves willingly."

And then, while the whole of the ville folk watched
in rapt fascination, the first of the marionettes appeared
above the lip of the cabinet.

K hadn't thought about that since he had awakened
from the trancelike sleep to find that the children were
gone. Whether that was because it had been hidden
from his conscious mind by some exterior force, or
simply because he hadn't wanted to face it, he couldn't
tell. But now it suddenly came to him with an awful
clarity.

The marionettes had spoken in natural voices that
couldn't have come purely from Mr. Jabbs alone. The
one that was female had sweet, fluting tones that would
surely have been beyond the pockmarked man's capa-
bilities. More than that, the mellifluous tones of the
man and the sweetness of the woman spoke simultaneously. They danced an obscene, orgiastic dance as
they spoke of the beginning of the world, and the prop-
agation of the species through incessant copulation to
create a race of slaves that would serve them throughout time. Then, seamlessly, the marionettes changed so
that they were three: a woman and two young boys. The
woman danced around the boys, then, without warning, took a rock and smashed in the skull of one of the
boy marionettes. Was that really blood and brain that
seemed to spurt from the wound and splatter the children at the front?

Then the scene changed once more so that a group
of marionettes was gathered around a stone table. They

were clad in feathers, and one wore a mask like a bird. They took a young woman and spread-eagled her on the table as the marionette with the mask raised high a knife before intoning something in an unknown tongue, then plunging it into her chest before cutting her open, pulling out the heart, holding it high to the sun, then eating it.

How could one man make all these marionettes move and talk at the same time? Come to that, how did the blood seem so real?

Now, sitting alone and recalling it for the first time, it seemed to K that he was, for the first time, understanding what had happened. It was as though the marionette show wasn't that at all—rather, it was an illusion. Mist and mirrors to suggest something that was enlarged in their minds by whatever had clouded them enough to allow the strangers to take hold.

And so the procession of brutality continued, with blasters and grens laying waste to humanity in the name of furthering worship to the dark gods the strangers seemed to serve. The carnage fed these creatures, the chilling made them strong. To serve them would mean a glorious afterlife of that pain that tilted on the edge of ecstasy—like the moment he had seen in tortured men, where they gave in to their suffering and embraced it.

And the younger the blood, the more it fed the creatures.

Now he understood what they had been saying. And now he knew why he was too scared to go after the children himself. Blind NORAD, anyone would be if they had seen that! And all his people remembered the show, if only beneath the level of consciousness so that they weren't aware of that memory. Look how hard he had been forced to look for the party that followed the mercies into the darkness.

Now K understood all this and one thing more. He and his people had known that the strangers wanted the children, and they would do anything to get them. Anything. And he knew that the fear of what that might entail had made him—and the others—cave in. He could remember, now, the way in which they had mutely stood back and watched the strangers lead the children out of the ville after calmly packing away their toys.

Stood and gladly watched them walk away into the barren earth. Knowing full well what they were doing, and doing it willingly.

K sat alone and wept. For himself, for his daughter and for what he had done.

Chapter Nine

By the end of day two, Ryan had little doubt that the time had come to mount an attack. The first evening had seen the light of the palaces dim swiftly come the night. The children were put to bed, and the adults who acted as their guardians were soon to follow. There was a cursory sec patrol, but in truth it seemed that those who lived in the palaces were secure enough in their location for such patrols to be treated as little more than a formality.

Fine. That suited Ryan and his people very well.

But the watches of the night carried on, so for those keeping watch the atmosphere grew more oppressive. Nothing actually happened, but that was what was creeping over them. Was it this quiet because there was nothing to worry about, or was it that the strange mind-bending forces that had almost stopped them from getting this far were aware of their presence, but were merely biding their time?

Now there was a question, one that played in the minds of all of the companions as they stood their watch.

Come the morning, they resumed their jobs in the same manner as the previous day. All of them were, in their own manner, jittery both from lack of sleep and from the phantom that lurked over their shoulder. It was unspoken for most of the day, but loomed large over their every move and thought.

The day itself, over on the side of the canyon where the sun beat down on the bleached stone of the palaces, proceeded exactly the same as the day that preceded it. Every detail was the same, and it was almost as though it followed the movement of the sun so that everything even occurred at the same time as the previous day— all of it, right down to the midday sacrifice, as another willing victim was led to the slaughter, ritually butchered on the makeshift altar over the site that had been marked out in stones. From the distance of the canyon's yawning mouth, the companions watched in horrified and fascinated silence as the chilling was enacted again.

It had to mean something, but what? And what, if anything, did it have to do with the stone circle that was proscribed beneath? It was Doc who voiced that question, though he wasn't the only one to be thinking it.

Ryan was brusquely dismissive. "It doesn't matter what they think they're doing. That's their weird shit to worry about. All we need to think about is what it means to us in practical terms. How much are they going to want to defend their rites? How much do they want to hang on to the children, for whatever reason they want them?"

"How hard are they going to fight us?" J.B. said, his face screwed up as though he'd bitten on something foul, which kind of summed up the way he was feeling.

"Plenty," Jak said simply.

There was little doubt that he was correct. It looked

as though this rite had been going on for some time, and that it was of no little importance was reinforced by the way in which the activity around the circle they were building seemed to increase after the sacrifice had been made. It was as if it gave strength and impetus to their action, whatever the end result was intended to be.

By the time that night had started to fall, and the lights of the palace began to dim with the setting of the sun, Ryan had made up his mind. There was, really, only one course of action that was left open to him. He gathered the companions, abandoning his watch and moving them toward the back of the cave, where the torches they possessed were used sparingly to light the darkness. Though the roof of the cave was relatively high, still it would have been stifling to use naked flames for any brush torches. And although it was cool, the buildup of heat in such an enclosed space would have been as stifling as any smoke produced. Come to that, the chances of smoke escaping and alerting those opposite to their presence—assuming that they weren't already aware—was too great to risk. So they had sparingly used the old flashlights they carried with them, one at a time and only when strictly necessary, to conserve the batteries they carried.

It was by the light of one of these, shining up and throwing their faces into stark relief, that Ryan gathered them in a circle. When he spoke it was low and insistent, communicating the urgency he was now beginning to feel.

"I don't know what those coldheart crazies are up to over there, and I don't really give a shit. Whatever twisted schemes they've got is their bastard business. But I do know this—K is going to pay us well to get his ville's kids back, and we need the jack to get supplies. Now mebbe we can get the kids, and just mebbe we might even be able to do something that can set the rest of the youngsters over there free before the crazies chill them. Mebbe. But if we're going do it, then we've got to act quick."

J.B. nodded. "Yeah, I'd go along with that. Looks like they keep on doing everything the same way, day after day, which makes them kind of easy to predict. The only thing that changes is that weird shit circle they're making. When that's done—"

"Exactly," Ryan agreed, "that'll be when they really start with whatever it is that they want to do. I'm willing to bet that it involves the kids, and that it's not going to be pretty. So we need to get at them now."

"Especially if there is some kind of exterior intelligence that has some power over them," Doc said darkly.

Jak spit noisily. "Nothing do about that. Not doing anything now, so strike before does."

"I'm with Jak on this," Mildred agreed. "If it's playing cat and mouse with us, then let's get going before it decides to stop playing and start killing."

Ryan turned to Krysty. "What do you reckon?" he asked her simply.

"I just don't know," she said, shrugging. "If it's some kind of old intelligence, or just some mutie power they have, then it doesn't feel like it knows we're here. It's like it figured that we just couldn't get past the shit back out there, and so doesn't bother this close to home. Bit

like the way they don't recce their own land properly,"
she added wryly. "Complacent bastards, too sure of
themselves. Mebbe that's how we can get them."

Ryan grinned. "That's the kind of talk I like to hear.
We need to get our shit together and start as soon as
possible. I've been thinking about the best way to hit
them."

TIME WAS OF THE ESSENCE, but there was no way of hurrying what had to be done. The distances that they had
to cover were large, and they could only do it under the
cover of dark, and by foot. Those who had traversed the
canyons in the days before skydark had generally used
burros as transport. The surefooted creatures could take
the mountain paths down the sides of the canyon at a
rapid pace without risk to life or limb, and could then
cross the rocky terrain that formed the canyon floor
before beginning the slow, painful ascent of the other
side.

Human feet were slower and less sure. Moreover, the
two groups into which Ryan had divided his companions were hampered further by the need to move only
under the cover of darkness. There was no way that
they could make their target in a quicker time, and they
would have to risk the remote possibility that, in the
course of a further two sacrifices, they could lose some
of the young they were charged with recovering. The
irony of making the target and not being quick enough
to save the baron's daughter was one that would have
no doubt been lost on the baron. No way would they
get paid: come to that, it was doubtful it would even

be worth returning with the rest of the children unless they were ready for another firefight.

But that was a chance they would have to take. The only way to get to where they wanted was to move in the dark and hide and rest during the hours of daylight. Whether they had slipped under the defenses, or whether the mind—or minds—that had created the illusory defenses was aware but biding its time was something they couldn't consider. All they could do was stay triple red at all times, and deal with the obstacles that they could see—the patrols that ventured forth in the morning to patrol and recce the area.

Having already watched them for two days, it was a marvel to J.B. that they even bothered. It was a thought that had occurred to all in the group, but somehow it seemed to irk the Armorer more than the others. Maybe it was the sense of military tactics and ways of fighting that had become second nature to him, but it just seemed so, well, stupe.

The purpose of a patrol was to scout to see that the perimeters of your territory were safe from incursion. But these people seemed to just do it because it was expected of them. Twice he had seen it from the cave, and now on the first morning after they had started their journey down into the mouth of the abyss, he watched from a secured spot while the sec party rode out from the palaces of light and down into the canyon, circling before returning to their starting point.

And that was all it was: a circuit that took them around the empty space, a perfunctory and pointless trip across the barren rocks and down into the area where the creek ran and dribbled through the dry stone and bare gorse and scrub. The riders looked impressive on their white mounts, but the horses, despite their sure-footed stance, weren't sturdy and weren't good fighting stock. Neither were the riders, by the look of them. They were tall and thin, as befitted the build of their steeds, and they looked ahead with a blankness that shone from glassy eyes. Like everything else in that bizarre city on the ledge, it seemed that the riders did everything as though to a ritual and one that was performed almost in a trance. Perhaps it had been so long since anyone had ventured this far into the canyon, or since anyone had even been able to get past the mind-bending defenses that lay in wait across the plains, that they had grown complacent.

As J.B. lay in hiding with Jak and Krysty, watching the riders go past and then come back again, sightless and unseeing, he wondered if it would really be as easy as it seemed to take the settlement. Sure, they were seriously outnumbered, but Ryan's plan was simple enough and took account of the ritual nature of everything in the city of palaces. They lived and worked on rigidly defined lines, and Ryan had figured a way to slip between these and cause the necessary chaos to extract their target and get out. But how had they managed to survive so long? If the story K had told them when he offered them the job was anything to go by, these cold-hearts weren't so bastard slack when they were in their own territory.

So who was to say that they wouldn't be able to

snap out of their usual ways when the first sign of danger hit?

Anyway, he grumbled to himself as he shifted uncomfortably under the shelter of a rock cluster that formed a natural windbreak close to the sluggish and most narrow section of the creek, it just didn't seem right that they rode out this way without noticing anything. What if they were more alert to what was around them than they seemed? From J.B.'s point of view, it would make more sense if they noted the presence of intruders and lured them into a trap.

Which meant that he and the others should be triple red about this whole operation.

Ah, hell, maybe he was just feeling really cranky. Considering that they knew they needed to move quick, as the stone circle looked near completion, they couldn't move with anything like the speed he would have liked.

Moving out of the cave and down the side of the canyon under the cover of darkness had been hell on wheels. The narrow paths were slippery and covered with loose shale underfoot. In daylight it should have been hard enough to move with any kind of speed, but under cover of dark it was near impossible. Especially as they had to keep as quiet as possible. In the still of the dark night, even the slightest sound of loose stone or a whispered curse as a foot fell loose could reverberate across the empty space between themselves and the now-silent city.

Parting at the mouth of the cave, Ryan had led his party one way while J.B. was deputed to lead his in the opposite direction. In theory, at least. As Ryan's unspoken number two, J.B. was nominal war party leader. He was to direct his section in their part of the plan. But in practical terms there was no way he was going to take the lead down the steep and treacherous paths. Not when he had the excellent night vision and the far more sure feet of Jak in his team.

The albino youth was a ghostly white vision under the wan light of the moon. His dark camou jacket and pants blended in with the landscape, leaving only the occasional shimmer of the metal patches on his jacket and the flowing white mane of his hair to mark his passing as he skipped and hopped over the uncertain terrain, picking out the safest path of descent. Following in his wake, Krysty found it hard to keep pace. J.B. held back a little, watching them skip ahead. This was partly because he was finding the going hard, and partly because he opted to take some stock of the situation.

Below them the floor of the canyon was shrouded in darkness, only the distant gurgling of the water giving any indication of depth to the dark. Ahead of him, the white dot of Jak's head bobbed up and down in the dark. It wasn't so bright under the pale moon, but still stood out like a beacon to the cautious Armorer when compared to the blackness that spread around. If anyone cared to look, their curiosity would soon be aroused by the sight of Jak's head.

Lucky for them, then, that as he looked across at the far city, J.B. could see that it was completely at peace, almost as though everyone within had bought the farm the moment the sun dropped over the horizon.

Dark night, he thought. If these coldhearts felt that secure in their homes, then it had to be more than just arrogance. The Armorer stopped momentarily and looked along the side of the canyon they were traversing, peering into the shadows to try to pick out where Ryan, Doc and Mildred were making their own descent.

J.B. realized that the other two were slipping away from him and picked up the pace to catch them.

It wasn't the smartest thing he had ever done. His mouth was dry, and his heart pounded as he felt his balance sway on the unsteady ground beneath him. A couple of times he felt the uncertain ground give, and his feet slip from under him, leaving him floundering on the edge of black space. It was little more than some built-in desire for survival that kept him from plunging into the abyss and reaching the canyon floor a damn sight quicker than Jak or Krysty.

After a couple of hours of a descent that seemed interminable, he felt rather than saw the paths beneath him start to grow more level. It was only when he realized he was looking straight ahead rather than down to track Jak's bobbing white mane that he realized that he was now running along the floor of the canyon.

He relaxed, which was an unwise thing to do, even though it was an unconscious and natural reaction to his sense of relief. Immediately, he stumbled and fell, his foot catching on a rock embedded in the soil. The ground rushed up to meet him at speed as his momentum carried him face-first so that he felt a crunching impact when his face squashed itself against the earth, his glasses flying away from him.

Cursing, he lifted himself up, his body momentarily aching from the impact and lungs protesting at the way the air had been driven from them by the way his ordnance bag had caught him under the ribs. Groping around in front of him, he managed to recover his glasses. Luckily, they weren't damaged. He placed them back on the bridge of his nose, thankful that he could still see okay, and that the lenses were in one piece.

He could also see Jak and Krysty ahead of him. It was then that he looked up and realized that the difficult descent had taken most of the night, and now the first light of dawn was upon them. They had to find shelter, and soon. He risked a glance across the floor of the canyon, and in the distance he could see three specks moving across the ground, parallel to the path forged by Jak and Krysty ahead of him.

If he could see Ryan, Mildred and Doc in this light, then they could also see him. And that meant, undoubtedly, that anyone who chanced to look down from the city on the ledge would also be able to see the six of them as they moved across the canyon floor.

J.B. picked up the pace, aiming to catch Jak and Krysty as soon as possible. He could see that the albino teen was searching for a place for them to take shelter during the approaching day. He needed to catch up before Jak actually found one good enough to hide him from the Armorer.

As he blew hard, gaining ground, he wondered if Ryan was realizing just what a stretch it would be to realize his plan. They were partway there in one night, but they only had one more night to make the target.

Once they were up the other side of the canyon wall and on top of the shining palaces, there was nowhere for them to hide. They had to strike immediately, hoping that it was still before the majority of the populace had risen: and hoping, maybe, that they still had the strength after the ordeal of making that last stretch.

RYAN WAS CURSING as he curled into the uncomfortable ridges of the stone hollow that he, Mildred and Doc were using as their hide until the light began once more to fade.

How many hours they would have to lie here, hidden and cramped, before they could cover the second half of the ground between themselves and the city of light was a matter that occupied the very forefront of his mind. Making it this far had been tiring in itself. To cover that distance was hard enough. To try to do it over unfamiliar territory and in the dark made it even harder. Each of them had fallen several times, and Ryan could feel the warm trickle of blood here and there from the small cuts and contusions that had come with each tumble. Each pulled and torn muscle would soon start to stiffen up. To have to lie in this place would only make it worse.

He was sure that there would be no patrols from the mysterious palaces during the remainder of the day. But if they moved out of the cover they had found, then they would be in plain sight of the populace as they went about their tasks up on the ledge. Now, Ryan was sure that they were all moving in some kind of drugged or hypnotic trance, but not so much that half a dozen people moving across an otherwise barren landscape wouldn't be noticeable.

The companions would have to stay there, secreted away in a position that could only impair their chances of making the second half of the journey without problems.

The sun continued to beat down. The only good thing about their having to stay in cover was that the heat wouldn't deplete them even further. Although the floor of the canyon took them deep down, it was as though the bleached stone on the side of the canyon where the palaces lay acted like a mirror that reflected and magnified the heat, pushing it down into the depths where they now lay, so that it was trapped.

Heat was supposed to rise, Ryan thought. Yeah, right... That was why he was sweating so that it dripped into his eye, stinging like a bastard, and why it chilled him every time he raised a cramped arm to wipe it away.

Time crawled by. Mildred and Doc were visible to him, and they communicated in a series of whispers. Even though they were some distance from the city of light, they were wary of how sound traveled across the empty space. So they kept their voices low and their communication to a minimum. They would try to rest as much as possible, and at the same time take turns on watch.

The day passed painfully slow. Doc could be heard gently snoring at one point, awakening himself with a grunt and a muttered apology. Ryan slept fitfully, dreaming odd dreams that were disturbing enough to jolt him awake so that he found himself staring wildly around, for a moment unsure of his surroundings.

As the sun crept across the sky and the shadows crept equally across the floor of the canyon, the intense heat started to subside, although there was still enough to make them feel as though they were baking. Above them, Ryan could hear the city halt when it came to the time for another blood sacrifice to whatever gods or forces demanded the chilling of a youth. Then there were the mundane and indistinct sounds of the rest of the day's business, which gradually wound to a close as the darkness and the first whispers of cool night air began to seep down to them.

Just that alone made Ryan feel refreshed. His limbs still ached and cramped, and the desultory sleep had done little to wash away the tiredness that crept through every vein, but even so just the fact that they were now able to come out from their hiding place and begin the second leg of their mission was enough.

He had wondered how J.B. and the others had been faring during the day. Little better than his people, he was pretty sure. Mildred had been complaining with the occasional low grumble about both the long wait and how uncomfortable she felt. Doc had said little, but the tone of his voice on those few words uttered had spoken all that needed to be said.

Ryan had tried a few times to get a look out from their shelter and across the space between where his people lay, and where he was pretty certain that J.B. and the others had landed. There was little between them in which to hide, and he was certain that the only glimpse he had caught of their movement would place them by the creek that wound across the canyon floor. But despite that, his view was too oblique or their place of hiding was too well chosen, for he had been unable to catch even the slightest flicker of movement.

Which was little more than he would expect.

So he was both pleased and frustrated as he led his people out into the cold and dark night, sure now that they were safe from prying eyes. There was no nocturnal patrol, and the silence from the palaces above betrayed the secure and steady habits of the inhabitants of the shining white city. Even as they emerged into the night, Ryan could look up and see the mysterious palaces shine like polished bone in the moonlight.

With the windows shaping darkness within the light, the buildings seemed to form faces so that they were like skulls grinning gap-toothed down onto the six who would seek to go against them.

For a second Ryan stood silently, looking up and wondering just what it was they were really fighting: was it just the will of a bunch of people who had lived too long in a rad-blasted zone that had enabled them to become muties who could make their beliefs seem real? Or was there something else at the back of it, something that had a real and tangible evil?

He shook his head. There was no time for this. He looked away from the city on the ledge and cast his eye across the flat base of the canyon floor. Three dark shapes, one at the front outlined by an equally bone-white shock of hair that moved like a beacon in the night, were moving swiftly across the remaining

distance between their hiding place and the ascent to
the city.

Ryan grinned to himself. J.B. was right to get them
moving, as there was little time. Before they knew it,
the sun would start to rise once again, and they would
be trapped halfway up the canyon wall, at the mercy of
the morning patrol as it rode out.

Doc and Mildred were out of their cover and ready
to go. Ryan gestured to them to follow, and didn't spare
another glance for their companions in the distance.

What had to happen next was simple: J.B. and his
people were to move in and hit hard, locating their targets and extracting them with the minimum of fuss
and the maximum of aggression. To aid the ease of this
action, Ryan and his team were to cause a distraction
in the city and divide and occupy any sec that they may
have.

So they had to cover the ground. Fast. Even as they
moved off, he could feel that it would be a strain to
get into position before the sun was in place. But it
was something they had to do. With Doc and Mildred,
Ryan felt that in some ways he had the lesser of the
forces. Doc was keen, but his body was ravaged and
slower than either Jak or J.B. And Mildred was a good
fighter, but again no match for Krysty. Not being born
into these times was something that neither could help,
but it had undoubtedly counted against them in some
unfathomable way.

Still, that was why he had chosen them for the decoy
action, so to fret about it was useless. Instead, they

should concentrate on making their target in time to put their strategy into action.

Yet as they made the ground, keeping pace—he hoped—with the other group, there was something that nagged at him. The sec force they hoped to distract: how, exactly, did it operate? He had seen nothing that resembled a sec force as they knew it. That should make it an easier task. But if they had no conventional sec as such, then what exactly would they be facing?

And how could they prepare to fight that which was both unknown and unpredictable?

Chapter Ten

Jak looked up at the canyon face. The sun was starting to ascend and the heat beginning to grow again. Above, across the clear air of the canyon, he could hear the sounds of people stirring and starting to go about their business. It wouldn't be long now before the patrol rode out, seemingly sightless and on a ritual ride that took no note of whatever was going on.

Except that the companions couldn't take that risk. Maybe the sec team on patrol wasn't as sightless as it seemed.

He looked back down to where J.B. and Krysty followed in his wake. The Armorer was taking the rear position, and was struggling a little. It was a steep ascent at this point in the journey, and the ordnance that J.B. carried with him was weighing him down a little. Krysty was blowing hard, but making good time. It was one hell of a task they had set themselves, but as Jak looked up to where the lip of the city's ledge was protruding above them—almost, it seemed, within touching distance now—it was one that now seemed more of a possibility than it had a few hours before, when the dark before the dawn had echoed in their hopes and fears.

He tried to stare across the vast, yawning chasm to

catch a glimpse of the companions who were climbing on the far side. They had to be in position at more or less the same time. If his people got to their point too soon, they would risk discovery with every second they had to wait.

The albino teen was suddenly filled with a feeling of dread, accosted by the smell and sense of chilling that lurked like a miasmic mist over the bone-white stone city.

He wondered if the others felt that same sense of foreboding.

"Jak, what is it? We need to keep moving."

He turned and found himself staring into Krysty's eyes. His own face and gleaming red eyes were as inexpressive as always. At least, that was what he hoped. But perhaps not. He could almost feel the doomie power of the redheaded beauty reach out through her own orbs and look into him. He could see that her sentient hair was flicking in an irritable fashion as it gathered close to her scalp. There was a depth to her words—the way she said them as much as the words themselves—that told him much.

"Place get you if stop," he murmured. "Yeah, keep moving...hit hard and run."

"I don't know about run, but otherwise yeah," J.B. said, grunting as he reached them, the initial puzzlement at seeing them halt evaporating as he caught a feel for what was going on mixed perhaps with relief that the nagging feelings he had experienced weren't his alone.

Jak turned, took a step up along the narrow rock path and squinted at the city, so close they could touch it.

"Wonder how others doing?"

"RYAN, MY DEAR BOY, I would hate to stand accused of jinxing our good fortune by saying as such, but this has been a lot easier than I had feared."

Doc was blowing hard between each word as he spoke, but the vulpine grin that spread across his features betrayed the truth of his assertion. Ryan would have to agree. They had emerged from their shelter feeling tired, stiff and aching. Yet the floor of the canyon across to the bottom of the roughly hewn rock track they had chosen for ascent had been surprisingly easy. The terrain was flat, and despite the dark there had been no hidden obstacles—dips in the ground, ridges of rock to trip them or loose stones to turn an ankle—to slow them or cause injury.

The path itself was partly natural, yet had also been assisted by man. Over the untold centuries since the mysterious palaces had first been built by an unknown hand, that very same hand had laid the foundation for the path that had enabled the dwellers of those palaces to move up and down the side of the canyon. It was shallow, with a gradient that spoke of mule transport, and therefore didn't require that the three companions now ascending use too much effort to make the climb.

The one-eyed man could see the buildings above begin to stir into life. As people began to move within them, it was as though the stone itself came to life, as well. The companions were close to their target, but they needed to move faster now if they were to create the necessary diversion.

"Pick it up," he said sharply. "You're right, Doc, but we can't waste time congratulating ourselves."

"Of course not, my dear Ryan," Doc agreed, suddenly solemn. "How long until the sec patrol rides out? I wonder."

Mildred looked at the sky, trying to judge time by the sun. "Not long now."

Ryan smiled wryly as he looked at his wrist chron. "If they have anything like this, then they'll be in the next few minutes. If they don't, then fuck knows…"

He wondered if the other group was thinking the same thing.

JAK, TOO, was looking at the sun. If he was any judge, then the sec patrol would ride out soon enough. He lowered his gaze to scan the path ahead of them for anything resembling cover. There was nothing. Like the path they had traveled on the far side of the canyon wall, there were a few outcrops and some sparse scrub, but nothing that would give them any kind of shelter or provide cover.

He hoped that Ryan's group was making good time, and that just maybe they could create their diversion before the patrol started its circuit of the canyon. Maybe that way they wouldn't have to face them down, because right now all he could see was that they would have to face off the patrol and raise an alarm before they reached the top of the path.

Beckoning to Krysty and J.B., he picked up the pace.

The path they had to travel was steeper than the one Ryan's group walked, and the effort was beginning to take its toll.

When they were at a point that granted them maximum exposure to any oncoming force, Jak heard the sounds of people approaching on horseback. There was the unmistakable clatter of hooves on rock. He turned back to face Krysty and J.B. and could see from their expressions that they, too, had heard the oncoming patrol. With a calm eye that belied the situation, the albino teen scanned the area. There was nowhere to hide; the fight would have to begin here.

"Frosty, now," he growled. There was no answer from his companions, but then again he didn't expect it.

The sec patrol rode out of the city and toward them, descending the narrow path at a speed that seemed to be amplified by the fact that there was nowhere to hide. The horses came within sight of the three companions, the men on their backs surely now able to see the trio that blocked their passage. And yet the horses didn't alter their pace. There was no speeding up to meet the oncoming foe, nor was there a decrease to take stock and prepare to fight. It seemed almost as if the staring, trancelike sec men on the backs of the steeds were truly as sightless as their gaze made them appear. Their mounts were receiving no instruction to change their pace, and so kept coming at the same steady rate.

"Dark night, they don't even see that we're here," J.B. breathed. "What kind of people are they up there?"

The three companions had their blasters drawn, ready to fire, but held back until the riders were almost on top of them. To start a firefight would be to alert the city above of their presence. But taking out the sec without a sound would be a much better option.

Jak swapped his Colt Python for a leaf-bladed throwing knife in each hand. The mounts were so close on him now that he could almost feel their hot, rancid breath.

And then he had a revelation—was there even a need to fight?

"Back," he said simply and softly, stepping to one side of the narrow path so that he was tight against the canyon wall, the rock digging into his back as he impressed himself upon it.

Krysty and J.B. needed no bidding to follow his lead. Both of them were almost instantly in tune with his thinking. The sightless eyes of the riders truly saw nothing and went on their way as part of some ritual of the morning, the significance of which had been lost over the decades—perhaps longer—that they had been practiced.

The horses cantered past the companions as they huddled against the rock. Dust thrown up by the pounding hooves billowed in a cloud over them, choking and stinging lungs and eyes. Yet they held their nerve, keeping silent and still so as not to disturb the steeds, which were seemingly only a little more alert than the automatons who rode their backs.

The horses continued on their path down the narrow pass and onto the floor of the canyon, on the set circuit that they had completed since who knew when. The companions watched them go.

"Black dust! This gets weirder all the time. I'll be happy when we get in, grab the kids and head out," J.B. said softly.

"You make it sound so easy like that," Krysty said wryly. "I can't see that happening quite so easily."

"Only one way to find out." J.B. shrugged.

Jak's eye teeth showed sharply in a humorless grin. "Let's get fuckers," he said before turning and starting toward the apex of the passage with a renewed vigor.

"FIREBLAST," RYAN BREATHED. "They're done for..." Inwardly he cursed himself for not taking that path himself and putting his companions in harm's way.

He halted in his progress along the path that he traversed with Doc and Mildred. The three of them stood and watched, hardly daring to breathe as they watched the riders mount and start off toward the path where they knew their companions were currently standing.

Doc looked up at the sky, studying the sun.

"They are earlier than yesterday. Not by much, I grant you, but earlier nonetheless. Enough, dammit, to make a difference when you would rather there was not."

"Screw that. I just hope they can get the fire off first," Mildred stated. "It'll wake the bastards up there to the fact that we're here, but at least they'll have a fighting chance."

Ryan was transfixed. He knew he should be insisting that his trio continue their ascent. If there was to be a firefight as the riders hit the oncoming companions, then at least he could get his party into position to provide distraction and covering fire as the city of palaces was mobilized.

He knew that was what he should be doing, yet he couldn't. He was transfixed by what was going on across the void, a mute observer who was powerless to affect the outcome.

Ryan was almost holding his breath as the horses reached the section of the path where he was sure that his three companions were located. He was only aware of that when he realized that the burning in his lungs was the air that couldn't be released.

And then he blew out, relief and disbelief mingled as he saw the horses descend onto the floor of the canyon without so much as a pause. He had expected the sounds of blasterfire to rend the morning quiet, to alert the waking city to imminent attack, and to adrenalize the stasis in which he and his people now stood.

But there was nothing. No blasterfire of any description. No pause. No sign that the riders had even noticed that there was anyone in their path. He had no idea what the hell had happened. Had the other three managed to find—in the most unlikely of locations—some place in which to hide? Or was it that, in some bizarre way, the riders had managed to pass them without even knowing?

Although the latter was the least likely of explanations, it seemed that somehow that was the case.

"Son of a—" Mildred whispered, breaking the silence.

"I would not claim to understand what occurred," Doc murmured, "nor would I wish to lay claim to any spurious notion of explanation. But I will say that to stay here now would be folly. If, as it appears, our friends have somehow managed to avoid the odious riders, by whatever means, then it falls upon us to tarry no longer and to continue, lest we let them down and betray the luck that they have so obviously been privy to."

"Man, you talk too much," Mildred said shortly, "but you've got a point. Let's get moving, boss man."

Ryan nodded. "Double quick," he said. "One thing for sure, though—more weird shit is going down, so we need to be triple frosty for anything that we get. No letting this shit throw us off what we got to get done."

"I hear you," Mildred agreed. "Come on."

Neither Ryan nor Doc needed further prompting. They set off at a redoubled pace along the path leading up to the city on the ledge. Certain that their companions weren't only safe, but had almost definitely redoubled their efforts to reach their objective, the three companions on this side of the divide knew that they had to move fast if they were to start their diversionary tactics before the primary party could make its move. Under the existing conditions, with no real ability to maintain contact, it was up to Ryan's people to make the first move. Only once they had started their diversion would the other three make their move. But they couldn't stay poised and in anticipation for too long. It was only by luck that they had evaded detection this far. To tempt fate would be folly.

Ryan could feel the anxiety gnaw at his guts as they marched. Could they go faster at the risk of reaching the target area exhausted? It was hard to hold back even a little, but he knew he had to.

It was the only chance they had of making this work.

J.B. WATCHED THE RIDERS go down into the valley, wiping his eyes as the clouds of dust began to fade in the backdraft created by the horses.

"Dark night!" he said once more, his capacity for anything other than exclamation taken away by the sheer weirdness of this experience. It was like no other kind of fight they had ever—willingly or unwillingly—entered into. "It'll take them about an hour before they make the circuit and hit where Ryan and the others are. Time enough for us to get in and out. Let's move it."

Jak merely grunted his agreement and continued his climb. Krysty, at his back, wondered if Ryan and the others would still be on the ascent, or would assume that the riders had somehow vanquished them and be on their way to find out. It was something that wouldn't ever have occurred to J.B. and made him wonder what was going on in Krysty's head. She had been the one most affected by the weird mind games of the trip to the canyon, and now it seemed as though it was making it hard for her to focus. It should have been obvious from the fact that there had been no firefight that Ryan and the others wouldn't assume the worst, and would carry on the mission trusting to the companions on this side to make the ascent unharmed.

He said nothing to her except to assure her that Ryan would continue, but kept to himself the doubt about her being one hundred percent on the game. It was a worry that, as they reached the last few hundred yards and could now smell and hear the city just ahead and above them, was a concern.

Jak indicated that they should halt and hold back. They were at a slight bend in the canyon wall, enough to shield them from view and also to block their own view of the city as it awoke to the day.

The smell was appalling. In contrast to the gleaming appearance of the buildings from a distance, close up they could smell the blood and rotting flesh, the stench of dirt and feces, and the strong ammonia of urine that hadn't been cleared. In the rituals of the day, there was obviously little room for simple cleaning.

No, the ville elders had higher, better things to occupy them. The ritual slaughter was part of that. And that was what made them truly dangerous.

"What do we do now?" Krysty asked quietly.

"We wait," J.B. replied simply. And trust in Ryan, he added to himself.

RYAN, DOC AND Mildred now found themselves in a similar position on the far side of the city, except that they didn't have the luxury of cover. Their path, though winding in its progress, now led them on a straight line toward the first of the mysterious palaces. Like the fighters on the far side, they were struck by the disparity between the appalling stench of the city as opposed to the gleaming beauty of the old buildings.

Any such further reflection was driven from their minds by the appearance of a man in front of them. He was wearing a multicolored coat, and his pockmarked, blank visage was betrayed only by the burning fire that made his black eyes gleam, hinting at a barely controlled savagery. Without even having time to consciously think about it, Ryan realized that this was the puppet master who had worked his insidious magic before the world went black for Baron K and his people.

More than that, as he stared at them without blinking, it seemed as though his hand merely twitched, and a blaster appeared in it. Long-barreled and heavy, it was a revolver that J.B. would have pinned down in a second. Ryan, for his part, took an educated guess at a Colt .44, accurate in a strong hand and liable to make a nasty hole in a man, even at the range that loomed between them.

How the hell had he managed to get that into his fist so bastard quick? Ryan was a good draw, but even so he had barely pulled the SIG-Sauer from its holster, and was in no position to fire first.

He should have been. The blaster should already have been in his hand before they reached this point. Something was slowing him: tiredness, torpor or some outside malign force, perhaps. It didn't matter. It was about to cost him his life.

Or at least, that was what he thought before the quiet of the morning was shattered by the sharp crack of Mildred's Czech-made ZKR. At his back, Mildred had been faster, and more alert. She was also a far better shot, at this distance, than any of them.

The barrel of the Colt .44 jerked up in the air, then drooped downward and fell as the pockmarked man's lifeless fingers let free their grip on the blaster. It fell to the ground, hammer cocked, and exploded into life as it hit, the slug harmlessly gouging out a chunk of the rock floor. As for the former wielder of the blaster, his impassive face showed a sudden and almost comical surprise as a small round hole neatly appeared in the center of his forehead, a small trickle of blood bubbling around the bottom edge of the hole. It was only when he crumpled and hit the ground that the wet slap of the back of his head hitting the rock revealed that the exit wound from the small-bore caliber of the ZKR had made a more considerable impact on exit.

"Come on," Ryan yelled, charging forward, as much to rouse himself from the momentary shock of staring death in the face as to whip up Mildred and Doc. The time for subterfuge had passed. Now they had to hit and hit hard, hoping that Jak and the others were ready in position.

As the pockmarked man hit the deck, Ryan was already past him, blaster now in hand and his mind refocused on the task ahead. Doc and Mildred were at his heels, each knowing what had to be done. They had to hit hard and get out fast. Their task was to cause chaos and pull back so that they could rendezvous with Jak, J.B. and Krysty…and hopefully the children of the ville.

The crack of the blaster had attracted some unwelcome attention. Ryan had hoped that they would be able to create chaos before they drew fire, but it was obviously not going to be their day for luck. For, as they moved from the canyon and onto the ledge of the city itself, they could see that there were already armed assailants coming to meet them.

The city extended for almost five hundred yards along the ledge. To create a diversion that would be of some use to their companions, they would have ideally liked to have made some ground along the ledge before having to tackle any opposition. It wasn't to be.

A wave of young men and women exited one of the buildings. There was no time to scan their faces to see if there was anyone among them who could be in their target group. The young people poured from the doorway and the windows of the building, yelling incoherently. They weren't armed with blasters, but they carried the tools they had been using to construct the circle and the makeshift altar that had been the sacrificial site.

Wave upon wave descended on them. The sheer weight of numbers threatened to overwhelm Ryan and his people before they even had a chance to move. Nonetheless, survival was paramount. With a muttered curse Doc put paid to the charge with a blast from the LeMat. The shot spread out over the distance between them, the hot metal scorching as it rent flesh and bone. The screams of agony cut through the cries of attack and caused the crowd to pull back, allowing the three fighters to move forward with a little more ease. Mildred and Ryan used their handblasters to pick off the more dangerous elements—those who would have the extra courage to move past the pack.

They had to move in a manner that was by its nature perilous. The clear pathway ahead took them along the lip of the ledge. One charge regardless of personal safety could take them over the edge and back down the way they had come. Yet this was the only way that was unobstructed, taking them as it did over the sacrificial circle with a sudden drop in temperature that only registered subconsciously but nonetheless spurred them onward.

Now it was getting harder. The noise had brought out more people from the buildings, so that the ledge was swarming with hostile opposition. Ryan felt as though they were being pushed to the edge, with nothing but empty air at their backs. Among the faces that blurred into a mass in front of them, weaving in and out of the younger crowd, Ryan could see older men and women, with a harder edge to their eyes that made them stand out. They were moving faster, and with more purpose. Soon, they would be on the three companions, and it would be too late to take action.

The one-eyed man cast an anxious glance to the side of him. In just a snatched second it was almost impossible to tell how far along the ledge they had come, but the back of his brain worked furiously. From where he knew the circle lay after their forty-eight hours of observation, and from how far they had moved beyond it, he was able to make a rough guess that told him they were almost central to the city itself.

He could only hope that Jak and the others had taken their cue from the first blasts of the firefight and had moved into the city on their part of the mission, using the cover that Ryan and his team was providing. Fireblast! he thought. It certainly seemed as though they had drawn most of the populace down on them.

Even as these thoughts went across Ryan's mind, he was picking off those of the mob in front of them who would dare to step forward. Flanking him, Doc and Mildred were doing the same.

But that couldn't continue indefinitely. Indeed, even in the short time they had been firing, the crowd had crept palpably closer.

Why hadn't the older, harder-eyed members of the crowd blasted them? They carried blasters, after all. Ryan could see that as he stared into the mob.

No, they had other ideas—capture and keep. Well, he had no intention of having his heart ripped out while it was still beating. It was time to create the real diversion, spread confusion and get the hell out. If they could…

He turned to Mildred and yelled at her. It came out as a wordless imprecation, but she knew what it meant. Letting her ZKR fall, she dipped into a pocket and her hand emerged with two gas grens.

In one fluid movement she pulled the pins with her teeth and tossed the bombs high and far into the crowd, noting with an amusement she hadn't the time to feel the looks of confusion and bemusement on the crowd as the grens casually dropped into their midst.

And then, with a dull thump, they detonated.…

Chapter Eleven

"Now!"

As soon as the first crack of blasterfire had sounded, Jak led his companions into the middle of the city. They moved swiftly and with an assurance that almost seemed to make them invisible. Calculating that the sudden chaos caused by the diversionary attack would provide cover, they made their move. As the people began to pour out of the buildings and onto a ledge that was actually far too narrow for the numbers that were now jostling shoulder to shoulder with the interlopers, it became apparent that to move with any attempt at subterfuge and hesitation would make them stand out among the chaos that reigned around them. So to move swiftly and decisively, as though belonging in that space, would be by far the best thing to do.

It was difficult enough to keep an eye out for one another as the young people rushed aimlessly around them, let alone to try to spot the ones they were searching for. But they had little time, and in the middle of the panic, their sense of purpose seemed to give them the calm to focus on what they needed to do.

While the kids were thronging around them, too, they had the advantage that the elders of the city wouldn't be able to spot them so easily. Those who had emerged were concentrating on moving across to the area where Ryan, Doc and Mildred were mounting their raid. For now, Jak, Krysty and J.B. had free rein.

It soon became apparent from the way that the groups of young moved around them, only parting to let them through in certain patterns, that despite the influence they may be under, they were still bonded and ran together in the groups by which they had been abducted. So it was that, in the midst of the formless shouting and the stench of fear that added to the already overpowering odor of the city, they could see individually that their prey would most likely still be gathered in an almost feral pack.

J.B. doubted that would make it easier, and was beginning to doubt the sense of their course of action, when out of the milling throng the solution almost literally bumped into him. There, in the middle of a pack of kids ranging from about twelve to eighteen, was a tall, rangy girl with tangled flowing black hair, a chiseled nose, and eyes that were almost as wild and dark as her mane.

He'd never seen the girl before, but she was so much like her father and the description he had provided that there was no doubting that she was Baron K's daughter. And, by the same token, those around her had to be the rest of the kids who had been taken, and who they had been dispatched to find. She was about to brush past him when he reached out and grabbed her by the shoulders, swinging her around so that she looked him right in the face.

Or should that be looked right through him. Her eyes

were sightless and piercing, focused on something that only she could see. For a moment she was still, and then she started to squirm, her mouth contorting in a formless wail of anger and frustration as she tried to pull herself away.

J.B. could see that whatever else she may be, she was in no fit state to be receptive to anything he might have to say. He tried to hold on to her, even though it was like trying to keep a grip on water, and turned to yell for Krysty and Jak, hoping that he could make himself heard above the general melee. He called, staring around and hoping that he would be able to catch sight of them. And that it would be quick. In response to the girl's wordless cries of distress, those who had been moving in a pack were turning on J.B., jostling around him. They weren't hostile—they moved too slowly and in too much of a stupor for that—but nonetheless they still had weight of numbers, and he tightened his grip on the girl as he felt fingers and hands clutch and pull at him, trying to separate him from the girl.

Dark night! he thought. Jak and Krysty better hurry. He could see two tall, older men moving through the throng with a greater deliberation. Although he had never seen them before, K's description had been vivid enough for him to know they were two of the men who had visited the ville and spirited away these youngsters.

If they reached him, then the game was up.

"Come on, J.B., don't make a big deal of it. She's only a little girl after all."

He felt two pairs of hands ripped away from his arm and chest before he heard Krysty's wry tones.

She joined him at his side, pushing back the kids who threatened to overwhelm them.

"They don't look like they want to go," he muttered through clenched teeth, still grappling with the girl as he started to drag her back the way they had come.

"Whatever these coldhearts feed them, it makes them subservient enough," Krysty agreed. "Only one way to handle this."

Before the Armorer had a chance to realize what she was about to do, Krysty pulled back her arm and delivered a roundhouse punch to the point of the girl's jaw. J.B. saw the light go out in her eyes before her eyelids dropped and the rest of her followed suit.

"Aw, now I really didn't want to do that," he complained. "Now I'm going to have to carry her back the way we came, and she's going to be bastard heavy after a while."

"I get the feeling that's going to be the least of our worries," she remarked, looking across the milling crowd at the heads of the two tall men as they moved closer. Their grim, hard stares left no doubt as to their intent. "Shit, I wish Jak would show himself," she added in an undertone.

And then a wry grin crept across her face. The albino teen might not have shown himself, or indeed been visible, but his presence was more than adequately felt. For as she looked across at the two men, first one and then the other vanished swiftly from view. It was as though they simply crumpled and folded up on themselves. Why this should be would have been a mystery if not for the fact that a spray of red shot from the throat of each a fraction of a second before they fell. A spray that seemed to draw the eye to the briefest gleam of metal, the merest flash of bone-white skin and dark fabric that was there and gone before it could be truly registered.

"Come on, let's move," she said to J.B., using her elbow to deflect one of the youths who was trying to grab her from behind, and both feeling and hearing the satisfying crunch of bone on bone as the grip was loosened and a slack-jawed voice groaned in surprise.

"Easy for you to say," the Armorer said as he hefted the girl over his shoulder in a motion that was impeded not by her deadweight but by the actions of those who still sought to claw at him. He lashed out at them but was still thwarted in his intent by the necessity of only using one hand and a foot.

Krysty understood what he meant. As soon as she had freed herself enough to move, she was at his side, helping him to free himself. She would be able to take care of one side and ride shotgun through the crowd for the hampered J.B., but she would require Jak to make his way through the crowds and assist her if they were to have any chance. Right now they were doing little more than treading water, and at that were in danger of sinking beneath the tide of slow-moving but insistent youth who milled around them.

If she hadn't been so busy punching and hacking her way through this tide, she would have expressed relief as the path suddenly opened in front of them, cleared by the flashing blades of Jak, a knife in each fist as he fought his way through.

"What you waiting for?" He grinned as he saw them.

Krysty cursed, which only made him laugh, but was thankful as she now found herself able to forge a path forward for herself and J.B. The Armorer had his hands full—literally—as he carried the girl with one arm and fended off grasping hands with the other. If she regained consciousness before they reached the path to the canyon, and some kind of clear way where they could outstrip the slow-moving horde, then he was in real trouble. If she struggled, she would take him down, and then they would be on him before he could protect himself.

Without having the need to speak, the three companions had made a decision that the baron's daughter was the primary target. The kids who had been clawing at them and trying to stop them were also from the ville— the way they moved as a pack made this obvious—but they were beyond help. Whatever malign force was at work in the city, it had them firmly in its grip and there was no way that just the three friends could extract all of them, unwilling as they seemed to be.

Get the girl away first and worry about the others later: that was the best option. They couldn't harm them, as they were all equally precious in terms of the jack they were worth if the companions were to take them home. And as they fought their way through this particular pack, that was why they used fists and boots, not blasters. Jak had palmed one of his knives, and was using it to slash a path but only if it hit fleshy areas and not organs. The other hand was empty, the knife secreted away as mysteriously as it had first appeared.

Now the grens had exploded, and gas drifted chokingly across the lip of the city. There was precious little breeze in the canyon other than that stirred by the mass movement of the people who had come out in answer to the first crack of blasterfire. But it was enough to push the mist of noxious vapor over to where Krysty, J.B. and Jak were struggling to make their way off the ledge. The first drifting wisps of gas started to tickle at the backs of their noses and throats, causing them to cough and wretch. They knew they had to move fast, before it took hold of them.

They were fortunate in two ways: first, the gas was sucked into the lungs of the milling crowd, unaware and perhaps even unknowing of what they were breathing in, causing them to falter in their attempts to stop the intruders. Second, the echoing crack and roar of blasterfire at their backs spoke to them of the diversionary tactics that were taking place. Doc's LeMat and Mildred's ZKR were each, in their own manner, distinctive sounds that could be picked out from the general melee, while Ryan's SIG-Sauer was lost in the blur of handblaster and longblaster fire that answered the war party's cover fire.

This latter firefight had undoubtedly attracted the majority of the older inhabitants of the city—they seemed, after all, to be the only ones who carried blasters in the gleaming palaces—and so left the second attack party with only the youngsters to fight their way through. Which, considering the burden that was handicapping J.B., was a major blessing.

They were in sight of a clear path, a steep rocky incline that would enable them to gain distance on the shambling crowd on their backs, their slowness now accentuated by the gas that was starting to decimate them as it took hold, paralyzing those who breathed too deeply and making them drop to the rock floor.

In sight, but not close enough. Suddenly, a bolt of pure pain shot through Krysty's head. She screamed, falling and flailing as she lost control, knocking J.B. to one side.

The Armorer stumbled, staggered and fought to keep his balance and on his feet. But it was to no avail. The weight of Baron K's unconscious daughter on his shoulder was enough to tip him. It was just bad luck. If Krysty had been at his other shoulder, then perhaps he might have been able to use the weight of the girl as a counterbalance. But she was in the perfect position to tilt him in such a way that her weight only added to his momentum. As he fell, he let go of the baron's daughter, but too late to thrust out an arm and break his fall.

The unconscious girl's flailing knee caught him in the side of his neck as his ribs impacted hard on the rock floor, driving the breath out of him as though with a hammer. That was bad enough, but the real damage was done by the knee, which caught his carotid artery. If felt as though the impact blocked the artery for a second, depriving his brain of blood and causing him to black out momentarily. That was all, but it was enough to cause his vision to blur and mist as he fought back nausea and the taste of bile in his throat. Desperately, he tried to get to his feet, but muddled messages from his brain wouldn't let his limbs respond.

He knew he was down, and he was sure Krysty was, too, after that scream. That only left Jak to pull it out of the bag for them.

He couldn't see what was happening to his left, but the rising swell of triumphant moaning told him that Jak was falling beneath the sheer weight of numbers. The occasional scream told him that the albino teen was going down fighting, as he would have expected, but that wasn't enough. Jak was overrun.

They all were. He wondered vaguely, through the mist of pain, what had made Krysty scream and collapse in such a manner. It was completely without warning, and the suddenness of it had been the major contribution in their downfall. He wondered how Ryan's side of the operation was doing, and what they would do if they got away and found that his companions hadn't succeeded. He wondered again about what had made Krysty suddenly act as she had. He tried to fight the flashing lights and throbbing pain in his head, to make the limbs that felt simultaneously like lead and like elastic work as he wanted them, rather than at random.

And then some bastard kid kicked him in the head. The little fucker moved slowly and sluggishly like all of them, but to J.B.'s frustration he was even slower, even more sluggish. The kid's boot connected with his temple and the lights flared brighter for a second before going out totally.

"WHY THE FUCK are we doing this?" Murphy moaned as they traipsed across the wasteland, the flat rock spreading across the horizon ahead of them.

"Because the baron says we have to. And are you gonna tell him you really can't see why the fuck we're bothering when it's his daughter we're tailing?" Taggart, the crater-faced and rake-thin sec man who had fought with K for almost as long as Murphy, shrugged and spit on the ground as he spoke.

Murphy sniffed. "Yeah…'cept we're not really trailing her, are we? It's the other kids, too, though you wouldn't think any of us had fucking kids except him. And it ain't even them, is it? It's the fucking outlanders.…"

Taggart shot him a sideways glance. Like Murphy, he had felt that it was some kind of a slight that the baron hadn't let them go after their own, but had taken advantage of outlanders with some kind of chilling background. If a man was so inclined, he could take it as a slight on his own abilities. K had explained it to them like this: why waste your own men on a vanguard action when you could send in outlanders you didn't give a fuck about? They could take the brunt of whatever the enemy had to throw at them, and then all your own men had to do was to mop up after and bring home the prize.

Taggart could understand that. Maybe you could still call it a slight on your own ability, but you could also call it a damn fine piece of tactics. There was always risk, but if you kept it to the minimum, then that was okay by him.

But he figured that Murphy didn't see it that way. The big man took it more personally because he had a kid of his own among the ones who had been spirited away by the weirdos. Taggart didn't have kids, so it didn't hit him that way, though he had enough of an imagination to put himself in that position. For Murphy it was more a matter of a man taking back his own. More than that, if there was going to be any risk to the kids on getting them back, he wanted to be the one who took those chances and assessed that risk. Not leave it to some outlander.

So that made him kind of jumpy. And complain like fuck, of course… Taggart was starting to get really pissed at the complaining, as it never seemed to stop. For that reason alone, if for nothing else, he hoped they reached the end of the line soon.

It was a wish he shouldn't have made.

Trailing the one-eyed man and his people hadn't been that easy. They had kept the original party in view from a great distance once they had gained ground. In the same way, Murphy had kept his own men at a similar distance. It was obvious that the mercenaries were shit hot, and would soon know if they had people on their tail. But at the same time, they had to keep some kind of eyeball on them. Now and again they were slipping over the horizon, and it felt like they were coming dangerously close to losing touch with them.

And then, when that seemed to be happening, they would come into view again and Murphy would have to halt his party while the outlanders seemed to just wander around in circles like they were doing something really weird and unexplainable before starting to move forward again, causing Murphy to let them get out of sight again.

Those weird moments when they seemed to be just moving in circles just doing weird shit sent a shiver down Taggart's spine as he watched them through the binoculars he had slung around his neck. These were his prized possession, won in a firefight years before, and Murphy knew better than to ask to use them. But sometimes Taggart had wanted to hand them over as he found himself at a loss to explain what the hell was going on. There seemed to be no reason why the outlanders were acting in such a strange manner, and yet there was something about it that he couldn't explain that somehow chilled him to the marrow. It was like they were doing real shit—stuff that was for real—but there was actually nothing there for them to be doing it to... Hell, it was so hard to explain, especially without coming across as some kind of stupe or crazie, that he kept quiet about any ideas he may have about what could be going on. Something to do with the way that they had all been weirded out back in the ville, but he couldn't explain it, so he opted to say nothing and look like a crazie himself.

Now the outlanders had moved out of sight but not over the horizon. Instead, it was as though they had suddenly dropped down into the earth. It was pretty obvious that they had found something like a crack in the earth, and had gone down on the tail of the weirdos and the kids.

It was time for the sec force to catch up to them. Accordingly, Murphy had gotten his boys to pick up their pace as they followed. Like the two groups they were pursuing, they were on foot. They carried emergency rations to lighten the load, but still it was a bastard of a trek into lands that they wouldn't otherwise traverse even with pack horses or wags. The heat and the hard rock beneath their feet took their toll, even at the pace they had previously set. Now it was faster, and they felt more and more drained. Frustration and exhaustion chipped at their patience, making them determined to get this action over and done with as soon as possible.

It made them edgy and blunted their caution. None of them apart from Taggart had paused to ask why the one-eyed man's people had stopped to act so strangely. Now that they were in even more of a rush to make up the ground, they were ill-prepared for what was about to happen to them.

They weren't to know that those who had gone before had experienced the anomalies of sudden canyons or rock walls springing up in front of them. They weren't to know as these forms of psychic defense weren't to be practiced on them. Instead, the intelligence that defended the mysterious palaces of light from all interlopers reached into the psyches of the men now approaching and took a different path, one that was, nonetheless, equally as terrible to the approaching sec men.

Perhaps it had intelligence able to assimilate the way in which it had been breached, or perhaps it just had a variety of mental games that it randomly selected. The intent was, in truth, irrelevant. It was only the result that mattered.

As they trudged closer to their goal, it seemed as though the very ground in front of them started to rise up and form a barrier. Bizarrely, as they found themselves instinctively shifting their balance for an upheaval that didn't come, it seemed that the earth crumbled and split asunder, re-forming without any tremor to indicate the vast forces that had to be causing such a schism. The dirt spilled and spun through the air, and yet they weren't covered with so much as the slightest film of dust. That alone should have struck them as weird, if not for the fact that they were dumbfounded by the suddenness of the action in front of them, and the way in which it seemed to cut off their path.

Murphy and Taggart exchanged bemused and fearful stares.

"What the fuck is that?" Murphy whispered.

Taggart had no words. He just shrugged as he looked along the length of the wall of rock that had sprung from nowhere with an uncanny and breathtaking speed. The barrier seemed to stretch as far as the eye could see in every direction. Somewhere at the back of his mind, connections were forming with some of the strange movements he had seen through his binoculars. Some of it had looked as though the mercenaries were attempting to climb something.

This? But why hadn't he seen it then? He looked down at himself, brushing away dirt that wasn't there. He smiled to himself.

"It ain't real, that's what it is," he said cryptically as Murphy shot him a puzzled glance.

"You gone stupe or crazy?" the big sec man asked.

Taggart shook his head, almost imperceptibly. "Neither. Though mebbe that's what someone or something wants me to be. All of us. Listen, how the fuck could that have come out of nowhere, with no dust to cover us? No fucking earth moving underfoot, either," he added, stamping down to prove his point.

Murphy sniffed and looked at the men around them. They looked scared. He didn't blame them much. He felt pretty much that way himself.

"Okay, so what is it, then?"

Taggart barked a short laugh. "Hell, don't expect me to tell you what it is. I can only tell you what it ain't. No dirt, too quick… It ain't real. Look."

Acting and sounding more fearless than he really was, Taggart stepped forward and punched the rock wall in front of them, not realizing that belief was the thing that powered the illusion. Even the slightest suspicion that it may have substance gave it so, a circular loop of logic that both sustained and powered the illusion.

And hurt his hand. Like hell. He yelled in sudden pain and anger as his fist appeared to strike rock. Despite the gravity of the situation, some of the men beside Murphy couldn't stifle their laughter at Taggart's cocksure confidence ending in such pain and humiliation.

He glared at them, spit in fury on the ground, then turned back to the rock wall.

"Blind NORAD, I know you ain't really there," he yelled in fury before aiming a petulant kick at the wall. His anger, and the certainty that the wall couldn't really exist, drove any doubts from his mind—with the inevitable result that his foot passed easily into the seemingly solid edifice, creating a hole of emptiness around its passage.

He yelled again, this time in triumphant glee. "Ya see?" he shouted. "Not fucking there, man."

He walked forward, waving his arms so that it opened up a large space of empty air around him as he entered the rock edifice.

"Shit—just some kind of…" Murphy trailed off, not really knowing himself how to describe what he was seeing.

"Doesn't matter what it is. Just matters that we can walk right through it and carry on," Taggart said with an almost smug air, surrounded by empty space that framed him in the wall and gave him an almost messianic aura. "C'mon…"

Murphy looked at the men around him. They looked bemused rather than scared at this point, and also seemed to be looking to him for a lead. He stared at Taggart. It seemed impossible, but it was there in front of him. Then he recalled the weird shit that had happened, and the way it had messed with all of their minds, when they were back at the ville, and suddenly he understood in a way that he couldn't have put into words.

"Fuck 'em," he muttered as much to himself as to the men gathered around him, and strode forward confidently into the wall. It parted around him, forming an empty space that felt strange and unreal, as though the air was sucked out and then blown back in as he moved into the space where the rock had stood moments before.

"C'mon." He beckoned to his men. "We can't let them get too far ahead of us. We need to see where they went down," he urged, goading his men to life with a reminder of what they were supposed to be doing here.

The others followed. Their first steps were tentative, but as they neared the rock itself, and could see that nothing had happened to Murphy and Taggart, their confidence grew—so much so that as they all reached the rock wall it seemed to part and fall apart around them.

And then it was gone, almost as if it had never been.

"How d'you work that one out?" Murphy asked Taggart, relieved and also unable to hide his admiration.

The gaunt man grinned, unwilling to give away his secrets. He would hold this one to himself and use it to get the upper hand when they returned to the ville.

That was the second mistake he would make. And his last.

There was a shimmering of the air around them, and then it seemed as though the rock had re-formed around them. Except that it wasn't solid, but rather seemed to be in a series of shifting and mutable shapes that moved at speed around their heads. The rock appeared to come alive and form into a series of faces and bodies that were fluid and yet awful, their twisted torsos and contorted, silently screaming faces staring sightlessly into the very souls of the men contained within the boundaries of their flight. The image seemed to move in repetitive and intricate patterns that formed a web within which they weren't so much contained now as trapped. For that fraction of a second that each stared into the face of the other, it seemed that the imaginary faces—for what else could they be—were staring right into the souls of the sec party. Every fear and doubt rose bubbling and unbidden to the surface.

And then the first man opened his mouth to scream. As he did so, one of the chimera in flight took advantage of the fact, and darted down his throat. He tried to swallow and then found that he couldn't. Choking, he doubled over and then, as his companions watched in a mute and horrified awe, he straightened and arched his back so that it seemed as though he might topple backward. But before he could do that, his chest split asunder in a spray of bone shards, pulped organs and a mist of blood forced from its previous resting place by a tremendous force. Only his spine, now raggedly exposed, along with the remains of his rib cage, kept him upright before the weight of his head and remaining shoulder tissue caused it to implode.

The shock of seeing that, and also of knowing that the force—whatever or whoever it might be—had the capacity to inflict physical damage if not real substance of its own was enough to make whatever resolve the remaining men had crumble to the dust that had failed to cover them moments before.

Each man screamed in fear. Murphy knew he would never see home again. The ville didn't mean much to him, but his family did. The same was true for a couple of the others. For another two it meant that they would buy the farm, alone and unloved, in the middle of nowhere, with nothing and no one to mark their passing, or even their brief tenure in this world.

For Taggart, there was the bitter knowledge that he, and he alone, was responsible for their demise. If he hadn't been so willing to score points with his little knowledge and the way in which he had used it; if he had been just a little more thoughtful about the consequences of any action that they might take, then he might not have opened them up to the force that was now invading their minds and—he was sure—actually making them cause this to happen to themselves.

It was too little realization, and way too late to make any difference. He could do nothing but acknowledge that fact as he felt his own insides rip themselves inside out as the cold flow of a chimera oozed down his throat.

Each man, as he bought the farm, unleashed a deep emotion and psychic wellspring that reached out across the wastes in frantic scream, searching for a recipient who might, in some way, understand.

Krysty was recipient enough. The moment she fell down screaming was the moment that chilled the sec party K sent on her tail.

Chapter Twelve

The grens had done their job. The clouds of smoke and gas that they had generated were drifting along the lip of the city, their progress stirred and quickened by the movement of the confused and choking mass. The young were still trancelike in their movements, except that now—in their confusion—they were doing little other than confusing the elders, who were wary of firing their blasters into the throng lest they should injure or chill the youth that they held so dear. Given a moment in which to ponder why this should be, Doc would perhaps have been chilled by the thoughts and memories that were stirred by the ritualistic behavior he had seen.

Right now, however, he had more pressing concerns. The gas was drifting uncomfortably close to where he was standing, alongside Ryan and Mildred. They had kept fairly close together so that they wouldn't lose sight of one another as the crowd began to press, regardless of the instinct that told each of them that to spread out would make for a harder target. More important than that, perhaps, was the fact that they were uncomfortably close to the edge of the lip, and a straight drop into the canyon below.

A thorny problem presented itself. There was pre-

cious little noise coming from the far side of the city,
where Jak's party would have encroached. The lack of
blasterfire boded well—it was an indication that they
hadn't been spotted by the elders of the party, and also
that they had no need to pull and fire their own weapons. Hopefully that also meant that they had identified
and closed on their prey. And that the risks that Ryan's
party were undertaking were therefore justified.

Doc would certainly hope as much as he tried to
keep his breathing as shallow as possible, holding a
kerchief to his face to try to cut out the worst choking
excesses of the gas. Like the companions who stood
beside him, he knew that the gas would eventually seep
through the pores of their skin if they took too long
before departing. It was a calculated risk. The youth
were breathing freely and without thought. The elders
might not be aware of such things as gas grens. Even
if they were, it was to be hoped that the confusion surrounding the rest of the area would deflect them from
avoiding at least some effects.

Or it may stop them firing. There was little room
to dodge the fire, and all that the three fighters had
really been able to do was to keep low and hope that the
gas and smoke it created, along with the melee around,
would prevent any kind of accuracy in the fire of the
elders.

Thankfully they were poor shots. Under normal circumstances, Doc would have expected them to have
been mown down by now, but instead they were able
to pick their targets through the mists and cause the
maximum of disruption.

But even so, there was only so long that they could continue before the clouds of gas became too much to risk. They could only hope that they had given Jak's party enough time to achieve their aim and get the hell out. For it was time for them to do the very same thing. Ryan barked an incoherent command, biting off his words as the gas caught the back of his throat, stinging and raw. That was how Doc imagined it, at any rate, comparing it to the parched tissue of his own.

Being the person nearest to the path that they had taken to reach the ledge, Doc had to lead off. The way ahead of him was blocked by the fallen youth, and he had to tread carefully between them to reach the relative safety of the path. Some were unconscious, either from gas or from blaster wounds; some had already bought the farm; others had just fallen, and were struggling to stay conscious. These were the dangerous ones, and it was hard to differentiate them under the circumstances. Were they just lying still, gathering themselves, or were they beyond being a risk?

As nimbly as he could, Doc stepped between them, cradling the LeMat in one fist while the other held the kerchief to his nose. He had the blaster loaded and ready to discharge, but he was unwilling to waste a charge on what would be—of necessity—a small target area. He didn't look back, but he just knew that Ryan and Mildred were at his back, following him while laying down cover. He could almost feel the ordnance whistling past him—and indeed some of it probably was, and it was little more than providence that kept him upright—but was comforted by the crack of the SIG-Sauer and the ZKR, blasters he knew so well.

Through the choking fog and the bile that rose in his already aching craw, he could see the multicolored coat of the first man to be hit by blasterfire. The puppet master, now little more than a lifeless puppet himself, and almost obscured by the bodies that either lay around or stumbled over him. Perhaps it was that catching his eye that distracted Doc for just a moment, but a moment was all that it needed. He felt his foot hit a body and stumble, his ankle turning on the irregular shape beneath—a body that was still moving.

Doc's reactions were slowed both by the distraction of the chilled man to one side of him, and also by the seeping effects of the nerve gas gren. That was enough. Before he had a chance to pull away, the young boy beneath his foot had grasped his ankle and lower calf with both hands. Whether he was trying to pull Doc down, or to somehow use the older man to lever himself up was something that was open to debate. The effect, however, was the same no matter what. Doc fell toward him, the ground coming up to him with an alarming suddenness. There was no time even for him to loose off a shot from the LeMat. Before he had a chance to fasten and squeeze on the trigger, he knew that he was too close to the lad beneath him. To fire at such range would have caused the charge to explode and almost certainly injure him as well as the intended target.

He used the butt of the heavy blaster to try to club at the young man, whose hands were now scrabbling over Doc's body. The old man couldn't tell whether the lad was trying to attack or to help him, or if the wild scrabbling was little more than the desperation of one trying to escape the effects of the gas. It didn't matter; if he didn't escape, he would soon be claimed by the nerve agent, too, as the kerchief slipped away from his mouth. Despite his best efforts he swallowed a mouthful of the noxious fog. He choked and spit it out as best he could, but the tendrils snaked down into his lungs.

He could almost instantly feel it weaken him, though whether that was an actual physical effect or pure fancy he couldn't tell. Regardless, it caused him to weaken and for the young man to gain a greater hold on him. His efforts to club his way free were hampered by the lack of purchase with which to get a good swing and bring some force to bear. It seemed as though all might be lost; all for one moment of distraction.

However, Doc had, in his panic, forgotten who was at his back. He felt an iron grip close on his frock coat, tugging him upward and out of the grasp of the weakened youth as though he were nothing more than a babe.

And no sooner was he clear than the crack of Mildred's ZKR sounded in his ear. Beneath him, as he dangled almost horizontally, he saw the bewildered face of the young man fade to nothing as a hole drilled itself neatly in his forehead.

Then, before Doc had time to register any more, he was upright and on his feet once more, a push in the back from Ryan signaling that they had to move...and fast.

It was only as he moved forward once more that Doc

realized the action had been so sudden and shocking that he hadn't even taken a breath, which, in the circumstances, was perhaps as well.

Still stumbling, he made his way onto the path that led downward. At his rear, he could hear the random crack of the SIG-Sauer and the ZKR in reply to a few stray shots that were coming their way. But these were few and far between. The gas grens had done their work, and the people milling around on the ledge that constituted the city of mysterious palaces now found themselves shrouded in a chem fog or on their knees, choking and desperately trying to drag in breath.

In the midst of this, the elders had obviously devoted their attentions to salvaging the youth that meant so much to them. To drive away the clouds of gas and to get the youth back into shelter was a prime directive, and one that would take their attention away from their attackers. They could be dealt with later. Now, they had more pressing problems.

That was the way it seemed, and that was exactly the way that Ryan and his companions had been hoping it would pan out. They needed to get back down the path quickly, and into some kind of cover. No doubt the elders of the ville would mount some kind of sweep later on. That could be handled when it occurred. Now, they needed to regroup.

But first the descent. Doc had no idea what it felt like for Mildred and Ryan, but if it was even a fraction of how it felt for him, then he wouldn't wish it on his enemies, let alone on his friends. He skittered down the path, thankful for the shallow incline as he struggled to keep his feet. Ground that had seemed so solid beneath his feet on the way up now seemed to shimmer like quicksilver beneath his soles as he slipped and stumbled down a path that had seemed so wide on the way up, but was now so narrow as to almost fail to contain the width of a foot.

Balance swaying as the forward momentum pitched him at bizarre angles with every uneven pitch and yaw of the surface, he fell first sideways into the rock wall of the canyon, scratching and grazing his face, the dull clunk in his head seeming to be beyond concussion, and then righting himself with too much force so that he seemed to proscribe an arc that took him out and down over the edge of the path, his torso seeming to swerve and pitch into space at such an angle that he thought he'd surely fall into the void.

But no. At the last moment, his instincts somehow caused him to twist and turn so that he was able to come upright again while keeping his feet. His lungs burned with fire and threatened to burst in his chest as he tried to gasp in the air needed for the effort of keeping one foot in front of another at such a furious pace. Air sucked in through lungs and throat scorched by the inhalation of gas....

Behind him, to a lesser degree as they were fitter and had absorbed less of the gas, Mildred and Ryan were finding it hard to keep up with Doc, who seemed to be moving at an almost preternatural speed as he headed for the end of the long path. Like him, both were aware that they had ingested small amounts of the gas, and that this had affected their nervous systems and therefore their perceptions. But unlike Doc, both found it easier to keep under control.

So it was that they were able to pull up with a greater ease as they hit the level, while Doc kept wildly running in any direction until he caught a foot on a lump of rock and fell flat on his face.

The shock did the trick. As Doc looked up, his head spinning and ears ringing from the unexpected impact, he could see that Mildred was looming over him, while over her shoulder he could see Ryan racking the chamber of the SIG as he looked up at the city they had left behind.

They were alone on the floor of the canyon. No one had even tried to follow them. Following the line of sight past Mildred and Ryan, Doc could see that there was now only a thin, wispy cloud of gas across the city, gradually dissipating to reveal the youth being herded back into the gleaming palaces by the elders. Even as he watched, he could see the area in front of the mysterious buildings clear and empty out as though no one had ever trod the earth. Even the corpses—and there had to have been some, to judge from the volume of blasterfire—had been taken in.

He became aware that Mildred was talking to him. The words sounded distant and muffled. He looked at her, and had to have been slack-jawed and vacant-eyed—heavens, he could feel it himself, so lord alone knew what he actually looked like—before she delivered an open-palmed slap across the face.

Bizarrely that seemed to work, as the ringing in his ears cleared and he was suddenly all too aware of what was happening around him. Mildred's slaps, of late, were becoming all too frequent, he thought.

"Jeez, you old buzzard, you really had me worried there. I thought we'd lost you totally. And to tell you the truth, I didn't really like the idea of having to leave you here and shoot you."

"Ah, to hear your kindly voice again," Doc rasped as he pulled himself to his feet and dusted himself down, frowning at the sound of his voice and the manner in which it made his throat ache. He spit green phlegm, almost fluorescent where it was tinged by the gas. He looked across the barren floor of the canyon. In the distance he could see the creek that wound through the vast space. Beyond and to one side he could see the foot of the path that had been taken by Jak, Krysty and J.B. His eyes scanned toward the city on the ledge.

There was no sign of their companions. He looked across at Ryan, and could see that the one-eyed man was also searching for any sign of them.

"Should we be concerned that there is no sign of them?" he asked, his words and tone a mild reflection of the concern he was feeling.

Ryan sucked on a hollow tooth. "Wish I knew. It took us some time to get disentangled from those bastards up there, so it's possible that they were way ahead of us and are already at the meet."

Doc breathed in slowly. Even a quick worker like Jak would have had to be moving phenomenally to get in and out so fast, but then again there was little about the albino hunter that would surprise him.

"If that is so, then I would suggest we find out as

soon as possible. I am sure that I am not alone in feeling a trifle exposed out here in the open. Those scumsuckers may have taken refuge for the moment, but I'm sure they'll want revenge…and their captives back, of course."

"Damn right," Mildred echoed. "I'm just surprised that they haven't tried to use that mind-bender of theirs on us."

"Yet," Ryan added softly. "Come on." He indicated that they should follow as he headed toward the sheltered spot halfway across the floor of the canyon that they had made their rendezvous from the safety of the cave, way up on the far side…something that seemed to be a million years away, though it was less than forty-eight hours prior.

They headed off across the floor of the canyon. Even though the depth of the crevasse and the shelter from the skies offered by the overhang of rock meant that shadow and a chill swept across them, they were still sweating. Doc felt as though his blood was bubbling with heat. He was aware that part of this was due to the residue of gas still pounding around his system. But more than that, it was the effort that they had put into both the diversionary attack and the subsequent flight. They had covered a lot of ground, and there was still more to go.

Each step jarred and racked his already aching body, but Doc was driven on by the need to attain shelter. Partly because he would be happy to see his companions and know that his fears for their safety were unfounded; and partly because he felt sure that some kind of retribution would be coming their way, and he would rather view the attempt from the relative safety of shelter than from out in the open. He was hideously aware that it was daylight, and that anyone could look down from the ledge on which the city sat and view them with ease…pick them off with ease, given the right weapons.

And then there was the illusory beast that could interfere with their perceptions and plant phantoms in their path. That was the last thing they would need. It couldn't harm them, of course—or could it? he wondered momentarily—but it could certainly delay their passage and so make them easier to round up by a vengeful group of city elders.

And he didn't like to think what they might do.

These thoughts passed back and forth through his mind as the foreground of his attention was taken with the simple act of putting one foot in front of another and trying to keep pace with Ryan and Mildred as they moved swiftly across the canyon floor. Doc, his hair plastered to his forehead with sweat and the sour of bile in his mouth as breath came hard, was keeping pace… but only just. But despite the effort causing him to feel as though his heart would burst, he also found that the conflicting streams of thought were distracting him from the sheer frustration of the distance they had to cover. The canyon floor was vast, and it took time to cover the ground between where they had started and the point that had been designated as the rendezvous.

Doc finally looked up and saw that no one was watching from the lip of the city, and then let his eyes follow their path upward to see that the sun had moved across a great chunk of sky without his noticing, and he realized they had been running for some time, and what's more they had been able to do it without being observed.

There was some hope. Could it be that these cold-hearts were so used to their isolation that they had no idea of how to deal with someone invading their space?

The cheering thought made him ignore the ache in his muscles and the dry, burning ache in his lungs as he surged forward to try to catch Ryan and Mildred. They were now almost at the place where they had agreed to meet after they had each taken their leave of the city on the ledge. It was close to the creek that trickled peacefully across the valley floor, oblivious to the savagery and combat that had been occurring so close by. A small crop of rocks that Jak had noticed from the security of the cave a few days before, it formed a natural shelter, open on one side and yet hidden from clear view by a rise in the ground and some scrub that grew straggling around it. Draping over the leading edge of the crop, making it hard to view clearly from above unless you were at the right angle, it was only possibly from the far side of the canyon to see that the rock formed a roof over a dip that was a natural corollary to the raised ground on the far side. It was a small space, but enough for several people to gather and shelter until the dark of night gave them a chance to escape.

As the three companions reached it, they were on the blind side of the opening, and it was with hope in their hearts that they reached the scrub and rounded the overhang, hoping that Krysty, J.B. and Jak would be there, along with the baron's daughter and however many of the kids they had been able to rescue.

"John—" Mildred panted as she slid around the edge of the rocks and into the gap, almost expecting to see the Armorer waiting to greet her.

The word choked and withered in her mouth as she saw the space was empty. Ryan and Doc were now level with her.

"Fireblast!" Ryan spit. With the other three not being there before them, there was little doubt that they hadn't made it down from the ledge. If they had been running behind the three companions, then there was no way that they could have missed seeing them as they traversed the floor of the canyon.

They had seen nothing. No one. Their companions hadn't made it down from the city on the ledge.

For a second, the implications didn't sink in. Then, when they did, the three of them sank to their haunches in the shelter of the rock overhang. For some time they were silent, each unwilling to voice their thoughts.

Of course there had always been the possibility that it could go wrong. That was a given any time that they entered into any kind of a fight. But there was something about this that seemed to have an air of finality about it. In any of the actions they had embarked on in the past, their separation wasn't a finality. There was always the chance that the others might be out there, struggling to fight their way free.

But this felt different.

The emptiness of the canyon, which had been so very welcome as they made their way to the shelter, now became oppressive as the full import became apparent.

"No…" Doc shook his head slowly, giving voice to the misgivings that all three of them shared, but had been wary of vocalizing, "I cannot believe that it would end like this. If they are gone, then so be it. We shall make those bastards pay for what they have done. Not just to our own, it is true, but certainly primarily for their sakes. If, I stress…for we are assuming the worst, are we not? Their not being here and our not having seen them means that they have in some shape or form bought the farm. But this may not be the case. They would go down fighting, it is true, but perhaps they did not go down at all? Perhaps the sheer weight of numbers and some misfortune that we cannot know have led to their being captured. In which case, we are back to the beginning. We have to free our targets, as we have come to do, but we also have to free our companions. It makes our task harder, of course," he added with a shrug, "but then again, when was the last time that anything came easy for us?"

With which he shrugged again, allowing himself a beaming smile that he didn't truly feel, but that was intended to emphasize the desire to go on.

It worked. Ryan agreed with a brief nod. "Come sundown we start over. We're not beaten yet, and I'd bet any amount of jack that J.B., Jak and Krysty aren't, either."

Mildred shook her head and snorted. "Doc, there are times when I could kiss you…" Then, noting his alarm, she added, "Don't worry, I was just saying…."

Chapter Thirteen

The dank, fetid charnel house stink of the place was the first thing to wake Jak from his dreams, where there were dark, savage shapes that came at him from all angles. They sought to eviscerate him piece by piece, no matter what he tried to do to escape. It was as though he had to track dark shapes in a dark room, using only the sounds and smells of their passing by him to know where they might be. At every turn it seemed as though they would get him. With every move he made they came closer and closer, gaining ground on him, striking out with razor-sharp claws or knives—he could not tell which—that grazed and scored at his clothing and at his flesh, drawing beads of blood from livid red weals that stood out on his white skin. The sharp jabs of pain distracted him until he could no longer tell what was in front or behind him, and they swooped in closer, closing for the chill....

The shock of their blows, falling like a rain of savage pain, jolted him awake. In his dreams he could smell the open flesh and the blood that welled from it, could smell the decay as it crept up on him and overwhelmed him, as though there were something in each blow that was making him rot at an alarmingly fast rate.

It was only when he was fully awake that he realized

that the smell came from around him. It wasn't his own body he could smell, but the contents of the room.

It was gloomy, but considerably lighter than the room he had been dreaming about, and so he was soon able to focus on what was around, groggily shaking the sleep from his head.

Lifting himself onto one elbow, he could see that he was now inside one of the gleaming palaces they had watched from the outside. In contrast to the splendor of the exterior when seen from afar, the interior revealed a different story. It looked like the sun hadn't only bleached the outside of the building, but had also acted as a cleanser of which the interior had been in sore need. The walls and floor were caked with what could have been excrement, could have been blood, and might well have been a combination of both. Human or animal: or, again, both. It was impossible to tell, although the fact that the young people who had overwhelmed them had been reeking suggested that it may be the former.

Jak could see meat hanging on hooks from poles that had been clumsily embedded in each wall, straddling the divide of the interior space. These lumps of badly hacked meat could have been horse, or maybe some other beast that they had so far not seen, or they could have been human. The butchery involved was so poor as to render them indistinguishable in any shape or form. They had been hanging for some time, to judge by the smell and by the clusters of flies that swarmed over them and appeared even to be incubating on them.

He was on the floor, on a pile of rough sacking.

There was little else in the room, which was presumably used as some kind of storeroom. There were other bundles of sacking and rags strewed around the room and on two of them were J.B. and Krysty. There appeared to be no sign of a guard. They were alone within the room, and although the stone door was closed, there was a window lintel carved into the stone close to the edge of the doorjamb. Anyone standing outside would be just about visible because of the closeness. Instead, Jak could see people going about the business they had watched from afar, with no concern for the three prisoners, even though the door showed no signs of being locked or barred—indeed, showed no signs of anything except a slab of carved rock—and there was nothing in or across the window space to keep them in.

Saying nothing—he could see that J.B. and Krysty were both still unconscious, and he didn't wish to call attention to himself as of yet—Jak got to his feet. His head was swimming, which he put partly down to the stench that made every breath an ordeal of holding down the rising bile; and partly perhaps because he hadn't yet recovered from the concussion that had rendered him unconscious. He stood for a moment, gathering his wits as much as was possible, before taking a step forward.

That was when he realized that something else was going on. His legs felt like lead, and moved only in a slow, jerky and awkward manner, something akin to the way in which he had seen the young people moving when he had been observing them from the far side of the canyon. One step, then another, and he realized that the effort was making him sweat. It was as though every movement demanded an effort that was sapping what strength he had left. It seemed to take him hours to get across the few yards that lay between himself and J.B. It was a perception of time belied by the way in which the people moved beyond the window, seemingly unaware of the titanic struggle that was taking place within the room. It was as though time slowed down for him as every fiber of every muscle demanded the utmost concentration to be willed into movement. The effort of just moving each foot made his head feel as though it would burst, and lurking at the back of his mind was the dread of the door to the room opening. If it did, he would be defenseless, unable to respond with any speed to whatever may happen, and in truth possibly lacking even the energy to move.

It was with something approaching relief that he eventually found himself standing over the Armorer's prone figure. Sinking slowly to his knees and feeling the sheer flood of relief at this resting position, Jak reached out and prodded J.B's still and seemingly unconscious body.

It was as he did that he noticed the marks on his hand. Why he hadn't before he couldn't say—perhaps simply because he had not looked, his concentration being so tightly focused on other matters. But now that he did, he could see that there were long scratches on the back of his hand, livid red welts with beaded scabs of dried blood. Like the wounds in his dreams... Perhaps that was where they had come from. What was real and what was dream? he wondered. Had he really been attacked in such a manner, or had the scoring of his body somehow penetrated his unconscious and been manifest in such a manner?

No matter. It wasn't the wounds themselves that were the relevant factor, but rather the strange paste that seemed to have been painted over them. It was pale green in color, and flecked with dark vegetable matter. A paste of herbs… Suddenly things began to click in Jak's mind, and the way that he was feeling made sense. The scratches had been made to speed up the absorption of whatever ingredients went into the paste, and it was these herbs and the combination of them that were now causing the disorienting effects that Jak was feeling.

Maybe it couldn't change the effect it was having on him, but it could certainly explain it, and so make it easier to cope with. And so make it easier for J.B. and Krysty when they regained consciousness and he was able to explain it to them.

Feeling as though it had taken him several hours to work this out, although in truth it had probably been little more than a few moments, Jak continued to reach out toward the Armorer and prod him.

J.B. moaned softly and shifted slightly on the sacking that contained him. Jak kept prodding, and gradually the Armorer came around. Again, this seemed to take place over several hours although it was probably only a few moments. Eventually, J.B.'s eyes flickered open and gazed blearily up through his spectacles at Jak.

"What…" The one word seemed to drain him, and

as he tried to raise himself he winced at the pain in his head. Jak held out a hand to stop him, and started to explain. It was slow and halting, and Jak felt as though his voice was slow and gloopy, like molasses rather than the running water of normal speech. He wasn't even sure that J.B. would be able to understand him, yet despite this it seemed as though the Armorer was taking in every word.

J.B. kept himself supported on one arm and raised his free hand so that he could study it. His, too, had the scratches on the back, and the greenish residue of the paste that had been painted over them. He frowned. As long as this crap was in their systems, J.B. knew, then the coldheart bastards who ran this ville had them exactly where they wanted them. Regular topping up of the drug in their systems would keep them in this state, and while they were, they found themselves in no position to resist such action.

All they could do was roll with what was going on and try to look for a break. He said as much to Jak, and felt the same kind of weirdness about his own speech as Jak had found with his.

The Armorer looked around the room and, ignoring the way his voice sounded to him as he knew Jak had to be able to understand it clearly, said, "Only the three of us here. That's good. The others must have been able to get away, otherwise they'd be here...or up there," he added, indicating the pole from which the shapeless slabs of meat were dangling.

Jak nodded. "We try get out, they try get in," he said simply.

J.B. grinned. "Yeah, except we'd better keep that as quiet as possible."

Jak said nothing, but the thought ran through his head that if the coldhearts running the ville could slow them with their herbs, then there was little doubt that they could come up with something that would make them unable to do anything except tell the truth. He'd seen it before.

While this ran through his head, he gestured toward Krysty, who seemed unaware that they were talking. She hadn't stirred the whole time, and it was only because his acute hearing could detect the sounds of her breathing that he didn't fear for her life.

"Better hurry, tell her before anyone comes," he said.

J.B. barked a hollow laugh. "Much as we can hurry."

The two men started to move across the room toward where Krysty lay. It was slow, torturous and seemed to take an eternity. Every step was like running up the side of a mountain, taking more effort from them than it seemed possible to give. How could they cope with the intrusion of any of their captors while they were in this state was something that both concerned them, and about which they didn't care to think. Instead, all they could really focus on was reaching Krysty and bringing her back to consciousness. There was nothing they could do to make their situation better at this stage, but at least somehow they knew that they shared the weight of the problem if they stood together. That sense of comradeship would be enough for now.

As they got close to her, J.B. looked through the window. If they were making enough noise to raise an alarm as they struggled across the room, then there was no one who was apparently watching them to hear them. Outside, the residents of the mysterious city seemed to go about their business oblivious to the inhabitants of the room; oblivious, indeed, to the disruption that had so recently disrupted their routines.

Recently? J.B. wondered about that as he caught sight of the shadows that formed on the far side of the canyon, and the way that the light reflected on the lip of the ledge that housed the city. It had been early morning when they had started their ascent, which would have made it about the middle of the day when they attacked. If the light outside was anything to go by, it was now early morning once more. They had been unconscious for at least eighteen hours. It felt like nothing. Possibly it was even more than that. How many times had the sun risen and fallen since they had been shut up in the room?

These musings were interrupted as Jak tugged at his sleeve. They were within a few steps of Krysty, and it was as if she had somehow been able to hear their approach and respond.

"She's coming around."

RYAN WATCHED THE CITY on the ledge with a mixture of feelings: frustration, anger and an impotent sense of rage. Why the nuking hell had he decided to accept this mission? If he had been aware of what these people were capable of, and the extreme isolation of their position, then he would have thought twice. But that was the key. It hadn't sounded like the kind of mission that would end this way.

The truth was that the dwellers on the ledge were in a superb defensive position. Now that they were alerted to the fact that they had an enemy within striking distance, they were well suited to close down any avenue of attack. To come from above would entail scaling down a ridge of rock that was almost sheer, and would leave any attacker exposed to those who could simply fire from below. To come from the floor of the canyon entailed leaving yourself open to being fired on at will from angles that gave a superior range of fire.

If J.B., Krysty and Jak were still alive, then they were being held in one of the buildings. There had been no sign of them during the watches that had been established two days previously, when his party had attained the safety of the rendezvous point. Since then, three patrols had been sent forth by the dwellers on the ledge. Those had been the armed, and the mounted parties that they had observed before had a subtle change in their behavior. Where before they had acted in a ritualized manner, as though drugged in some way and performing actions of which they had little awareness, this time they had been only too well aware of their actions. The three companions had used their cover well, keeping themselves hidden while still being able to observe the city.

When the riders had left the palaces, their bearing and the speed at which they spurred their mounts had been telling. They had galloped down the path, and instead of proscribing the circuit that had served them so well for who knew how long, they had begun to comb the floor of the canyon in a methodical manner. Instead of simply riding the route, they had stopped then doubled back on themselves before splitting into two groups and crisscrossing the bottom of the valley. Instead of silence, they had called to one another, and this time they had spoken in a tongue that was all too recognizable. Whatever the language they used when the rituals on the ledge took place, this wasn't the one they used to communicate in an everyday situation.

Each patrol had been relatively easy to avoid. The sec teams were angry and alert, but they were inept. The canyon had kept these people protected for so long that they had little idea of how to cope with an intrusion. That, and the way in which it had been only the numbers of youth that had driven the companions back before, was what gave Ryan hope. He thought of the fighters he had with him: Mildred was strong and dependable, with good tactical skills and a crack shot. Although she wasn't a tall woman, she had a deceptive strength. Doc was another matter. The heart of the old man could never be doubted, but his body was battered and fragile because of the ordeals he had been through.

His mind was another matter altogether. Doc's psyche had taken more of a beating over the years than his body, and so was liable to fragment and crumble at any moment. His heart was dependable, but his body and mind weren't.

Ryan felt disloyal even thinking that. He knew his companions were tightly bound together, and would stand or fall for one another. Nonetheless, the reasons for splitting them into groups before had now left him with a fighting force that was less than ideal. It felt wrong to think it, but given the free hand he would always have opted for Jak, J.B. or Krysty over Mildred and Doc.

And he was more certain than ever, after what they observed, that it would be necessary to pull out every last effort if they were to get their people back, let alone try to achieve the main aim of their mission. Fuck that. Freeing Baron K's daughter would be something that they would only do if the chance arose. Finding their friends came first.

Not that he could hold out much hope at this moment. So far, there had been no sign of any of them. While his group had kept watch from cover, it seemed that the city on the ledge had settled back into its routine, and was continuing as though nothing had happened. The attack had been just a hiccup in the routine that seemed well established.

The one thing that their attack had caused was a break in the ritual of sacrifice. The time of day when it happened had coincided with their attack, and so by the time that the gas had cleared and the ledge had been cleared of those who had fallen, it was late in the afternoon, and the sun was already beginning to make a path beyond the uppermost ridges of the canyon. Two large bonfires had been built on each edge of the ledge, by the paths that led down to the canyon floor, and by the light and heat of these the young had worked into the night, clearing the debris left by the assault and then going back to work on fashioning the large stone circle on which the sacrificial altar had been temporarily erected each midday. They had been urged and spurred on by the harsh imprecations of the elders—two in particular, one of them being the immensely fat man who had practiced the ritual slaughters, and would appear to be the senior of the elders.

Once they had finished for the night, the fires had been extinguished, and apart from the smell of wood smoke that drifted to the floor of the canyon, it was as though nothing out of the ordinary had occurred that day. Even the time and manner in which the gleaming city had greeted the shine of a new day's sun had been just the same as usual.

The only thing to mark any anomaly had been when the midday ritual had been practiced. For instead of one young person being put to the knife, the fat man had sent two youths—a male and a female—to the altar, one to wait patiently while the first climbed willingly on the altar to have her heart ripped from her body before taking the place of the still-warm corpse to succumb to the same fate. Mildred had watched this, calling on the other two despite the fact that it was their rest and her watch, and had wondered out loud why the youth would allow themselves to be led to their deaths in this way. Seemed, in fact, to welcome what was about to happen as though it were a privilege.

"What, I wonder, is their ultimate fate if they think this is such a wonderful thing?" Doc mused. "Do they know, and is that why they think nothing of this?"

Now, as Ryan played over these things in his mind, he could see that the altar was being set up again for another willing sacrifice. The point of this slaughter escaped him. Even if he knew what it was, he doubted that he would understand or sympathize.

It was back to normal. The crowd gathered as always, and the fat man stepped forward with his knife. From the crowd, a young woman came forward and lay prostrate on the altar, almost welcoming the blade as it carved into her, her last scream as the beating heart was pulled from her chest being almost ecstatic and orgasmic, rather than the fear and agony that Ryan would have expected.

And then it was over, and the altar was being taken down again as though nothing had happened.

"There is much significance in the fact that they feel the need to make the sacrifice on that spot."

Ryan was suddenly aware that he had been so engrossed that Doc had been at his elbow, watching with him, without his even being aware of the fact. He turned to the old man, and the look on his face had to have spoken the question in his mind, for Doc continued in a conversational tone that seemed incongruous in view of what they had just witnessed.

"Why would they be building that altar every day and then taking it down again? Why not just leave it there? Because they are building that circle beneath..." Ryan stayed silent, letting Doc answer his own questions as he could see the old man was using this to vocalize his own thought processes.

"So it would seem that the circle is the most important thing," Doc continued, "leading us, of course, to wonder why they then feel the need to make the sacrifices on that spot, rather than somewhere else. I think this may have to do with the fact that these are not just sacrifices to whatever foul gods they may worship. Rather, they are partly a way of trapping the energies of those who are the victims, though such is their willingness that to call them victims may be inaccurate. Rather, it would seem that they almost view themselves as honored in some way by being killed in such a way."

"Why the fuck would anyone feel that way?" Ryan asked softly.

"Because, my dear Ryan, they think—or are led to think, either willingly or by coercion—that their actions are leading to a greater good, and indeed may be just a quicker route to the same end."

Ryan looked at the old man quizzically. "What do you mean?"

Doc shrugged. "In truth I am not sure what I mean. I may be completely wrong, but I have heard of such things before. A mass sacrifice of some kind—either by your own hand or by the hands of some outside agency—that leads to your life energy being somehow transmuted to another, better place. Maybe they don't mind being sacrificed because they somehow see it as getting in first…as it were."

Ryan shook his head slowly. "That's just so incredibly stupe that I can't even start to tell you—"

Doc interrupted him with a hand. "My dear Ryan, I agree with you completely. But our views count for naught—it is their views that we should be considering. And if they achieve their aim with the young by some kind of coercion, then are they attempting to practice this on our missing companions?"

"In which case we need to move pretty quickly," Ryan said.

Doc shrugged. "You will find nothing in the way of disagreement from me. Nor, I think, from Mildred when she rejoins us. The only problem is this—just how do we go about it?"

AT ABOUT THE TIME that Ryan and Doc were pondering this dilemma, Krysty was in the midst of one entirely her own. Had the nightmarish images that had accompanied the pain that had sent her reeling into unconsciousness been real or some kind of appalling vision?

She had been surfacing from sweet oblivion when she had felt J.B.'s hand on her shoulder and heard his voice whispering her name. He sounded as though he had a mouth stuffed full of rags like the ones she could feel beneath her cheek as she opened an eye. She resented the return of the real world, for as soon as it came to her, so did the sights of the sec men being disemboweled by the wraiths that flew around them, and down into their bodies. Gaia, she hoped that was just a nightmare, but the fact that it had come unbidden into her mind in the first instance warned her that this may not be the case. She recognized the faces of men she had seen back in Baron K's ville, even though she didn't know their names.

Had they been following the companions for some reason? She wouldn't put anything past a baron like K, although it had done him little good if this was the case.

Far more worrying in this instance was the fact that these men had—if the vision was true—been ripped apart by the psychic force that had previously only erected simple obstacles.

Did this mean that it had intelligence? Or whoever controlled it, at least… But why then hadn't it come after them when they reached the canyon? Unless it was merely a remote defense, and couldn't, for whatever reason, progress farther than its own defined paths. Which, she figured, would make it a real bastard to try to get past on the way back. Assuming they ever got that far…

She raised her face and looked at the Armorer and Jak, who was standing just behind J.B.'s shoulder. There was something awkward and unnatural about the way they were standing, as though they were having trouble controlling their limbs. She did, too. Krysty tried to raise herself and found that her left arm, trapped beneath her, refused to move. Then she noticed J.B.'s hand, which still lingered on her shoulder. She saw the marks and the remains of the green paste.

Jak, noticing her gaze, raised his own hand slowly and awkwardly, revealing similar marks. Without even pulling her hand out from under her, or trying to raise her free hand, she cursed and knew that she had the same wounds. Herbalism and the use of such pastes and tinctures for medicinal purposes had been one of the strengths of Harmony, and why the ville had been able to survive. By the same token, she knew that these things were also used for unsavory purposes.

She was aware that J.B. had been talking to her, and

the way in which his voice stopped and he looked into her staring, unfocused eyes revealed his realization that she hadn't heard a word he had said.

He began again. "Krysty, listen for fuck's sake. It's hard to talk or do anything. We were poisoned by some shit they put into us. Means they can do what they want. We need to keep it frosty, look for a way out."

She could have laughed, if not for the fact that it would have taken too much effort. The chances of their being able to take advantage of any such way out, even if it should present itself, was nothing short of laughable right now. She shook her head, a movement that seemed to take forever and made her sweat as if she'd been running for hours.

"Ryan," she said simply, not wanting to waste energy or effort. "Our only chance."

"Mebbe," J.B. replied. "Not sure if they got away. Probably. Don't know what's happening to us, though."

"What is?" Krysty asked.

Before J.B. could form any kind of answer, a voice from behind them took the initiative.

"You, my dear girl, like your fellow meddlers, are experiencing the first stages of the road to enlightenment. A road that you would be only too happy to pursue with us once you had the chance to see what it would mean. Unfortunately, though, time precludes us from being able to educate you and make you see, as we have done with the others. So you'll just have to be shown the short, brutish way. Not my way, if given a choice, but I find myself bereft of choice at this stage."

They turned to see a figure that they found only too

familiar: the grossly fat man they had observed talking in an unfamiliar tongue before he ripped the heart out of an unfortunate young person. Now he was standing in the doorway of the palace, the rest of the denizens of the city going about their business behind him, paying no attention to what he was doing. Neither was he guarded by anyone. He stood alone, leaning heavily on a walking stick. At his waist, sheathed in leather, hung the knife he used for sacrifice. He smiled slightly as he noticed that all three pairs of eyes were trained on him.

"You'll notice, of course, that you haven't been stripped of your weapons. They'll be useful to us, not against us. You'll also notice, of course, that I have nothing other than my knife, which would normally be of little use to me against three younger, fitter people such as yourselves. Indeed, normally I would think twice about coming up against you even if I had a blaster. But I have none. And I don't need them. In fact, I feel comfortable doing this."

With which he turned his back on them and closed the heavy stone door, shutting out the light and noise from outside. As he turned his back, their natural instincts were to reach for their weapons. Krysty tried to move for her Smith & Wesson, but found that it was virtually impossible for her to move a muscle without immense effort. She realized that in the time it took her to get even halfway to where the blaster was holstered, the fat man would have been able to move across, take it from her and shoot her between the eyes if that was his wish. In the same way, J.B. struggled to move toward his weapon with little success, while Jak attempted to palm one of his leaf-bladed knives. He struggled to move with anything approaching speed, and was so clumsy that the blade slipped from his grasp, landing on the floor of the stone room with a reverberating clatter that did nothing other than disturb a cluster of flies on a nearby lump of rotting meat.

The fat man turned back to them, his face wreathed in an indulgent smile. "You see," he said calmly, "there was no point in your doing that. Although perhaps it might have shown you that any attempt at resistance is futile. You should give in to your fate. It could be a lot worse, you know."

"And wh-what's our fate?" J.B. stammered, the impotent anger he was feeling doing nothing more than make speech that much harder.

The fat man leaned forward on his stick, looked up at the ceiling and wrinkled his nose in thought, though it did appear to them as though he had only just noticed the smell that was making them gag with each hard-won breath.

"You have arrived at an important time," he said softly, almost with reverence. "We've waited a long time for this moment. It's the culmination of many generations, and the reason why we are here."

Krysty rolled her eyes. It was a familiar story, and one that seemed to fuel half the shit that they got caught up in as they crossed this blighted land. She didn't need to hear the details: come to that, she didn't want to, although she had little doubt that she was about to, regardless of her desire. It seemed to her that every tin-pot baron who had a piece of territory, every group of maniac stupes who thought they were better than anyone else, they all had a story to back up the fact that they believed they were right and everyone else was wrong. There was always a better place, either in this world or in the next, that could only be attained if you followed these sets of rules, or those sets of teachings.

And most of them were shit: half-baked and half-assed, handed down through generations that had no accurate means of recording them so that they got distorted and perverted until where they had come from was lost to history, and all that was left was the made-up and half-remembered bullshit that meant one set of people needed to do some kind of territorial pissing on another to reach the so-called promised lands.

She remembered Dr. Jean, Atlantis, Mad Joe Corrall, the Sunchildren, the Pilatans...Gaia, that was just some of them. Really, it was anyone who thought he or she was on a mission of some kind, and would call upon any kind of justification to ride roughshod over others to get their own way... This fat bastard was going to be exactly the same. He was no different, she knew, maybe even worse. After all, Krysty couldn't think of any of the others who had used drugs to reduce their chosen few to puppets who would follow their will. They may use tech to persuade them and indoctrinate them, they may use their own charisma to persuade the weak that they were the figurehead needed for those who couldn't make their own decisions. But none of them had stooped so low. They may have used such tactics on subjugated populations, but never on their own people. Not those who would form the core of their populace.

But then, she had never seen any of those she re-membered—the well-intentioned like the Pilatans, the misguided like Corrall, the mad like the Sunchildren—actually sacrifice from their own.

That just said that there was something even weirder and nastier going down here. And, along with Jak and J.B., she was going to hear about it, whether she wanted to or not.

Chapter Fourteen

"It's hard, Ryan," Mildred said quietly as they changed watch.

The one-eyed man followed her gaze up to the city on the ledge and took the binoculars from her. Focusing them, he could see what had prompted her. It was now midmorning, and for the second day of their observation it seemed that their companions had now become fully absorbed into the body of the populace. He could see J.B. and Jak helping a group of young men construct the temporary altar that would serve for the coming sacrifice. Just as he had watched them help build it the day before, and then take it down. Just as he had watched them assist the construction of that bastard stone circle. Krysty, meanwhile, had been with the younger women, milling around and doing something that looked like clearing the ground surrounding the circle, and daubing on the ground.

"They might be faking it," Ryan mused.

"Yeah," Mildred added, "maybe they're going along with it until they get a chance to make a break."

Doc had joined them, roused from his uneasy rest by their hushed voices. He had been taking the night watch as he found it hard to get any sleep, but even this measure hadn't exhausted him. His mind was uneasy—

more so than usual—and there lurked at the edges of his consciousness a memory that was itching to break out. It was important—that much he knew—but it so far escaped him. Nonetheless, his restless waking hours had been filled with thought. He had been listening to Mildred, and as much as he felt he was bursting some kind of bubble, he was also impelled to voice what he felt sure was the truth.

"Do not deceive yourself, my good Doctor," he intoned gravely. "I fear that the case is far more serious than you would care to diagnose."

"What?" Mildred looked at him with a mix of puzzlement and anger. Doc smiled indulgently, which did little for her mood.

"Consider this—have you ever known any circumstance under which our friends would happily stand by and allow such a sacrifice to take place, even under duress? Let alone seem to take part, as happened yesterday?"

Mildred took in a sharp breath. Thinking back, it had been puzzling to her but she had been prepared to rationalize the participation. Sure, they would—any of them—take the long odds over the short term, but even so…

"I thought as much," Doc said, taking her silence as the answer he required. "I think we must face some facts. Our companions may be under some kind of influence, either of a chemical nature or some kind of psychological or psychical nature. This would not be the first time…for any of us, so we should be wary of what action we take next. We are as susceptible as they, and furthermore if they are under such an influence, then it is more than possible that they will have been turned against us."

"You think they might be sent out to track us down?" Ryan asked. "That wouldn't be the first time it's happened, either."

"I remember it well. This time, though, there is more at stake than the sport of spoiled, wealthy barons. These people have a purpose that would at least purport to have a higher aim. They have sent scouts out to search for us who have been unsuccessful. They may assume we have gone, or they may have something else in mind for us."

"Like expecting us to go back for them," Mildred stated. "Nice. We get screwed either way. They buy the farm, or we walk into a trap. Some choice."

"They are acting in a way that seems so familiar to me," Doc continued, as though he hadn't heard Mildred. "The sacrifices to the sun—that time of day in particular seeming to be so important—date back to ancient religions and ways that happened in the southern continent of the Americas before even I was born. And I heard of something from the whitecoats…seems like a lifetime ago, though I suppose in some ways it is far more than that…down in the south of here…Guyana, someplace that had only just been discovered when I was naught but a boy. A man who was a preacher— Jim Morrison, I think they said—saw the doors of perception open to a greater world and made those he preached to drink a liquid laced with poison so that they could ascend together. He was not the only one.

There were strangers in the night who had an obsession with UFOs, and believed that to leave the earthly body behind was the only way to travel…"

"What in blue blazes are you talking about?" Ryan snapped, his patience wearing thin.

"No, it makes sense," Mildred interjected. "It's something that's happened throughout the late twentieth century, so why shouldn't it carry over in legend and tales that are passed down? The idea that by buying the farm together they can obtain absolution and find a better place than this isn't a new one. It's just what my daddy used to preach in another way. And we've seen that it still survives here and there in Deathlands."

The old man said nothing, but nodded slowly. "I know to what you refer, my dear Mildred. And I am not proud of what happened. Perhaps this may be my chance at absolution, finally. Perhaps I am reading too much into it. But one thing is for sure—if I am right, and I would urge that we use that as a working supposition—then we cannot rely on the aid of our friends if we are to save them. Furthermore, time is an imperative, and we must act quickly, whatever the course we decide upon."

J.B. PILED PETRIFIED logs on top of each other so that they meshed together to form a solid structure on which they could balance the stone slab that served as an altar. In contrast to the sun-bleached and shining stone of the buildings at their rear, the slab that he helped lift into place was dark and stained, generations perhaps of blood soaked into the surface, streaking and discoloring the stone so that it was mottled. Like the petrified logs, it spoke of being there for a time long before the current settlers. It was as though they had been drawn here with their beliefs and ways, led by some primal instinct to a place that would satisfy their needs.

This percolated at the back of J.B.'s head while the frontal lobes carried him through the mundane tasks that he was programmed to perform. He was, quite willingly, helping to build the altar for another sacrifice, and would then help to dismantle it while the gore was still fresh and throwing up steam from the ground it stained around the altar. Then he would return to assisting with the construction of the circle that would be the vessel of deliverance. On one level he was happily looking forward to it, yet at the back of his mind, that part of the Armorer that was made of steel was fighting against it, reminding him of who he was and what he was doing.

Yet still he continued with the tasks set for him. Both he and Jak were dexterous, more so than many of the youngsters they had been placed with, and so had soon picked up the knack of constructing the altar. The logs knitted together in a pattern, stacked so that they interlinked and provided a solid base. There was pride to be taken in being able to do this and pave the way for another release of energy to the gods, feeding them so that they would come down and deliver salvation.

Pride, and yet also revulsion: for he knew that this was bullshit, and that he needed to get the hell out, Jak and Krysty, too: as soon as possible, for the final revelation—as the fat man put it—was closing in. And when that came down, there would be nowhere to hide. They needed to find Ryan, Mildred and Doc and get the hell out.

But he couldn't make his body respond to the screaming that came from the back of his brain.

For Jak and Krysty things were much the same. Jak didn't rationalize his thoughts in the same way as the Armorer, but as he went about his tasks, that part of his brain that wasn't in thrall attempted to force its way out, to make him use the weapons that he still carried against those who would seek to control him. But despite a mental effort so intense that it drained him, he couldn't force his will to overcome the directions that had been put in place. He took petrified logs from the youth, passed them to J.B., and then helped the Armorer to lift the slab and put it in place. With each movement he tried to silently plead with J.B. to help him somehow to break free, all the while knowing that J.B. was feeling the same, and was equally powerless.

At a distance, Krysty watched them as she went about the proscribed tasks for herself. She was joined with a group of the female young. They were clearing the ledge of stones and rocks, smoothing down the paths and the expanse of dusty stone so that they could spend the time after the sacrifice expanding the painting that they had started the day before. At any other time, she would have been fascinated by the designs and symbols that they were putting down on the floor of the city. Some of them made no sense to her, but others harked back to a time before the nukecaust. Some of them she recognized from things taught to her by Mother Sonja as being ancient symbols of power drawn from a number of old ways, religions and spiritual traditions. Some of them went back thousands of years, their origins shrouded in mist even before the nukecaust came along and wiped out most of the records that existed.

The one thing she did know was that many of these symbols and pictorial representations they were painting on the rock floor spoke of absolution and ascendancy. Something that didn't bode well unless they could get out of here, and soon.

She wanted to draw on the power of Gaia, which had served her so well in the past. Krysty was able to tap into the power of the Earth Mother and channel it through her body so that it gave her a preternatural strength. Sure, it left her exhausted and weak as a new-born babe after the event, but that didn't matter. When it came to mopping up, she would have enabled herself, J.B. and Jak to free themselves and reach Ryan, Mildred and Doc. She had faith in them to back her up once she had engineered the break they needed.

She had been trying. It was a matter of focusing, drawing on her inner reserves and opening up her being. She had an invocation she spoke to herself. It had never failed her on those occasions when she had felt compelled upon to call on it, in her hour of need.

But somehow she wasn't in touch with the power.

She thought that she knew why: it didn't help, but it did at least explain it, and indicated that she would have to find another way to try to break free. The key was in something the fat man had said to them the day before, as they were about to be put to work.

On his first encounter, after he had introduced himself and annoyed her with his inflated sense of importance, he had stopped short of explaining the belief system that he thought justified his tyranny. Instead, he had intimated that they would soon understand without his needing to tell them, and had abruptly left.

Alone in the room, the three companions had attempted to move with anything approaching their usual ease and speed, and had found it impossible. Even speech was difficult, and within a few minutes—minutes that seemed like hours—they were exhausted and forced to admit defeat.

They stayed silent for some time, until the stone door opened and the fat man entered, accompanied by two other elders. One was a woman as skinny as he was fat, with a pinched, sour face and a look of contempt for them on her face. She was carrying an earthenware bowl with—incongruously—a plastic spatula laid across it. Behind them was a tall, gaunt man with staring eyes set deep in a gray, drawn face. He closed the door and leaned against it, his arms folded, his seemingly relaxed demeanor betrayed by the stark intensity of his eyes.

The fat man moved toward them.

"Ah, it still seems to have a good effect," he said to the old woman, reaching out and thumbing back Krysty's eyelid, the better to examine her eye. She tried to bat his hand away, but her movements were slow, clumsy and without strength. He pushed her hand back with only a flicker of amusement.

"Of course it has good effect," the old woman snapped, ignoring Krysty's weakened defense and concentrating on the fat man. "Are you implying that my work is poor?"

The fat man smiled that irritating smile—the one that Krysty would have loved to smash down his throat—and said smarmily, "My dear lady, that was the last thing on my mind. I was merely contemplating that these are stronger, healthier and older specimens than the ones we usually give you to treat. That may have made a difference to the proportions you use."

"Hmm, so you think I wouldn't take that into account?" She sniffed. "You don't think much of my intelligence if that is the case."

The fat man chuckled. "I could say nothing that would please you, Martha, and perhaps that is just as well," he said, shaking his head.

"Then let me get on with my work," she snapped.

"Very well," he said simply, taking the knife from its sheath. The blade was stained and worn, the metal dull and tinged with the remains of many sacrifices. But the edge was honed and bright, a noticeable thinning of the metal to a razor sharpness indicating how many times it had been whet over the years.

Krysty flinched as the fat man took her wrist, pulling her arm roughly to him. He chuckled again, and she knew this was because the slowness of even this instinctive reaction showed how vulnerable she was.

She despised him even more for that, if that were possible.

With three deft flicks, he opened up the wounds on the back of her hand. Blood welled to the surface as the skin parted. He had been subtle, and the cuts were no more than skin deep, but that was enough. He kept hold of her wrist while the old woman stepped forward and used the spatula to paint the cuts with the green paste that was in the earthenware bowl. Now that it was fresh, Krysty could feel it sting as it soaked into the exposed flesh. It was painful in that out-of-proportion way that only the surface exposures that sliced nerve endings could be. She could almost, in her altered state, feel the herbs being absorbed in her blood. She could certainly smell them. There were some that she could identify, and others that were unknown to her. But of those that she could pinpoint, she knew that they affected the motor functions of the brain, and also caused near hallucinatory and suggestive states. She eyed the gaunt man standing by the door with a rising fear.

The ghost of a nod greeted her as their eyes met, as if he could already see into her mind, and confirmed her darkest fears.

The fat man let her hand fall and moved over to Jak. The albino teen had given up on the effort to stand and was now seated by Krysty. He made a token effort to move as the fat man grabbed at him, but in truth he was only too well aware that he could make no real resistance. The burning anger in his red eyes said everything. Despite that, he couldn't stop the fat man taking his hand and opening the scabbed lines just as he had done with Krysty. The old woman, wordless and yet still giving out an aura of disapproval at having to deal with such matters, painted the tinctured mix on the back of his hand. Finally there was J.B. The Armorer was still standing, and had attempted to edge away as his companions were painted with the herbal mixture. He had managed only a step and a half, shuffling at a speed that was all he could muster, and seemed all the more pathetic for this fact. He, too, had the lines on the back of his hand opened up, and was briskly painted with the mixture.

"There. You can go now, Martha," the fat man said with satisfaction, dismissing the old woman with a wave of his free hand, while with the other he sheathed the knife. The old woman gave him a withering look, one with which she also favored the three captives, before turning her back and leaving through the door the gaunt man opened for her.

Closing it at her back, he moved forward until he was level with the fat man. His eyes swooped over the three of them, seeming to capture them all in his mesmeric gaze.

That was it. Krysty realized what was going to happen next. To gain their full cooperation, without the need to take the time to persuade them of the rightness of their arguments, they would resort to that age-old type of brainwashing known as hypnotism. Her uncle, Tyas McCann, had used it for entertainment purposes back in Harmony, but had often warned of the dangers if it was put to bad use.

"Good, I see that you are all paying attention," the

fat man said quietly, but with steel in his tone. "My friend and associate Delroy here is a very persuasive man. I have no doubt that after you have been looking into his eyes for some short time, you will find that you have little desire other than to agree with what we are saying to you."

Mutie power: Krysty was enough of one herself to recognize it when she saw it. She tried to turn away, but the mix of herbs that was in her blood was sapping her of the will to look away. More than that, she could feel that the gaunt, dark man with the gray face had a strength that was equal to her own, but could exceed her will and powers under this kind of duress. She couldn't turn her head from him, and so couldn't see how Jak and J.B. were reacting to his gaze; but she was in little doubt that they were already unable to look away.

The fat man waited a few moments, studying them until he was sure that his associate had them fully under control.

"Good... Now, you will listen to me, and I will explain to you why our cause is a just one, and why it will benefit you to join with us. Of course, you will have no choice to begin with, it is true. But, even in the short time that is left to us before the day of redemption, I'm sure that you will actually come to see that our way is right."

There was something about the way in which he said the words that spoke of his complete belief in the path his people were following, no matter how dark, evil and wrong it may seem to those on the outside. It was as if he was warming to his subject, and becoming almost evangelistic as he continued.

"This area has always been special. Since the times before the first so-called native tribes rode across the old lands of Colorado, there has existed in this place a cradle of great power. The ancient races who first trod these lands and then migrated to the south knew this. That is why they built these shining palaces of wonder. They were partly to live and worship within, and also partly as a homage and shrine to the gods that gave them life and belief. The powers of the land, the sea, the earth, the air, the sun and the moon are the root forces in our existence, and those who forgot that did so at their peril. The ancients of all lands worshipped these forces as sentient beings who guided us, their children.

"So it was no wonder that when the modern world that they despised, and from which they wished to find refuge, began to collapse toward the inevitable so-called triumph of science that was the nukecaust, they sought to find a refuge in this place that had been an early shrine to the forces they followed.

"But they weren't the only ones to seek refuge here. When they arrived, they found that there were others who also made their way here in search of refuge. These were disciples of another kind of salvation…or at least, that was how it seemed. These people were survivors of abduction by beings from other worlds or other dimensions. They weren't sure, and they sought clarity. The one thing they knew was that something had happened to them, and that they were drawn to this place as one being possessed of great power. They didn't know if these beings traversed space, or time or both, nor did they know if the manner in which these creatures showed themselves was real or a mental image designed to make sense to those who lived in a scientific age.

"It soon became apparent that all parties had one thing in common—they worshipped and revered a primal force, and this force had led them to this place. Some of them had come without even knowing of these palaces of worship. They knew just this—whatever had called them here had done so for a purpose, and with the world as it stood falling around their ears, then to be here made perfect sense."

Krysty couldn't quite believe what she was hearing: a bunch of crazies, scared and running from society, themselves, and the impending nukecaust had landed up here because somehow they'd heard it existed, and it had the bonus of being completely isolated. That she could understand: the spurious rationalizations and the way in which they were willing to bend their beliefs to fit in with each other was another matter. Krysty knew that there was a power in the earth—Gaia alone knew that she had called on it time enough—and yet she had never sought to understand what it was, or how her mutie sense could tap into it. She figured that when humankind was in a good enough state to understand it, then it would be clear.

And yet despite knowing this in her heart, she found that the words of the fat man made sense to her. She could feel the eyes of Delroy boring into her, as they were to J.B. and Jak, and she knew that whatever she might want to believe, she was fighting a losing battle against the combination of herbs and hypnotism.

And still the fat man continued.

"This place was once known as the Mesa Verde, and many of the practices we have adopted come from the old ways—the ways of those who were before even those tribes that are erroneously called the Native Americans. The words we intone on our sacred ceremonies are theirs. The notion of giving energy back to the sun and the moon by sacrificing a willing young person whose lifeblood is transmuted back into the stuff of life itself by recycling is nothing new, merely something that has run throughout history. Indeed, it can be said that the nukecaust was just the unconscious desire of the old whitecoats and their sec to do such a thing. The difference between us and them, of course, is that we are aware of our actions, and therefore more in control of them."

That's your view of it, Krysty thought bitterly. And yet even as she did so, another part of her disagreed, feeling that it made perfect sense. She fought it, sealing off a part of her mind as best as she could, so that it couldn't get at the very core of her being, even if she was forced to act accordingly on other levels.

Meanwhile, the fat man droned on. Surprisingly, he had something to say that caught her attention on every level.

"The ironic thing is that in seeking to escape their fate, our forebears landed up in just such a place as would benefit them the best. The nukecaust was particularly harsh on this part of the land, and for some time our histories tell us that it was doubtful that any would survive. Many who were born had terrible deformities and didn't survive past infancy. And of those who had come here, many were sick and bought the farm. But those who survived adapted along with Mother Earth. Just as she became strong in new ways to survive the sickness, so did our people. Outlanders came to us, to keep our gene pool from stagnating, and as they had traversed the rad-blasted lands so they, too, were touched with the hand of the new nature.

"The power that lay within the land was now theirs—ours—to harness. We found that we had the ability to cloud the minds of others, to make them accede to our demands with little resistance. And that was when it became apparent that we were now in a position to achieve our aim."

Krysty forced herself to speak. It was slow, and it sounded as though her voice was being choked from her, but still she managed to say, "Talk so much, but say nothing. What do you want?"

The fat man shook his head sadly. "I would have thought a bright girl like you, with the power that I can tell that you possess, would have worked that out by now. We want to join with the power of the earth. That's where we belong. To become one with the sun and the moon. But to do that, we need power. We need to boost the psychic energies we possess to reach the critical mass. Only then, when that power is focused, will we be able to ascend and find our rightful place. But to do that, we needed the life forces that would grant us that power."

"Young life," Krysty rasped, thinking of the sacrifices they had seen.

"Absolutely," the fat man agreed. "You understand totally. That's good. It makes Delroy's task that much easier. You see, we didn't particularly wish to leave the Mesa Verde as we consider it our home, and we don't welcome interference. To leave invites such interference. But it was a necessity that we do this. And so we began to travel in small groups around the wastes, seeking settlements that were run by fools. That wasn't difficult, I assure you. My heavens," he added in a suddenly changed and confidential tone, "have you seen the mentality of some of the people who live out there these days?

"Personally, leaving aside the work, I feel we can only have been doing a good turn to those young folk that we took. But anyway," he continued, remembering himself and returning to his previous, more formal intonation, "we made it our task to travel forth and recruit for the great work. The elders of the settlements we traveled to would not understand, and anyway their energies were not those we needed. So we designed a show that would both explain to the young the meaning of what we were doing, and also recruit them to our cause. From there, it was simple. If they weren't willing at first, then they soon saw the truth in what we were doing. As would you, if there were time. But as there isn't, then we must rely on Delroy and his powers. Now, if you'll follow me…"

He turned and walked to the door. Despite the anger and revulsion that was within her, Krysty found herself rising and following the fat man. Looking around, she could see that Jak and J.B. were also on their feet and moving to the door. In that part of her mind that she had portioned off, Krysty was despairing of the fact that she was powerless to resist. Yet she could also feel that the rest of her mind saw nothing wrong in following orders. To be so separated was a strange and almost indescribable thing. She hoped that the others had also been able to cling to part of their own will and identity. The awful thing was that she found herself unable to ask...

That had been how long before? A day? Two? More? It was impossible to tell, for time seemed to move in such an elastic manner now that they were here. All she knew was that it was time for another sacrifice. The feeling came upon her, there was no need for words. Without prompting, she left her task and moved to the area where the makeshift altar had been built. She jostled for position with the young, despite the revulsion that rose in part of her psyche. She could see Jak and J.B., but couldn't read their impassive expressions. They, like her, seemed keen to gain a good view. The crowds parted to allow the loathsome fat man to walk through. A young woman followed, a beatific look on her face as she ascended the altar and lay ready to buy the farm.

The fat man yelled his incantation in a tongue that may well have been ancient, but could just easily have been of his own making and have no language as its base. It seemed absurd and sick as he raised the knife and brought it down into the woman's chest, carving open her breastbone before reaching in and pulling out her heart, stuffing it into his fat maw.

Krysty watched the girl rather than the fat man. Did she, she wondered, have a few seconds of life left after the beating heart was ripped out? Did she see him eat her life? And did she accept that as salvation? The scream she made as the knife hit was certainly more akin to the sound of pleasure than that of agony.

There was one thing for sure: whatever the cause, and whatever power lay in the valley—whether from the minds of those muties who lived there, or from some force in the earth, and beyond understanding— she could feel it surge as the girl chilled. It reached out greedily, sucking up the life force as it seeped from her, sending a charge through the crowd. It was a palpable, living thing, and she could see how its presence was so seductive.

So seductive that she knew she had to escape, as did J.B. and Jak, before its intoxication overtook them for real, and not under the duress of hypnotism.

For, unless she was mistaken, she could already feel that seductive pull telling her that to move with the crowd would bring her salvation and freedom from earthly cares and ties.

"FIREBLAST, I CAN'T believe they're just playing along," Ryan said as he watched the spectacle at the gleaming city. He could pick out J.B. and Krysty, though Jak was lost in the crowd because of his height. They were doing nothing, and once the sacrifice had taken place they went back to their business: Krysty returned to the paintings, joining other young women, while Jak and J.B. started to dismantle the altar along with some of the young men.

Ryan turned away in disgust, a bitter taste in his mouth that he spit out on the dry ground. He couldn't help but think that his companions were lost to them.

"We have seen this before, and we have been there before," Doc said to counsel him. "There is no situation that is beyond redeeming until we are under the ground. It is just a matter of strategy."

"Well, we'd better come up with some kind of strategy, and soon," Mildred said. "The longer we stay here, the greater the chances we get discovered, and the greater the chances that those bastards will get their hooks into our friends so that we won't ever be able to get them back."

"There is more than that," Doc murmured. "They are stepping up their activity. No matter what our agenda is, theirs is more urgent. And it has nothing to do with us, I am sure."

"But how…" Ryan mused softly. "Now that they're alerted to the only ways we can approach, how the hell do we find another way in? Two routes, both open, and both known to them… I tell you, I'm not full of bastard ideas on this one. How the hell can we tackle them?"

"I wish I could answer you on that question," Doc mused. "I fear that we will have to leave it to providence."

"What if providence doesn't provide?" Mildred suggested.

Doc grinned. "No. If I am any judge of brigands,

megalomaniacs and fanatics, they will not be able to proceed to fruition of their plans until they have eliminated the danger. Which, my dears, we are. All we need to do is try to be patient. I think providence might just be on our side."

Chapter Fifteen

After the sacrifice had taken place, and all those outside had returned to the tasks previously allotted to them, the fat man returned to his own palace of light. Like all the elders of the city—those who were either descended from the original stragglers who had found their way to this spot, or who had arrived through the wastes in the time since the nukecaust—he lived separately from the young they had brought into the city.

It hadn't always been that way. At one time, there was something resembling a traditional family unit within the city. There were more than enough buildings along the ledge for everyone to make a private home of their own. In this way they had continued for some time, until the fat man came of age. Called Gideon— which wasn't the name he always used on the outside, when they went hunting—he was born to believers in the notion that the old gods had originally come from the stars and would one day return to take home those who believed in their ascendancy. Because of that, and because of a childhood accident that left him with a shattered hip and too much time with nothing else to do, he had started to think about the different ideas, prophecies and beliefs that had brought them all to this place.

The hip eventually knitted, after a fashion, but his pursuit of an ideal that unified the myriad ideas shared in the city didn't go away. As he grew to manhood, he became known as a thinker and scholar, whose knowledge of history was deep. And so it was, comparative to the others who had been born since the nukecaust. But he knew that the sources from which he took that knowledge were sparing and incomplete. He attempted to bridge the gaps with informed and inspired guesses, and if he sometimes secretly believed that his guesses were way off base, then he kept quiet about it for fear of losing his position. For despite what appeared to be a towering intellect, he was aware that he wasn't physically attractive, and that the badly mended hip had left him with a decided limp that made movement difficult. As a result, his weight ballooned, and to be fat and immobile in a world of lean, mobile men was a danger. So he cultivated his reputation, and nurtured it.

Martha, the pinched old woman who excelled in herbs, had once been the most beautiful and desirable of all the women in the city. Many had wanted her. So had Gideon. He had won her with his intellect: not that she was interested in it, but like him she believed in power, and she could see that although there were many strong men, they would wither with age, whereas the mind of Gideon could take them to a preeminent place.

Two children who perished shortly after birth and thirty years of enmity, bitterness and a mutual dependency turning to hatred had put paid to that. Yet she still believed in the thing that had first united them: the grand theory.

Gideon had known that he needed something to cement both his own position, and his chances of getting Martha. His studies were showing some kind of link, but not one that he could identify.

Then it came to him: starting with the idle thought that one section of the city believed in worshipping the stars while the other believed they came from there, and would once return, he began to work on the theory that perhaps there was a link between the two in the form of space.

It wasn't long before logic, fevered imagination and a handful of old tracts and books gave rise to the unified theory of the city of light.

The people adored it. They adored Gideon. It would take many years to come to fruition, but then, what were a couple of decades in the history of the world? Nothing more than a blink of an eye. However, if they were to fulfill the theory—which was fast becoming a prophecy, such was their fervor—then it was necessary to harness the energy that could only be supplied by young, vital life force.

And therein lay their problem: they had a birth rate that ensured that it would be many generations before the city bought the farm and ended up as deserted as it had been for the many millennia before they arrived. It was steady, with only a small rate of decline. But it wasn't enough.

The people turned to Gideon again. This time, the man of supposedly towering intellect turned to his childhood. There were few books in the city that could be read and understood by the young, and during his period of convalescence after his accident he had read them all—taught as he was by his mother—so many times that he was sick of them. He wished to forget them.

But they stuck. And at that moment, he was never more glad for the childhood stories that haunted his dreams and nightmares. One came back to him: the Pied Piper who charmed the rodents, then took the children when payment was welched. Why bother with the first part? Just skip to the chase... They had the mutie powers among them to carry it out, so it was just a matter of working out a plan that would allow them to enter a ville to study and ingratiate themselves before going in for the chill.

There were those who objected that it would be easier to just ride in and blast the way out, taking as they went. Gideon smiled that beatific and patronizing grin, explaining carefully that that was wasteful. They would risk losing their lives, and wasting potential life energy in the cross fire. Besides, without a firefight, how many more life energies could they spirit away with each journey?

The power of thought triumphed over the power of brute force once more. That was an overriding concern and obsession throughout Gideon's life, and now that it was nearing its conclusion he didn't want to be proved wrong at the last.

So it was that he gathered the elders in the communal palace they now shared, having given up their separate palaces for the good of the whole, housing the hordes of young life force that they had brought to them.

"We are nearly there," he began in stentorian tones that echoed in the stone interior. They had kept the most opulent of the structures for themselves, and the building had ornately carved and high ceilings that added weight to his already impressive tones.

"The stars are finally coming into alignment," he continued. "There is only a matter of hours before they are in the right place, and the ceremonies can begin. These rituals are only to prepare the young, whose life force shall help propel us to our destiny while also being their salvation. We do not need them, for we know that our own beliefs are strong enough.

"But having come so far, we must not let anything come between us and our destiny. We have been protected for so long by the forces that we have harnessed to protect our perimeters that we have become slack. At the last we have allowed intruders to breach our defenses. I know that there were others in their wake who were repelled by the advanced measure we put in place, and that we now have three of the intruders in thrall to us, but the fact remains that we have some still at large. Patrols have been sent to find them, but to no avail."

"Perhaps they have run scared," Delroy suggested, his voice as dark and gaunt as his demeanor.

Martha snorted. "If they had run, they would have come up against our psychic wall. I have felt nothing, have any of you?" She waited impatiently while there was some muttering before continuing peevishly. "Exactly. They are still inside the canyon. Why we haven't found them is beyond me, but—"

"I think the answer to that is simple," Gideon interrupted. "We have never had to deal with such intruders, and so we do not have the skills in which they excel. That is reasonable, and I think no grounds for apportioning blame…"

Martha's mutterings suggested that she felt otherwise, but the fat man was aware of the need to keep unity among the elders so close to the goal, and so pressed on regardless. "I would suggest that we use those things in which we do have skill to trap them and nullify their threat. Delroy, I would like you and those who use their power to maintain the wall to draw it in so that it gradually enclosed nothing but the valley of the canyon."

"Won't that leave us open to any possible intrusions?" the gaunt man questioned.

Gideon sniffed. "So close to the goal, I feel we can take that chance. The continued presence of those irritating bastards is a greater threat. Pull the net tighter to catch them and draw them out. It will keep them occupied while we prepare, and it will also leave them open to being picked off as they emerge. Furthermore, to speed the process, I have a second measure… Bring the three intruders to me," he snapped, indicating to an elder at the back.

The elder—one of the incredibly tall men who accompanied him on life energy gatherings—nodded and slipped through the doors. While he was gone, the remaining elders discussed the fine details of what would occur on the following day. The circle was now complete, and the energies that had been released by sacrifice were now within the circle itself, adding to the power it contained and the beacon it became. As with any kind of ritual, there were mundanities of organization to sort out before the day itself came upon them, and these were now falling into place. The discussion was more by way of confirming that well-laid plans were in place and proceeding smoothly.

Gideon was pleased. Once the day had come and gone, there would be nothing left in this place to mark his achievement, but to have reached this point was monument enough for him. His monstrous ego was satisfied with the culmination of a plan conceived by himself and activated by the elders as a whole. To wield such power demanded no other statue.

Thus it was that their business was almost concluded when the door opened and the tall elder led in Krysty, J.B. and Jak.

Krysty looked around at the palace. It was opulent compared to the other interiors she had seen thus far, and certainly it had less of a stench, though it was still pretty overpowering. She also noticed that there were bowls of differing herbal mixtures everywhere. The scents from these intermingled with the stench, both disguising and adding to it in equal measure. Because of the differences in scents, she knew that these tinctures weren't for the same purpose as the one that was painted on their scratches. Nonetheless, they were used by the elders for whatever purpose, and meant that in effect they were as high in their own way as any jolt-head. Which would explain a lot, she figured wryly, if not how to extricate themselves from this situation.

Her train of thought was interrupted as they were brought in front of Gideon.

He sighed heavily. "Your fellow fighters are giving us problems. We cannot afford to have such problems. We are not fighters. We have some capability, but not your experience. Or theirs. However, we do have you, and you know them well. With your knowledge, we can send out men to crush them." He looked them over, and a sly smile spread across his face. "Now, I suggest that you tell me all you know of your friends. What their strengths and weaknesses are, and how best to combat them."

Krysty shook her head and looked at Jak and J.B. They, too, seemed resolute. Yet she could feel something within herself that she knew would also be flooding over their consciousness. No matter what the intent, the combination of herb and hypnosis was making her irresolute. She could feel her weakness growing, and the desire to spill her guts wash over her. She knew that Jak and J.B. would be the same. And that there was nothing they could do about it.

The fat man's loathsome face was wreathed in a smug grin. "Bring forward the guard. They should pay particular attention to this," he said, beckoning to some of the elders.

Despite herself, Krysty felt her mouth open and the words spill out. Detesting herself, and more so the influences that were making her do this, she told all. The fat man smiled. When she had finished, he simply indicated that Jak continue. And despite the loathing in his voice, he took up where Krysty had left off.

She hung her head. Forgive us, Ryan, Doc, Mildred....

NIGHT HUNG HEAVY over the canyon. In the depths of the valley, the companions felt safe in coming out of hiding. The shadows were deep and dark down here, and as the city on the ledge slowly extinguished its lights and settled for the night, there was little chance of their being observed.

"Man, I'm getting really stiff and ring rusty cooped up in that place," Mildred said as she stretched. "I don't think I can wait much longer, Ryan, no matter what."

"Patience, my dear Doctor," Doc mused as he flexed equally cramped and stiffened limbs. "A straightforward assault would not be a good idea. You know that."

"Yeah, but even so," Mildred began, trailing off as she caught sight of Ryan. The one-eyed man was standing apart from them, staring up at the ledge. "What is it?" she asked with an urgent edge to her tone.

Ryan turned to her. "Why can't we just go up there? It's the middle of the bastard night. They're so arrogant that they don't have any kind of defense, and when they sent out sec patrols they were shit. Fireblast, even a blind stupe stickie could have worked out where we were by now. Unless they do know, and they're just playing bastard games with us... But why the fuck would they do that? Why would they do anything? Look at it."

Mildred and Doc followed the direction of his arm.

The city looked quiet, peaceful…and completely defenseless.

"Weight of numbers, Ryan," Doc murmured. "That's why we haven't done it. Two ways up, two ways down. The slightest alarm and we're trapped on either of them. And then when we're up there—"

"We have the element of surprise if we go now. We didn't want to take out any of the kids last time, either, so we held back. Fuck the mission. K wasn't straight with us, so all bets are off. We get our people back. That's our only mission now. We go in, we hit hard, we get Jak, Krysty and J.B. and we run. Maximum chaos and we get the chance to run before they can regroup."

"If that were our only option, then perhaps I would agree with you," Doc mused. "But I tell you, Ryan, we are an irritant to them. They will come out and give us an opening. I'm sure of it."

"I wish I could be," Ryan said softly.

Mildred looked at him askance. "This isn't like you, Ryan. You feeling okay?"

The one-eyed man shook his head. "No. I'm not. I feel like…like there's something unbalancing me," he said, his tone suddenly changing as a realization dawned on him. "Mebbe they're not leaving us alone."

"Look!" Doc said, interrupting.

Mildred and Ryan followed Doc's indication. Deep in the shadows at the foot of the canyon, beneath the city, something stirred in the black, forming into shapes that detached themselves and seemed to make their way across the flat canyon floor.

"Cover," Ryan snapped, willing to take no chances.

As they took whatever scant cover they could, blasters drawn, the detached shadows became shapes that became recognizable silhouettes. Then, as they neared and the three hidden companions prepared to draw a bead, a flash of moonlight caught the three figures and revealed them as Krysty, Jak and J.B.

They came to a halt about five hundred yards from where their friends lay in cover.

"Hold fire," Ryan whispered. Then, throwing caution to the wind in a way that would normally have been out of character, he rose to his feet. "Krysty, J.B., Jak...how the hell did you get away?" He stepped out of cover and went toward them, blaster falling at his side.

Doc—his nerve ends twitching with some kind of crazy instinct for such things—looked up at the sky, then yelled, "Ryan."

The one-eyed man turned back to him, a puzzled expression on his face. Doc was gesturing upward.

"There is no moon, Ryan..."

Ryan looked up to the skies above the canyon walls. Doc was right. The night was clouded, and the scant sliver of new moon was only occasionally visible through the heavy, rolling cover. There was no way that he should have been able to see their three companions in such relief.

"What the fu—"

Ryan raised his blaster, but it was too late. As he watched, the three people in front of him suddenly grew in stature until they were five yards high, looming over him. Their features changed, morphing into some kind of demonic mask like those he had seen in old books and vids. Mouths open, they stooped down toward him, and he could feel the hot, fetid breath of all three as they closed on him. With a yell that was half anger and half unfettered fear, he threw up the SIG-Sauer and unleashed a volley of blasts that he knew was stupe and wasteful as soon as his finger twitched on the trigger.

These were phantoms. They could do him no harm, and they had no more substance than the wall, mountain and abyss that they had seen on their journey to this place. All he had done was waste three slugs and alert the city on the ledge that they had come out of hiding. Which, he realized, was probably the point. He cursed himself as he turned his back on the phantoms and ran toward cover.

"Doc, Mildred, take cover," he yelled, realizing even as he said it that it was a waste of breath, and that they had already taken evasive action.

He was wrong. Although both of them had momentarily been fascinated and frozen by the sudden change in the figures of their erstwhile companions, they had soon realized that these chimera were merely the vanguard of a further attack, and so had opted to regain cover.

As they headed for cover, they found that the ground rose up around them, forming a semicircle that started to close in on them, directing them back the way they had come.

"It...is...not...real..." Doc told himself as he came close to the edge of the rising ground. Figuring that belief was all, as before, he opted to try to break through the illusion by running through. It was, after all, the only way that he would make cover. He steeled his soul, and flung himself forward into the rising wall of earth and rock that was slow and inexorably coming toward him.

Whether the illusion was stronger and the force at the back of it more aware of the flaws that had betrayed it once before was open to debate: the only thing he knew was that he felt the impact of rock and dense packed earth as he hit it full-on. The momentum of the forward roll hit him hard and threw him back, dazed. The ground seemed to rise beneath him as he landed, pushing him back in a direction he didn't wish to go.

Mildred wasn't aware of that, but she had opted to try to take a different route. If she was unsure enough not to risk running through, then she could at least try to get over the top and beat the illusion that way. She ran at an angle to the rising wall, so that she might counter its roll and use that to aid her speed as she attempted to climb.

It was worth a try. Grunting with the effort she pumped her way up three-quarters of the wall, and was within reach of the ridge when it seemed as though the earth movement was sentient, and able to respond to her actions. With no warning, a wave shuddered along the length of the wall, taking her feet from under her and causing her to stumble and fall. As she did, the ripples of the wave rose to meet her, catching her under the chin and making lights flash in front of her eyes. She felt herself black out for a second, and when she fought her way back to consciousness it was to find that she was rolling down the ridge, her progress aided by a push from the wall of earth beneath her.

Ryan, meanwhile, was having problems of his own. As he tried to run from the demonic figures that loomed over him from behind, he found that the shadows around him were now beginning to take substance. He saw Krysty, Jak and J.B. All grew up from pools of shadow around him, and all were carrying blasters directed at him.

Blasterfire chattered at him: the staccato shrill of the Armorer's mini-Uzi set on short bursts, the crisp crack of the Smith & Wesson, and the muted boom of the Colt Python. Despite the fact that he knew these were nothing more than phantoms that couldn't hurt him, he dropped to the ground and rolled in evasive action, returning fire and cursing each time instinct made him waste another round. He knew that he couldn't hurt these things that were smoke and mirrors, plumbed as they were from the depths of his mind. And yet could they hurt him? He wouldn't have thought so, based on previous experience, but he could feel the shells whistle past him, could taste the earth their impact threw up as it showered over him, landing with a bitter taste in his mouth. What if the psychic force—whoever or whatever it might be—had found a way of realizing itself in some physical manner? With a renewed vigor he returned fire, wondering all the while if the spending of ordnance until they were defenseless in this way was its intent.

And then, as suddenly as the psychic attack had begun, it was over. The silence was almost deafening after the sounds of blasterfire echoed and died. It weighed down on them as they stood beneath the ledge, looking up at the sleeping city. Despite the noise and activity that had occurred beneath it, the city appeared to be as somnambulant as before.

"What the hell is going on?" Mildred whispered. "They must have heard that shit going down. Hell, I can't believe they weren't directly behind it themselves."

"Perhaps they were," Doc said mildly, looking to the rear of the group. "It may be ostensibly quiet, but I would direct you to where we have ended up after that little fracas."

Ryan and Mildred both turned to see what Doc had meant. The area where they had been hiding out was some distance away, and their chances of making it back there to cover were less than zero. The reason for that being apparent from the shimmering presence of other people on the floor of the canyon—real people, not phantoms. That was clear from the way that they moved slowly and cautiously, using what little cover there was on the ground, both rock and shadow, to slowly advance without leaving themselves open to attack.

"Well, look at that," Ryan said quietly. "Real live sec this time. Guess the weird shit was less to try to chill us than to give them cover to get down here."

"Uh-huh," Mildred agreed. "And I'll tell you something else. That covering shit has cut off any way back to our little hidey-hole. We're out in the open here, whether we like it or not."

"They knew where we were," Doc said flatly.

"If they knew, then why didn't they take us before?" Ryan said, backing his companions slowly into the cover of shadow provided by the overhanging lip of the ledge.

"Because they didn't know before." Doc sighed. "It was only a matter of time before the others gave us away."

"Doc, cut that shit," Mildred snapped. "They wouldn't do that."

"Not willingly," Doc murmured. "But perhaps they had little choice. We only have an indication of what these coldhearts can achieve, but is that not enough? They've had our friends long enough to inflict the necessary damage."

"Doc's right. We've got to face that," Ryan agreed. "But that doesn't mean that we don't get them back."

"Oh, heavens no," Doc replied. "However, we may not find them as we would wish... And furthermore, I would contend that if they have revealed where we were able to take cover, then they may also have revealed other things. Perhaps it would be as well to not go about things in our usual way, as they may be expecting that. To be a little circumspect would be politic, I think."

"Wise words, if long-winded." Ryan grinned.

"Hell, I'll second that," Mildred said.

"Then we take them, but we don't do it the usual way," Ryan said. "Fuck strategy, let's surprise the bastards."

Chapter Sixteen

There were six of them. With no moon to speak of, it was difficult to see out there, but the moving shadows were regular enough in their progress to give themselves away.

They had fanned out across the valley floor so that they were closing in slowly, surrounding the three companions against the wall of the canyon. From where they were sheltering, it seemed to the friends that the sec force was more intent on taking them alive—for whatever purpose—than simply chilling them. A quick spray and pray into the area they had surrounded, if coming from all six sec men, would soon chill anyone within the area.

"Want to take them all out, or mebbe keep one alive to question?" Ryan asked, a feral grin spreading across his features as the adrenaline began to pump.

"If we can get one, then it would be useful," Doc muttered, his jaw set hard. "I have a few tricks of their own that I can throw back, and it may get us some useful information."

"Okay, then," Ryan said. "If you get a chance, take one out and keep one alive. But don't worry too much about it."

Without another word, they began their assault. Reasoning that the sec force would expect them to behave in a careful and strategic manner—as they usually would—it was obvious that the only way to approach taking on the superior odds would be to use tactics that seemed random. It was a stupe and crazy way to fight, but somehow seemed entirely fitting to the madness that had beset them from the moment they crossed the line between the wastelands and the entry to this canyon.

Thus, it was the last thing that the sec force expected when Ryan charged out of the shadows, across the valley floor, firing random shots toward the area where he had seen two shadows move. It was only when he heard the crack of return fire that he hit the ground and rolled, coming up firing toward the area where he had heard the shots. He was gambling on their lack of skill with a blaster, and the fact that the other four sec men would be otherwise occupied.

Which they were.

Mildred was as direct as Ryan, but perhaps even less subtle, if that was possible. Stepping out of the shadow for a moment, before stepping back, she took range and distance, and lobbed underarm the two grens that Ryan had passed to her before his own charge. They were frag grens, and she had sighted the movement well. Her only concern was her ability to throw the correct distance.

She needn't have worried. The grens floated through the air begging to be shot down by a dead-eye. Mildred herself would have had no problem picking them off.

The panicky volley of fire emanating from the target area, with no discernable result, was another matter.

Standing back in the shadow, Mildred counted and then grinned as the night lit up with the double explosion. In the light of the blast, the fragments of spreading metal seemed visible in a way that they never had in daylight, and she could see where the two clouds of shards overlapped, leaving little room for escape.

One of the sec men perished in the blast. For a fraction of a second she could see him, lit up in relief as he stood to run before the blast evaporated him in a rain of blood, flesh and bone fragments.

That left the other sec man. He was able to make a partial escape, as she saw him run, outlined by the light of the blast. It seemed as though, on the fringe of the blast area, he had been able to escape. But not quite. Some of the fragments caught him, throwing him forward. He writhed in the air as the hot metal penetrated him, his screams lost in the explosion.

Mildred was out of the shadows and across the ground before the afterimage had even faded from her retinas. She had pinpointed where he had fallen, and although it was doubtful that he would be any kind of a threat, she was in no mood to take that chance. With the injuries he had to have received from the blast, there was also no chance of him being any use to them. Another one down.

RYAN'S HEAD-ON ASSAULT, reckless and stupe, had been exactly what the sec men had been briefed wouldn't happen. As a result, their shocked fire, compounding their lack of skill and practice, had been high and wide, enabling the one-eyed man to hit the ground and return with a greater degree of accuracy. He didn't hit either of the enemy with his first rounds. He knew that because there was still fire from either location he had pinpointed. That was okay. They were no closer to getting his range than before, as the rising clouds of dirt from the pockmarked earth on either side and in front of him would attest.

He scrambled to his feet and started to run again, the Steyr held across his chest. He had been using the longblaster because of its greater accuracy at distance, but now that he was getting closer, he wondered if it was going to be too clumsy for close-up combat.

He didn't have to worry. His charge had scared the hell out of one of the sec men, who rose from the shadows in panic, shaping to fire with two hands clasped on his handblaster.

"Too much time," Ryan whispered to himself as he whipped the Steyr around and, while still in motion, loosed off two quick shots. The kickback from the longblaster held at that clumsy angle made his wrists ache, but regardless he was able to steady it enough for the shots to hit home. The sec man jerked in the air, his own blast going up into the sky as his fingers squeezed too late.

One down, then, with the other taking heed of his companion's fate and staying in the shadows.

"Right, you bastard, let's draw you out," Ryan snarled, taking the cover that had been vacated by the hiding sec man's now chilled companion. As the one-eyed man dived over the sparse cover of rock and shadow to take up the empty space, a slug whined off the rock, chips thrown up by the impact cutting into his leg. Despite himself, he yelled, as much in surprise as pain.

The inexperience of the sec man sent to hunt the outlander showed itself and sealed his fate. Taking the yell for a sign that he had a man down, the sec man came out of cover, moving swiftly across the space between the two outcrops of cover.

Ryan was waiting for him. This was a chance to take one of the bastards alive and hand him over to Doc. The one-eyed man lay back until the sec man cautiously edged around the rocks, reaching out with his foot to prod the prone man. Then, with a swift and savage kick that jarred pain in his cut leg, Ryan lashed out and took the sec man's standing leg from under him. Unbalanced, he stumbled and fell. Ryan disarmed him of his blaster and straddled him, ready to strike down with the butt of the Steyr.

He lashed out. It was clumsy and uncoordinated, but it was effective. Somehow, his foot came up high enough to catch Ryan between the shoulder blades as the one-eyed man pulled back his arm. The combined momentum of both actions gave the contact enough force to knock Ryan from his perch, and he pitched sideways, landing so that the Steyr slipped from his grasp. He rolled onto his back so that he could see what the sec man was doing. Scrambling to his feet, the panicked sec man was breathing hard and loomed over Ryan. Before the one-eyed man had a chance to move or to prepare himself the sec man had fallen awkwardly on him, trapping one arm beneath the one-eyed man's body with his weight.

The sec man was wild-eyed with fear and panic, and was lashing out with no thought. Blows rained down on Ryan, hitting him full in the face and on the temple as he turned his head to avoid them. He felt the taste of blood in his mouth, and could feel it trickling down the back of his throat from a blow to the nose, making him gag. Lights flashed as one indiscriminate blow to the temple caught him hard. With his free hand he tried to ward off the blows and land some in return, but he had no purchase. He struggled to free the hand beneath him, but it was starting to go numb as his own weight cut off the circulation.

And then the sec man found his throat. Ryan tried to lower his chin and make it as hard as possible, but still the sec man managed to gain a hold, thumbs on either side of his windpipe, feeling for the carotid artery. Even in the grim light, it was possible to see the wild eyes, and the grin of realization and triumph that spread across the sec man's face.

If he couldn't do something, then this was how it would end for Ryan. Desperation made him struggle harder, but it seemed to be futile. He could only pray to whatever he believed in that something in his luck would turn.

The sec man shifted his position, the better to gain a hold on the one-eyed man's throat. In so doing, he lifted his body for a fraction of a second.

It was all Ryan needed. Momentarily freed from the

weight bearing down on him, he was able to lift his knee, jerking it up with all the force he could muster. And, because he had lifted himself to shift his weight, the sec man had left himself exposed. Ryan's knee caught the sec man squarely between the legs, causing him to yell in pain and surprise, pushing him forward and over the one-eyed man's head. He landed in a crumpled heap three feet or so from Ryan, still in shock and clutching at his throbbing testes.

That gave Ryan all the time he needed. Before the man had even landed, Ryan had scrambled to his feet and had pulled the panga from its sheath on his thigh. Screw taking this bastard alive, he was too lucky. It was best to nullify the threat right now. Ryan took one step toward him and yelled wordlessly.

The sec man, his eyes still clouded with pain and confusion, turned at the sound, looking up. It exposed his throat perfectly. One flick of the wrist, and the panga blade sliced through skin, tendon, flesh and bone. Back to the spinal cord with one razor blow. The sec man's eyes flashed fear, then faded and went to black as the life spurted rhythmically from him and splashed onto the ground.

Ryan stepped back to avoid the grue as it hit the dirt, and turned to where Doc should be.

While Mildred and Ryan had been full-frontal in dealing with their foes, Doc had been a little more circumspect. Partly because to vary the approach would, he felt, cause more confusion; and partly because he didn't trust that the others would be able to take one of the opposition alive, given their methods of attack.

So it was that, as the others caused chaos and confusion in their chosen direction, Doc began to move slowly in the shadows. The LeMat was cradled in the crook of his arm, and his strategy was simple: draw out one of the coldhearts so that he may take the shot and be nullified. And the other would be wounded, captured, and then let Doc play their little games back at them. A grim smile played at the corners of his mouth as he kept low and made his way to the edge of the shadowland.

The two sec men in his third of the arc remained hidden. There was no attempt to go to the aid of their fellow sec men. Good. This meant that their directive was to take out one of the three intruders, and they were sticking to this. No doubt their lack of experience when it came to combat was leaving them in some doubt as to the best thing to do.

Doc decided on a diversion to draw them out. He picked up a rock and threw it away from himself and out into the light. It landed with a dull thud, eliciting a sharp crack of blasterfire from one nervous sec man. The flash of the blaster enabled Doc to pin down his position. He was hidden by a small outcrop with some scrub on it. Doc grinned to himself as he withdrew a bullet from his pocket.

He opened the cartridge and rolled it across the ground toward the sec man's hiding place, taking two rocks and striking sharply for a spark. It took several attempts, but he worked quickly and trusted to fate. The spark came and leaped onto the powder, fizzing a bright trail across the path it had made.

Of course, it was pointless from the point of view of attack. There would be no power of any kind in it. It merely acted as a firework. But attack wasn't the purpose. Doc gambled that the sec man wouldn't realize its futility.

He was correct. The cartridge continued rolling, the fizzing light of the fuse it made catching up with the source. The sec man, believing it to be some kind of bomb, stood in panic, firing wildly into the shadows and making himself a target silhouetted against the canyon's empty floor.

All of this took only a fraction of a moment, but it was enough for Doc to aim and fire. The standing sec man's scream was lost in the noise of the firefighting that was going on around, but there was no mistaking the way that he crumpled and fell backward, killed by the impact.

Even as the sec man fell, Doc was already hitting the ground himself, throwing himself away from what would now be a target area for the remaining sec man. The returned fire spattered against empty space and rock.

Doc was already half crawling, half running. He was at the edge of shadow once more, and would have to risk coming out into the open. There was no other way, as they had all been pinned back into the only cover—shadow—that had been available. The psychic force had done well to maneuver them into such a place, but the inexperience of the sec force sent to deal with them had given lie to that effort.

The sec man was still firing into empty space before

he realized that Doc had moved around to flank him, and was now in plain sight. He moved to adjust, but was too slow for the wily old man. As the sec man turned to fire, he opened up his body enough for Doc to get a good view of his torso.

Doc snapped off the shot from the LeMat, barely stumbling as he took the impact of the recoil in a stride.

His aim was true. The .44 round hit the sec man in the shoulder, shattering the pin of the joint and causing him to howl in agony as his arm flew at an unnatural angle before hanging uselessly at his side. He was pitched backward, his blaster flying away from him.

He had barely hit the ground before Doc was on him. The old man could see that he was in great pain. The last thing Doc wanted was for the injury to cause him to lose consciousness, so he took a kerchief from his pocket and stuffed the material into the wound, to try to staunch the flow of blood. While he did that with one hand, he quickly frisked the sec man for other weapons, throwing them away from him without any other concern than distance. That done, he slapped the man around the face, causing his captive's rolling eyes to suddenly focus.

"Don't you dare pass out on me," Doc hissed. "I haven't finished with you yet."

He checked the man's wounds and looked him over. Yes, he would live. The flow of blood had been staunched, and although the ball socket of the shoulder joint had been smashed beyond repair, and the man's arm would be useless if he was given the chance to recover, it wasn't by any means a fatal wound.

By this time, the noise of the firefights around had subsided, which Doc took to mean that some kind of conclusion had been reached. He had little doubt which way it had gone, and so didn't even bother to look up when he heard footsteps approach. He knew it could only be Mildred and Ryan.

"Anyone else alive?" he asked as they approached.

"Had to chill mine," Mildred answered.

"Same here," Ryan stated, "but I can see that you got lucky."

Doc snorted. "Luck, dear boy, had nothing to do with it. Your methods were necessary, but hardly conducive to taking prisoners. I considered it my role to preserve the life of one of these miserable wretches…at least for long enough to question him."

"Looks like he's in a bad way," Mildred said. "I don't have any pain meds in my bag." She dropped to her knees beside Doc to examine the captive. "You sure you can get anything out of him?"

"Trust me, I can," Doc said with a steel in his voice that momentarily took Mildred aback. She rarely heard that tone from him. Doc continued before she had a chance to frame any further questions. "Ryan, what is happening up there?"

Ryan looked up to the city on the ledge. "Fuck all, Doc. You would've thought that the noise would bring them out, if nothing else."

"Good. Perhaps they are contemplating their next move, or perhaps they simply assume their tactics have worked and they are waiting for their triumphant little men to return. They have that arrogance. No matter, it will serve us."

Doc looked down into the face of the wounded sec man. His eyes bore into the wounded man's clouded eyes, fixing him with a stare that couldn't be ignored or deflected. When he spoke, it was in a gentle voice that had a rhythm and pitch that was quite unlike anything either of the companions had heard from him before.

"You will listen to me and you will hear no voice but mine, for my voice is the only one that has any meaning. When you look into my eyes you will see yourself reflected in there because I have become you and you have become me and everything that you are I am also. Listen to my words and see that the questions I ask you have a great meaning, for you have much to do before your destiny is fulfilled, and I can help you to achieve that, but only if you cooperate and pay me the greatest heed. Do you understand me?"

The sec man—his already gaunt features now accentuated by the pain he was suffering—nodded briefly.

"Good," Doc said soothingly. "Now, you will tell me about the aims of your people and how I can help you to achieve that."

The sec man's voice, when it came, was slow and pained. At times, it was almost inaudible as he husked his way through the agony that was racking his body, and they had to lean in to hear him clearly.

"We come from the stars, and to them we will return. All life on this earth feeds back to great voids and it is there that we achieve the state of bliss that explains our being. Only then will we be whole. That is why we need to make the circle, to focus the life force and power that will take us on the journey."

"Why did you take the children from all those villes? What was the purpose?"

"The young have energy that the old lack. We are not all old, but some are, and there are not enough of us to charge the earth and bring on the power we need for the flight. So Gideon told us that we should go out and find the young, bring them back and show them the truth of our way so that they can join us. Their presence will boost the power."

"And what of our friends? What use are they to you?"

A brief smile flickered across the sec man's face. "They understand now, and they are with us. That is why they told us about you. They understand that your being here is all wrong. It is too close to the time. We could talk to you, but you would not listen. So they understand that we have to make sure you do not interfere with our plans."

"So they did betray us…" Mildred said.

"Yes, but not of their volition—you see how easy it is?" Doc snapped. "Now be quiet…" He turned back to the sec man, his tone returning to the way it had been previously. "Listen to me. You say that the time is soon—if I am to help you, then you must tell me when, and what it will entail."

The sec man smiled distantly. He was beginning to slip away into unconsciousness through blood loss, and Doc was aware that he had to get the information from him quickly.

"The time is now," he said. "We have waited years for the stars to align, and now they are in the right place. That is why we have worked so hard. But it is ready. Tomorrow the cleansing fires will come and make us whole again. All of us..."

His last words trailed away as the loss of blood took its toll. Death claimed him.

"We do not have much time," Doc said as he straightened and looked to the sky, which was turning from black to gray. "He said tomorrow, but I think we can safely assume that tomorrow has arrived. We have very little time. They must be stopped, you know... They will destroy all those lives if they can. Whatever they think is going to happen, it will mean a mass cull to achieve it. They will destroy the young. And Krysty, Jak and John Barrymore. Let them destroy themselves if they wish. But not those who have no say."

Ryan agreed. "It hinges on that bastard circle. They'll be preparing for that. Just mebbe, if we can get in there unobserved, we can use that as a cover. I don't know how we'll do it, but if we can chill those bastards, then the kids will be okay. They're jolted to the eyeballs, or hypnotized or something, but they aren't the real problem. Chill the elders and we can free them. And our friends."

"No time to worry about how," Mildred said briskly. "We'll have to make it up as we go along."

Doc looked at the carnage around them and sniffed. "Well, it has not worked so badly so far. Let's just hope that they figure it was us who bought the farm down here. They will realize eventually, but we need to make sure they realize too late."

IN THE SILENT CITY, Gideon waited for word. He was unable to sleep anyway, excited and agitated as he was by the prospect of their purpose finally coming to fruition. He had heard the firefight below, but had chosen not to leave the palace. He would know soon enough, when his men returned. They had to. They were twice the number of those they opposed, and they had been thoroughly briefed. He had left nothing to chance. He never left things to chance. The idea that his plan may not have worked hadn't thus far occurred to him. Things had always gone right for him up until this point. Why would that change now?

But the longer that time went on, the more that doubts began to creep into his mind. They had been able to neutralize the threat of three of the intruders, that was true. But these were the three that had managed to get away. In Gideon's ordered mind, this made the three that were still roaming the canyon floor the more dangerous. That stood to reason. Hence his desire to eradicate rather than try to co-opt them.

By matching them two to one, and also having a full understanding of the way they would fight—something they couldn't know—then he had assured the success of his own men.

Hadn't he?

The longer that he had to wait, then, the more that the doubts began to grow in his mind. With the culmination of everything so close, he couldn't allow for any margin of error.

He had heard gren blasts out there. None of his men carried grens, only blasters. He had believed that the man with the canvas bags carried all the ordnance of that ilk. Certainly the albino and the woman hadn't. He had made an assumption, and that may have been a grave misjudgment. And if that was so, then what else…

He left the central chamber and hurried up the stone staircase that led to the upper levels of the palace. Here he knew he would find Delroy, sleeping.

He shook the gaunt man until he awoke, his eyes bleary with sleep.

"How on earth could you sleep through that noise?" Gideon asked in an irritated tone. Then, before the dark man had a chance to reply, he shook his head. "It doesn't matter, it's just… Listen, I fear I may have underestimated our opponents in this instance. They may have got the better of our men—certainly, they have not returned as yet. I must have a contingency. Get the three intruders and bring them to me."

"Can't it wait?" Delroy muttered.

"There is no time. It's all too close to be risked," Gideon said cryptically. "Go, please…"

It was unlike the fat man to ask for anything. His authority had grown gradually over the years until, almost without anyone noticing, even himself, his word had been taken as law and was obeyed without question or need for request. The fact that he now felt it necessary convinced the dark man that this was a serious matter.

Without further comment he rose and dressed quickly before hurrying to Jak, J.B. and Krysty's quarters. He roused them and led them back to the palace, where he found Gideon waiting at the doorway, contemplating the silence that had fallen across the night.

"Bring them in," he ordered, adding, "Do you hear that?"

"I can't hear anything," Delroy replied, baffled.

"No, precisely..." Gideon murmured, ushering them into the palace and closing the door. He walked around so that he was facing the companions and Delroy as they stood in the middle of the floor. Their eyes were pinned from the herbal mixture, and out of focus from the influence that Delroy had applied. Gideon nodded to himself, grunting.

"How malleable do you think they are?" he asked. "Really, could you override any instinct they have?"

Delroy shrugged. "I've never been tested to extremes, but I've never had any problems. I'd say that even if they were buying the farm inside at what they were doing, I could still make them ignore every instinct and do it."

"Good. I was hoping you would tell me that. I hope that you are right, for all our sakes. Come around, there is something I need to talk to them about."

The dark man moved so that he was standing beside the fat man. They faced the three disoriented and bedraggled companions. Internally, each of them was fighting to keep some semblance of their independence and true identity alive, but the strain was great, and each doubted that the strength was there to keep up the effort.

While Delroy's eyes bored into them, Gideon started to speak.

"You are in a very privileged position, one that will take you to great glory, should you choose. I know that you will. Your erstwhile friends would seek to deflect us from our goal. They have already claimed the lives of some of your new compatriots in doing this. We cannot allow this to happen. You have been of great help to us thus far, and we appreciate your efforts. But we would ask one further effort from you. They will seek to stop us as the new day dawns. You must find them and stop them. Only then will you reap the reward—with us—that your new status deserves. Will you do this?"

Gideon looked at each of them in turn. One by one they nodded, their eyes clouded.

They would do this. But only each of them, in his or her own private hell, would know how much the clouded part of their mind made that one small piece of freedom still remaining scream, scream and scream again....

Chapter Seventeen

While the fat man had wasted little time in arranging a backup action to the plan he now believed had failed, he still hadn't been quick enough. Ryan, Doc and Mildred knew that their only hope lay in getting off the canyon floor and up into the city of light while it was still, paradoxically, swathed in the dark of night. Now that dawn had broken, they knew that the city would soon stir. By the time that this happened, they planned to be inside and hidden, to wait for the moment when they could take action.

They moved swiftly up the path that was nearest to the spot where the chilled sec man lay. It was the steeper path, but in their adrenalized state this presented no obstacle, and in truth it was the fastest route as it took the least distance. They moved without caution as they ascended. There was no point. If they were discovered, then there was nowhere for them to hide and they would have to fight it out. It was an impossible route to climb with stealth, so speed presented them with their only opportunity.

When they reached the top and were in the city, the gray light of dawn was starting to yellow as the sun crept above the horizon, signaling a new day. Perhaps the last day…

The ledge in front of the palaces was deserted. There was little time for them to take in the strange designs painted ornately across its floor. If they had, they would have seen that these formed a path leading to the circle; a path that was signposted with symbols and depictions of events taken from all the major predark religions and spiritual philosophies, accompanied by bizarre markings. The profane and the sacred were all tied together in pursuit of one goal—one that was marked by the large stone circle that now took up most of one end of the ledge. It was this that took their attention.

Without having to exchange words, each knew that this was where the populace would be herded at some point during the day. Here was where they would find their compatriots. Here was where the children of Baron K's ville would be taken. Perhaps they would be able to save both. Probably not.

Maybe they would be able to save neither. Also unspoken was the fear that Jak's, Krysty's and J.B.'s minds would be so clouded that they would refuse to cooperate. Would there be the opportunity to fight it out with them and with the sec force of the city?

It was doubtful, but all they could do for now was to find some place to wait until the city was awake. They would have to watch events unroll and wait for their chance.

There was no other way.

While it was still silent, the companions made a quick recce of the buildings close to them. Most were populated by sleeping youth. If they were really lucky, then they would find their companions sleeping, and be able to take them before the city had risen. But luck like that doesn't come along too often.

What they did find was a reeking room, full of unidentifiable meat hung on hooks, surrounded by clusters of flies, with a few piles of sacking and rags strewed about the filthy floor.

"Home sweet home," Doc muttered, wrinkling his nose in disgust.

"Don't knock it, Doc," Mildred said as Ryan ushered them inside and closed the door. "The way I see it, no one's likely to be using this place. Not when they plan on checking out today. Besides which, I can't say the smell here is worse than the stink the rest of this place carries."

Ryan closed the door behind them and went to the empty space that defined the window out on the city.

"No one's around," he said softly. "It's going to be hard to keep some kind of recce without being seen. But at least we can do something about them seeing in…" He moved across to where the rotting slabs of meat were hanging on the pole. He moved them so that they formed a barrier, at an angle, between the view from outside the window and the interior of the room. The movement disturbed the hordes of flies, who buzzed angrily around the room, causing him to swat at them as they flew into his mouth and eyes, before they settled contentedly back on the now-still slabs.

"Wonder where they're keeping Krysty, J.B. and Jak," he muttered as he rejoined Doc and Mildred.

IF HE HAD KNOWN of the irony, he would have been amused. While he and his two companions settled into the room where they had recently been sleeping, J.B., Jak and Krysty were out on the sloping path at the far side of the city, making their way down into the canyon and tracing the recent actions of those who now sought them.

They surveyed the carnage that had been left in complete silence, taking in the chilled and mutilated corpses of the six sec men.

"Good job," J.B. murmured.

"I'd expect nothing less," Krysty answered. The words sounded strange and alien to her, reverberating in her head as though coming from another planet...or from another person. For she didn't feel that she was herself except for some small element at the back of her brain that was crying to be heard. "They must have taken the far path, or else we would have seen signs of their passing," she continued, mush-mouthed and slow, saying things that only made echoes of sense.

"Know we told, too," Jak added.

"How?" J.B. queried, his brow furrowed.

Jak indicated the sec man with a neat hole in his forehead. "Tracks here like stood for time. Must made him talk."

"Shit, that means they know they've got to fight us," Krysty cursed, banging her hand against an open palm. "I was hoping we could take them by surprise."

"Yeah." J.B. grinned. "If they weren't expecting it..." He shrugged and let the rest fall.

"Right." Krysty looked up at the city on the ledge. "If they didn't take the path we came down, and they sure aren't here or they would have come out to greet us, then…"

"Uh-huh." J.B. nodded. "They're ahead of us. Up there somewhere, mebbe looking for us, mebbe hiding out."

"We've just got to find them…and finish them," Krysty said decisively.

"WE'VE GOT TO FIND them and get this finished," Mildred said as she paced the back of the stinking room. "I can't take this shit much longer. It's not just the smell or the fact that they screwed us over, even if it isn't their fault, it's just…" She trailed off, gesturing that she had no idea what was really at the root of her unease.

Doc was more forthcoming. "It is not you, my dear Doctor, it's this place. And I do not mean this room. I mean the city as a whole. There is something dark and evil about it, despite the shining grandeur when you first see it. There is a kind of darkness that has settled over it, like the kind of dark you find in the blackest of hearts. And that can leave traces, it can infect. I fear it would infect us if we stayed too long. Certainly, it is a contributory factor to whatever has allowed Krysty, John Barrymore and young Jak to succumb so easily to hypnotic influence. I would suspect that this place has always harbored the dark. Perhaps these people were lured here because of that, because it chimed with some resonance within them, or perhaps they just stumbled here and were infected themselves. Whatever the cause, it is building to a head."

"You mean, this ceremony thing?" Ryan queried. "I

mean, what the hell are they going to do? Get that fat bastard to work extra fast with that knife of his?"

"No…" Doc shook his head slowly. "The way in which this psychic force they can control seems to come from them and yet be apart… I wonder if it was always here, just waiting. If that is so, then perhaps it was here for a reason."

"That doesn't make sense," Mildred said heatedly. "In them and apart from them—it's got to be one or the other, Doc, it's—"

"No, hear me out." The old man raised a hand to stay her. "What if it was always here? What if the fact that they appear to have some kind of mutie ability that can tap into and work with and for it… What if that is what it is looking for? I mean, how else would such buildings come to be in such a place? How difficult that must have been, to carve the stone. And the age of them. What kind of civilization would be able to do that as far back as we know it was done?"

"What are you trying to say here, Doc?" Ryan asked, even though he wasn't sure that he wanted to hear what the old man might have to say.

"Simply this. There have been occasions throughout history when migrations to particular spots have occurred, either through the hand of man or spontaneously. Many of these sites have circles of stone associated with them. Now, I know that there have been many theories, many of them far more crazy than I am generally thought to be, but what if…what if there were some grain of truth in at least some of them? What if there is a thread that runs through these?"

"You know," Mildred said, "I don't know if this place is making me as crazy as you, but that makes a kind of sense. Religions always need gathering places, a focus of some kind. Without that, the worship—whatever form it takes—has no real power."

"Exactly. Power is the key, my dear Doctor. What if they have been attracted to this place because it is a focus not only for their power, but of some other power? A beacon, if you will, for some other entity or force, something that will come to take them."

"What exactly are you saying, Doc? 'Cause I'm not sure I like where this is going," Ryan said slowly. "It sounds like it's going outside of the kind of shit we can deal with just with blasters and our wits."

Doc sighed. "I fear it may be, my dear Ryan. That fool we dealt with last night was babbling on about the stars being in alignment. But alignment for what? Of course, all the major religions of the predark times had some affinity with the stars as a means of explaining the great beyond—that which is beyond explanation in essence..." He looked at Ryan's baffled expression and laughed. "Forgive me. I speak aloud what I should be thinking. I should not speak until I have a conclusion, but...I fear to voice what I think will happen."

"Doc, I think I'm with you, but I don't want to be," Mildred said softly. "I'm thinking about the dinosaurs and something I read once. Place in the east, too... Tunguska...must've been around the start of the last century before the nukecaust. Caused about as much damage as a single nuke, too. Why there, that was the question. Was it just chance?"

"I think not," Doc said solemnly. "I fear that there are certain markers beneath the land. Perhaps it is some natural thing that we cannot understand, or perhaps they were put there by someone we cannot comprehend when the earth was young. Why else would sacred sites always be in the same places, no matter what the belief at any time in history? And this place? Why would a society build a place so beautiful and then just disappear for no apparent reason?"

"Unless they were taken," Ryan said quietly. "He said that they needed energy, that's why they had the young. Energy for it to feed…"

"Or for it to use as a homing signal on the beacon," Mildred finished. "This is real bad. No wonder weird shit has been happening. No wonder we all feel so edgy. And it's happening today."

"Great." Ryan swore as he moved to look out the window at the city beginning to wake. "As if it wasn't going to be hard enough getting our guys back, now it looks like we've got to do it before some fucking space laser fries our asses."

"DARK NIGHT, I wish they'd let us get on with finding the others and get rid of them," J.B. grumbled as he, Krysty and Jak were led in front of the fat man by Delroy. As with the previous day, they found that the fat man was presiding over a meeting of elders. All gathered in the ornately carved room were looking intently at them as the fat man spoke.

"So, have you found them?"

"Not yet," Krysty snapped. "They took out your

men, which is no real surprise, and you sent us down there too late to catch them."

"What do you mean, too late?" the fat man asked. "Did you check the place you told us about?"

"Of course not." Krysty sighed. "They wouldn't go back there. There was evidence that they had questioned one of your men, and that they headed back up here."

"What?" The fat man's voice rose—partly in anger and partly to be heard over the mutterings of discontent from the elders around him. "You mean that they are here?"

"Looks likely," J.B. stated. "It's what we'd do, too. Truth is, we were about to start searching for them when you hauled us in here. If you want us to do as you ask, then you should let us get the hell on with it."

The look on the fat man's face showed his displeasure at being spoken to in such a manner, but he held his tongue. There were greater measures at stake than his pride.

"Very well," he said in a strangled tone as he attempted to rein in his temper. "Go find them. The preparations are under way. Time is short. They must not interfere. You chill on sight, understand?"

"Sure. What else," Jak said coldly. He meant it. His thoughts were echoed by the other two companions who stood beside him. Yet inside, there was a part of each of them desperately fighting to overcome that feeling.

"Go, get out," the fat man said dismissively, biting his lip. When they had gone, he faced a barrage of questions, fears and anxieties, gabbled so loud and so panicked that it was hard to just pick out one. He held up his hands. "It will be all right. We will achieve our goal. We have come too far for it to be any other way."

Outside, the three companions caught the gist of the conversation as the door closed on them. Around them, and across the ledge, preparations were under way. In some senses, there was little to be done. The vast majority of the work had been completed by the previous day, and with the grand ascension set for the time when there was usually a sacrifice to the gods, there was no need to erect the altar. Despite that, the youth—unbidden by the elders who were still cloistered, but well schooled enough in their tasks—cleared the ledge, made last-minute adjustments to the path of painted symbols, and aligned the stones of the circle perfectly, building the construct so that not a pebble was out of place.

The ledge was, therefore, milling with people.

"Here somewhere, but where?" Jak mused.

"They must have gotten here before most of the kids were roused, so they'd be looking for somewhere that was empty," J.B. reasoned. Then a sly grin crossed his face.

Krysty met his eye, and a smile crept across her own face. "Yeah...just about the only place that would be empty, right?"

With a renewed sense of purpose, they made their way through the crowds toward the room in one of the smaller palaces where they had been put on their arrival. It was the only place that they knew would have been empty when their former companions had climbed to the city. Empty because they had been down below on the canyon floor while everyone else was billeted for the hours of dark.

"Don't take any chances," J.B. said grimly as he shouldered and checked the mini-Uzi, setting it to short bursts.

"Don't worry about that," Krysty said as she made certain that the Smith & Wesson was cocked and loaded.

"Not expect us hit without talk," Jak stated, a vulpine hunger showing on his otherwise bland, white features. "Got advantage."

"So let's use it," J.B. said as he shouldered his way past the melee of young people. All three of them barged a path through the youth, who were so absorbed in their tasks that they appeared not to notice that they had been deflected in their path.

As they approached the building, Jak said, "Moved meat." He waved at the shapeless cuts that now hung in view of the outside, obscuring the view inside. "Not there before."

"Ryan, Ryan… What a giveaway." J.B. chuckled. "Just what we'd do."

The Armorer indicated that Jak should circle around a group of young women who were absorbed in painting on the ground. They would provide some kind of cover for him to come around so that he could take the window. Meanwhile, he and Krysty would take the door. He indicated to her that she should approach at a crouch, to take the lower section of the room when the door was hit, while he would spray at head height. She indicated understanding.

They headed toward the door from an angle, so as to minimize any chance of being seen from the inside. Looking across, J.B. could see that Jak had made his approach in parallel, and was now in position. He took a breath and indicated to the albino teen that he should go…

In a blur of movement, the Armorer put a shoulder to the door to throw it open quickly. Despite its weight, it was on a smooth pivot and opened with ease as he straightened and began to fire across the expanse of the room. From below him, Krysty pumped shots into space. The roar of Jak's Colt Python sounded as he crouched at the window space, using the ledge to pivot his own fire.

After several rounds, J.B. indicated that they cease, and he entered the room, whipping the SMG around so that anyone left standing would be caught in the arc.

"Dark night!" he cursed.

"What?" Krysty said as she followed him in. Then, as she took in the interior, she murmured, "Shit…"

"Where go?" Jak asked as he entered through the window.

J.B. shook his head. "I don't know where the hell else they could have gone. There was nowhere that was empty. Fuck it, they must be around here someplace." He kicked out at a pile of sacking on the floor, venting his fury.

"THIS IS VERY uncomfortable," Doc whispered to Mildred, "but I think it is working."

Mildred kissed her teeth. "You better hope it keeps working, Doc, otherwise we're going to have to take on our own before we get them away from here."

Doc nodded sagely. "I fear that their mesmeric influence is rather stronger than we could have wished for. It may come to something that we do not wish... but for the while, I thank Ryan for his idea and will try not to complain too much."

With which he fingered the sacking that the three companions had used to camouflage their own clothes. Realizing that they were in a position where, although hidden, they were also sitting targets should they be discovered, they had opted to move out into the general populace of the city as soon as it stirred. They had agreed that their actions could be second-guessed by their friends, who knew them too well to be trusted while they were under a malign influence. So the best way to outwit them and try to gain the upper hand would be to simply do the opposite of what would be expected.

Thus, as soon as the young had started to crowd the area outside their hiding place, it seemed politic to slip out and join them, using their mass and movement as cover. They would be too noticeable and stand out too easily if they just moved as they were. But to use some of the old sacking to cover their usual clothes would enable them to hide in plain sight and blend more easily with the ill-dressed and ragged youth as they milled around. Would they be spotted as outsiders by anyone other than their erstwhile friends? If they stayed clear of the city elders, they figured that they were safe. The young were shuffling, brainwashed and addled automatons, moving only to the beat of the drum that had been planted in their skulls by the elders.

It was a calculated risk, and their boldness was repaid by the nonappearance of the elders. For whatever reason that may be, it was something for which they were thankful.

Their plan of action had been to move between the groups, to look as though they were taking part in any of the activities they had been close to, and to search for their companions.

That plan was soon challenged by the appearance of their friends. They emerged from one of the larger palaces with a mien of grim determination about them. Doc had been about to move toward them when he felt Ryan's hand on his arm. It was a move that proved to be wise in view of their subsequent action. And now, as the three warriors watched, their former friends but now palpable enemies headed off to search the interiors of other palaces.

"How long before they figure we're out here?" Mildred mused.

"As long as it takes them to comb the interiors, and that won't be long. Question is, how do we tackle them? We can't take them out, or leave them, but if they're now against us…"

"They won't hesitate to fire first and ask questions after, right?" Mildred said.

"Exactly," Ryan said. "So how do we take them down and get them away without hurting them? We can try to break the hold once we're clear, but…"

Doc looked up at the sky. "I fear we may have a more pressing concern than that," he said softly. "That is no natural sun. Not unless there are two of them all of a sudden."

Ryan and Mildred followed his gaze, and both cursed softly at the sight that greeted them. For it was as if the sun itself had grown a satellite, one that seemed to be growing with every second. Even as they watched, it grew in circumference. It was only marginally less bright than the orb it seemed to shadow, and would soon equal or exceed in size.

"What the fireblasted fuck is that?" Ryan asked.

"I would not assume to know," Doc said hesitantly, "but I think it would be a fair guess that it is the vessel by which they hope to be taken to their better place. It is certainly fast, and considering the vast distance it may possibly have traveled—"

"How long have we got?" Mildred cut in.

"My dear Mildred, math is not my strong point," Doc said. "I am not a physicist."

"Neither am I, Doc, but I'm betting my math is better than yours," Mildred mused. "At the rate it looks like it's going, then I figure maybe a couple of hours at the outside."

"Not that long. There's no time to pussyfoot around them," Ryan said. "We're just going to have to take the firefight to them."

"I rather feared that you would say that," Doc said sadly. "I hope that we can make them see reason."

"No time for that." Ryan shook his head. "If only…"

"THE TIME HAS COME," Gideon intoned as the elders prepared for their time of ascension. Once the three companions in thrall to them had been sent out to deal with the intruders, it had been relatively simple for the fat man to quell the fears of those left within the building. The young were preparing for the final ritual, as they had been directed, and it was simply a matter of three against three. What could they do to ruin the event that the city elders had worked so long and so hard for?

Within the building, while the world outside prepared in its own way, the elders began their own preparations for the event. Gideon intoned verses in the tongue that he had compiled from the many documents of old religions and beliefs that had been left behind by the original predark settlers. It was no wonder that Ryan and his people had been unable to make sense of it when they had first heard it several days previously. It wasn't real language, but rather a bizarre amalgam of Sanskrit, Latin and Ancient Islamic tongues, spiced by the gnomic utterances purporting to be "Alien" languages as recorded by supposed UFO abductees, handed down through the generations.

While this continued, the elders anointed themselves with herbal mixtures and tinctures prepared by Martha. They dressed in robes that they had prepared and dyed over several months to be ready for the coming of the messenger, the one that would transport them to another world.

They knew this messenger was near. The air was beginning to crackle with static energy, superheated by a charged force that was beyond understanding. Although there was no rumble to betray a movement of the earth, small objects in the room began to rattle and hum as though an earthquake was taking place beneath them. This impression was then given lie by the fact that some of the objects began to levitate in the charged and changed atmosphere.

Not that the elders were aware of this. The art of self-hypnosis, the toxic effects of the herbs they had ingested or painted upon themselves, and the changed nature of the air around them had made them impervious to any of those things. All that they knew, once whipped up into an orgasmic frenzy by the rhythm and sound of the words intoned by the man who had shown them the path—and whom the changed nature of the air within the room had vindicated—was that their destiny was now upon them.

As the last notes of his intonation died away, they could hear the sounds of the young outside, echoing this chant, taken up as it had passed through the air and also into their minds by the escalating power of the elders' mutie minds. They were ready to be led into the circle, to gather together and harness the power that would propel them to their destiny.

The elders rose to their feet, led by the fat man. His limp seemed miraculously to have diminished, as though the air was suddenly lighter and carried him upon it. He threw open the doors of the palace and led his people out to the young.

When the doors opened, neither Gideon nor any of the other elders truly saw the ledge as it was. The circle as it had been built, the path toward it as it had been painted so meticulously: all of that had vanished. They were there for the young, who used them as they had been taught to build up the power within themselves by the intensity of belief in the ritual. The groups of young snaked along the path, gradually reaching the circle as they chanted, crowding and jostling as they bunched into the stone outline, their bodies hot and sweaty, stinking of their dirt and also—miraculously—stinking of the beatific reverence with which they had been infused.

To the elders, the young weren't people, but lines of energy and life, their separate physical bodies fading to nothing as the effects of the ritual and the changed atmosphere stripped away the corporeal plane and showed only the pure essence that would travel onward.

The sky was now unnaturally bright, the light approaching at a rate and range that seemed to fill all space. The sun was obscured, and all that filled the sky was the light from a distant star come to take its people home. The light was pure, and yet seemed to shimmer with life, flickering and shifting patterns of shapes that had no discernable form and yet were also unlike anything seen on this earth dancing in and out of the circle that was now so wide as to be nothing more than all-encompassing of the horizon. The heat was immense, and it felt as though any flesh left would be burned to the bone before the light had a chance to touch base with the earth and so diffuse itself.

All thought of the three intruders who had come to disrupt the ceremony, and their three companions who had been co-opted to combat their threat, was now banished from the minds of the elders. It was too late for them to stop what was happening. If they hadn't been dealt with, then it didn't matter. They would be absorbed into the belly of the beast and become one with the elders and their young acolytes as they began their journey to the next level. Intent didn't matter now: that was an earthly failing, and it was too late for such things.

All would be absorbed.

All....

JAK HAD CAUGHT sight of them first. It was hard to see anything in the melee—not just because the young were milling around and chanting, getting in the bastard way of his search, but because the light was so strong that it hurt his eyes. There was something about the air, too. It shimmered in front of him, making it hard to focus on anything. Shapes dissolved into nonsubstance in a way that he couldn't understand, even though he could see it in front of him.

But there was no mistaking Doc. Using sacking to disguise their clothes had been a good move, but Jak knew how they walked. He could spot the gait a mile away, and Doc was more distinctive than most.

With a satisfied grin he looked around for J.B. and Krysty. They had opted to stick together, and he was sure that the other three would adopt the same tactics in this kind of situation. But in the changed world that he now found himself walking through, it was hard to literally see where his companions had gone.

Jak turned and found himself staring down the barrel of a ZKR.

"Hey, Jak, looking for me?" Mildred asked before flipping the blaster in her hand so that the butt was now the offensive part of the weapon. She thanked God that Jak had expected them to act a certain way and was slower than usual because of the shit that had been pumped into him, one way or another. In the split second it took the albino teen to register that he had been fooled and to react, Mildred brought the butt of her ZKR blaster down and across, swiping him across the temple so that a raised red bump signaled the dulling of a light in his eyes before he crumpled.

She reversed the ZKR quickly and looked around. They had split up, knowing that their companions would expect them to stick together. Things were getting weird up here now that the light was so close, but she would happily have bet that it was even weirder for the three who had been hypnotized into joining the throng. That was what was giving them the edge.

She wondered how Ryan and Doc were doing.

Doc's tactic of reverting to his usual self—bar the sacking camou—was a risky tactic, but one that was bearing fruit. He knew that if for no other reason than Krysty had just stepped out in front of him, her blaster leveled at him.

"Should learn to hide better, Doc," she said through gritted teeth.

"Perhaps I wanted you to find me," he said calmly, even though he was aware that in her current mind-set she could just blow him away. But perhaps if there was something of the old Krysty still inside there somewhere.

"Why would you want that? You know I have to chill you. I have to, Doc. I don't want to, I really don't." She grimaced as though a pain was ripping up her head. Doc stepped forward, and she straightened, setting her jaw as she leveled her blaster on him as steadily as her shaking hand would allow. "Don't come any closer."

"Why not?" he asked. "If that is what you have to do, then why not do it now?"

As he spoke, he was aware of the risk he was taking. It was as though all that was around them melted away so that they were the only two people standing on the ridge. Nothing else mattered but the hope that he could get through to the real Krysty, could stop her chilling him.

But she could just do it, and he would have no chance of evading the bullet. However, he could see that there was an intense struggle within her. Her intellect and mutie power battled the influences that had been thrust upon her. He hoped his trust in her strength would be justified.

"I...have...to...do...it," she intoned slowly and through a mist of pain. "It's been imprinted, and it's so...strong...that...I..." She trailed off as the effort to speak became too much. It seemed to Doc that the pain in her head—the result of the struggle between her will and the will of others—was overcoming everything else. She crumpled, bent and clutched at her head with her free hand. The blaster wavered.

Doc took two steps forward, brushing a group of

young people—oblivious of his presence—away from him as though they didn't exist. He was almost within reach when she looked up and leveled the blaster once more. He stopped. But the expression on her face—imploring and desperate—told him more than the raised hand.

"Doc, help me…" she said in small voice.

The old man took the last step forward and pulled the Smith & Wesson from her now-limp grip. She fell against him.

"I could have—"

"But you didn't," he said simply, cradling her. "You are stronger than that, and the bonds we share are stronger. But this is not the time: We must get the hell out of Dodge, as they used to say, before we get fried. Come…"

She was only too willing to be led, weak and yet pushing herself to the limit as Doc led her to where he could see Mildred with the prone form of Jak across her shoulder.

"Good work, my dear Mildred," Doc said with a raised eyebrow.

"Not so bad yourself," she returned.

She turned to Krysty. "How are you doing, sweetie?"

"I've been better, Mildred," Krysty replied with a weak grin. "Where's Ryan—" a worried expression crossed her face "—and J.B.?"

The one-eyed man and the Armorer were, at that moment, in the middle of their own face-off. J.B. had been keeping a keen eye out for Ryan. Their former leader was the real danger in his view, and being the man who had ridden longest with the one-eyed warrior, J.B. had determined that he would be the one to take him down. Even though a voice at the back of his head kept asking him why.

Like Jak and Krysty, he was finding it hard to focus on what was real and what wasn't, the people around him fading in and out from real bodies to streams of light. He felt as though the air around him was light in all sense of the word, as though he could—if he didn't concentrate hard enough—find himself drifting away into the ether.

But there Ryan was, suddenly directly in front of him, and staring him down…

RYAN HAD SOUGHT OUT the Armorer. He knew that J.B. would want to chill him, and that the impulse would probably be beyond his control. That was okay. It was up to him, then, to reach the Armorer first and take him out of the equation until they all had gotten clear. There was no way they could stop what was happening, but at least they could try to escape before whatever it was decimated the area.

When he saw J.B. looking around, Ryan strode straight toward him, cutting through the crowds as though they weren't even there. He held the Steyr across his chest with one hand, and shrugged off the sacking as he walked so that he would stand revealed.

He was about a hundred yards from the Armorer when J.B. saw him. He leveled the mini-Uzi, and Ryan halted, standing his ground. He kept the Steyr across his chest. He was taking a great risk, but he figured that it was worth taking. J.B. was sweat-spangled, his hands shaking, and he seemed to be having trouble aiming at his onetime friend.

"Do it, J.B.," Ryan said calmly, but inwardly he winced as he saw the Armorer's finger tighten on the trigger. He flexed his muscles, ready to bring the Steyr down and across if he had to.

"Ryan, for fuck's sake, stop me," J.B. said, his voice sounding somehow distant and faraway. "I can't fight it much more."

Ryan needed no further prompting. He moved across and swung the butt of the Steyr, moving it in a perfect arc so that it snapped the Armorer under the chin, knocking him cold. After shouldering the longblaster, Ryan scooped up his old friend, keeping his eye on the sky as he carried him across to where, through the gradually thinning crowds of young, he could see the others.

The light was now so bright as to be incandescent, surrounding them all with an aura that made it hard to see where the shimmering outline of their bodies began and ended.

"It will be here soon. We must go," Doc urged.

Mildred looked at the young crowded into the circle. Somewhere in the middle of them stood the elders of the city, lost in their own worlds of imagining, and no longer a threat, but still the root cause of what was happening, and still in control of the youngsters.

"We can't just leave them," she said.

"We'll never find any of K's kids," Ryan snapped.

"Maybe, but that doesn't matter. Any of them…"

"There's no time, Doc just said as much—" Ryan began.

Doc stopped him with a hand on his arm. "But Ryan, who are we that we can just turn away? Some of us just lost ourselves, but still managed to find a way back. Does that not signify something? Something that we cannot ignore."

Ryan looked up, squinting at the brilliant light that was now so close that it seemed almost possible to reach up and touch it.

"I've got to be stupe to agree to this," he muttered. "Come on."

Putting the prone Jak and J.B. carefully to one side, with Krysty assuring Mildred that she would be able to move freely and assist, they moved to the outer edges of the circle.

The young people were unresponsive for the most part. Lost in the hallucinogenic effects of the herbs, along with the stimulus of the hypnotics, they were wrapped up in a world that the companions couldn't see. Ryan, Doc and Mildred pulled at them, trying to get them out of the circle, only to be shrugged off. They hit out at them, hoping that pain would break the spell in some way.

Some of the young caught the blows too hard, and were rendered unconscious. There was nothing that could be done for them; they would have to be left. They already had Jak and J.B. to contend with. They would have to be carried. Only the ambulatory could be led away.

It seemed a thankless task, but gradually a few of

the young were detached from the circle, and wandered
dazedly around as though seeing things for the first
time. One or two even asked—of no one in particular—what they were doing in this place.

There was no time for explanations. A small group
was gathered, the baron's daughter whose abduction
had set these events in chain nowhere to be seen, and
they were led away from the circle. Some wanted to
go back, to collect siblings and friends. To find them
would take too long, and they were dissuaded by any
means necessary, even if it meant a further blow.

With one eye on the encroaching light, Mildred
shouldered Jak while Ryan took up J.B., and with Doc
and Krysty leading the young, they started the descent
into the canyon. They took the steep path, even though
it was the most treacherous, as it was the quickest route
down.

The atmosphere was now beginning to feel fractured
around them. The air hung heavy, and the lightness of
a few moments before was now reversed into an oppressive pressure, as though the gravity had suddenly
increased, making every step more and more difficult.

But they had to get down to the floor of the canyon
and take shelter. The covered dip in the earth was an
hour away, and there was no way of knowing if they
had that time. They just had to keep going, one agoniz-
ing step in front of another.

It was the longest hour that any of them could remember. Every second was impressed on their minds
as though stamped by an invisible combat boot. The
air hummed, the rocks sang and the air shimmered in

waves around them. The refuge of cover seemed almost eternally out of reach as the light grew closer and more intense.

And then, without knowing how, they were there, under cover.

The rest was lost in a roar of displaced air that was less sound than sheer force, and a light that seemed to sear their eyeballs to the insides of their closed eyelids.

IT WAS NIGHT when they came out of hiding. The air was thick with a choking dust that settled across the canyon floor. The night was quiet, the sky dark, the moon a single sliver in a cloudless sky. The city on the ledge was dark and empty.

"Best wait till morning," Ryan said simply.

And when the morning came, he and Doc journeyed up the slope. Mildred and Krysty—now feeling stronger, if still a little washed out—stayed behind to look after the young and to tend to Jak and J.B. They were both conscious, but still disoriented if aware of what had happened to them. Which was more than could be said for the young. Many had memories that halted at the moment the puppet show began. They had no idea how they had ended up here, nor even of what had happened the day before, when they were rescued.

Perhaps, Mildred thought, that was just as well.

Up on the ledge, there was nothing to mark the passing of the elders and the young they had abducted. Nothing beyond the dust that was everywhere, slowly stirring in the morning breeze. All traces of humanity had been expunged. The stone circle and the paintings that had marked the path into it had been vaporized. The ledge looked just as it had to have been when the settlers had arrived in predark times.

"It's so peaceful," Doc said softly. "You would not think that such an awful event could pass without some kind of mark. It is as though no one had ever been here."

"Mebbe that's the way it is," Ryan mused. "If you and Mildred are anywhere near right, then mebbe this has happened fuck knows how many times before. And will again."

Doc snorted. "Perhaps that's why it feels so peaceful. The beast, of whatever hue it may be, has been satisfied for now."

They traveled back down to the people who were waiting for them. Ryan outlined what they had seen, and when he had finished, he saw that Jak was looking up at the ledge.

"Fireblast!" Ryan said. "Mebbe that's what makes the stone shine so bright."

The rising sun had reached a point in the sky where it was directly shining on the ledge. The stone palaces, built by an unknown hand, in an unknown time, and possibly to unknown gods, were shining like ivory, looking more refreshed than a few scant days before.

"The sooner we get out of this canyon and back to what passes for civilization, the better," Mildred said. "Meantime, we need to decide what we're going to do with these kids. They come from lord knows where. Some of them don't even know where their villes were. How we're going to get them back to where they belong, I can't even begin—"

"We won't bother," Ryan said, interrupting her. "Listen, they're changed. No way would they fit in. But I'll tell you what. K sent us to get his kids back. Okay, we didn't get them. But we got *some* kids. And he has a ville that doesn't have any. It's not the only ville like that, but the only one we know about. I figure any kids to keep his ville going will be welcome."

"You think he'll pay us for that? It's not what he asked for."

Ryan shook his head. "I don't give a shit what he asked for. Mebbe he will, mebbe he won't. Only thing that matters is that we managed to save some kids. Better than jackshit. For that alone we earned our keep."

After scavenging for supplies in the palaces of light, Ryan turned away and led his companions and the children into the wastelands.

* * * * *

The Executioner®
Don Pendleton's
LINE OF HONOR

American medics fall prey to terrorists in the Sudan in this latest exciting episode of The Executioner!

When several American medics are held captive after a Janjaweed war band takes control of their camp in Darfur, Mack Bolan launches his own rescue mission. But the Janjaweed group has become an unyielding force in the region, and as the enemy troops close in, Bolan realizes he could be leading his men into a death mission.

GOLD EAGLE®

Available in June wherever books are sold.

James Axler
Outlanders®

GOD WAR

An epic battle to the finish risks humanity in its cross fire in this latest Outlanders episode!

A deadly war of the gods has broken out and the bravest of the rebels, Kane, is humanity's last hope to halt it. Ullikummis, a son born of cruelty, has plotted revenge against his father, Enlil, the most sadistic of the Annunaki, a power-hungry alien race. Endgame has finally arrived…but who will be the winner?

Available in August wherever books are sold.